FAMILIES AT WAR

FAMILIES AT WAR

JOSEPH NICHOLAS KENNEDY

The
Book
Guild

First published in Great Britain in 2025 by
The Book Guild Ltd
Unit E2 Airfield Business Park,
Harrison Road, Market Harborough,
Leicestershire. LE16 7UL
Tel: 0116 2792299
www.bookguild.co.uk
Email: info@bookguild.co.uk

The manufacturer's authorised representative in the EU
for product safety is Authorised Rep Compliance Ltd,
71 Lower Baggot Street, Dublin D02 P593 Ireland (www.arccompliance.com)

This work is entirely fictitious and bears no resemblance to any persons living or dead.

Typeset in 11pt Adobe Garamond Pro

Printed and bound in Great Britain by 4edge Limited

ISBN 978 1835743 133

British Library Cataloguing in Publication Data.
A catalogue record for this book is available from the British Library.

This book is dedicated to Hans Scharpf and Tom Kennedy and all our families.

"Me miserable! Which way shall I fly
Infinite wrath and infinite despair?
Which way I fly is hell; myself am hell;
And in the lowest deep a lower deep,
Still threat'ning to devour me, opens wide,
To which the hell I suffer seems a heaven."

– John Milton, *Paradise Lost*

LICHFIELD

★
★

BIRMINGHAM

★ LONDON

BERLIN ★

BREST ★

★
PARIS

MUNICH
★

★
FRIEDRICHSHAFEN

★ MOSCOW

FRIEDRICHSHAFEN
★
★ ERISKIRCH

1 JULY 1938 – THE ART ROOM

THE THIRD-BEST PLACE TO WORK in the art room was occupied by Judith Lareine, a twenty-year-old English Jewess. She was looking out of the big bay window at Lake Constance, watching the little sailing boats fluttering their ways to and fro in the blue afternoon of the July sun. It was 1938 and certainly not the best of times for Jews in Germany. The worst were yet to come.

The room was really a community chamber of the Saint Nikolas Catholic Church, Friedrichshafen, which was used by its members for various cultural activities. It had an old wooden floor and always a musty smell of catechism and boredom. Herr Ganther, a resident, eccentric artist, had offered to teach artistic techniques and appreciation in an after-school course to students of the local grammar schools. Today, only three young people had turned up to finish their work.

School: it was the last day of their final year, and she had attained very good grades in her Abitur; an average of 1,3, which would be the equivalent of top marks in England. If they accepted the German Abi. Although she had had to repeat two years since 1932 (which was allowed in Germany), she had made such excellent progress in German in word and script that she had achieved a straight 2,0, or an eighty per cent mark. And she had worked hard to get it. In French she was also competent, having received private lessons with Brigitte Rollet since she was eight years of age.

It was a wonder that they had been able to finish at Abitur level; everything was changing in Germany. She could now choose any university she wanted to study languages at, but not in this frightening country that had become so horrible. What to do? Surely her father would soon finish his research work at Freiburg University, and they could go home. The storm clouds had now gathered. It would seem that, officially, she and Matthias would soon be enemies…

To her left and diagonally in front of her (at the second-best place in the art room) sat Matthias Krieger. He was carving what seemed to be the silhouette of a woman's face, simple, yet so delicately, exquisitely, formed. He said it was of and for his mother, who loved to sit outside their farmhouse of a night and observe the moon as it moved around and over the lake. Matthias was one year younger and slightly smaller than her. He was broad-shouldered, strong-armed with a sturdy, robust figure. She loved his curly, untidy, dark hair and his contrastingly strong but fine, delicate-looking hands, which she would like very much to feel on her body.

She had been to his house and had met his parents. They were nice, characteristically Catholic Swabian. They had welcomed her into their home in the polite yet reserved manner that was typical of the region. Matthias took after his father, who not only ran a small farm but also built roof frameworks for houses and sometimes boats. Just of late, they had won a contract with the German army to repair wooden transport carts. Matthias helped him after school, specialising also in making furniture. She very much liked the table he was making for a family in the town centre – of cherrywood with a centrepiece that could be folded out from underneath, thus enlarging it. She liked his quiet, thoughtful manner when they conversed. He was a creative, honest, hardworking, very gentle young man who was delightful to be with. He had an Abitur average of grade 3,0, an average mark, apart from mathematics, in which he had got a 2,0. He was unsure if he should study engineering (or even art), or stay on and help his father run the family business and at the same time qualify to become a master carpenter.

On Wednesday evening, whilst ironing her blouse to get ready for school the next day, she had been struck by the sudden realisation that she wanted to be with this artistic, yet sturdy, kind, somewhat reticent young man for the rest of her life. She wanted his babies. Of this, she was sure. Simultaneously, she felt a sense of foreboding that was darkening her mind.

To cap it all, to be indoors on a hot summer's day was not where she wanted to be at all. All the other members of the art group were down at the lake, where she should be – i.e. at Matthias's home by the lakeside in Eriskirch watching him work outside on his table for the Fischer family and then sitting under the oak tree by the lake. Talking and laughing, drinking his mother's homemade lemonade. Then into the lake, splashing, fooling about, and laughing again with lovely Matthias. Simultaneously, as she thought this, Matthias shifted about in his seat. He could now feel Judith's eyes on him. He turned slightly away from his carving to look over at her and was met by a cross-eyed gaze aimed straight at him.

He burst out laughing and said: "You look like a new Picasso portrait, Lady Lareine!"

"And you like something from Grosz and his horror paintings!" Judith shot back.

"Sssshh, modernists are perverts, don't forget!"

They both laughed and their looks lingered on each other. Judith stared at Matthias long and longingly, until he blushed bright red and turned back to his carving piece, to the sound of Judith's giggles. She looked at her painting of Matthias's house by the lake in the style of Gabriele Münter of the Blue Rider Group around Wassily Kandinsky. She was pretty sure that the expressionist style of painting was classified as degenerate by the Nazi government – she was taking a risk.

Old Herr Ganther, who always smelt of turpentine and onions, did not seem bothered and, after looking long and hard, he said: "Nice use of colour and an unusual perspective, Fräulein Lareine – I see that you have observed your subject with great care." This was Ganther's credo: do not just gaze; look and observe in detail and observe again.

At the biggest window, Hinrich Richter had claimed the very best position in the room. He was also the most beautiful boy in the school. Judith had thought so too, at first, admiring his long, elegant, athletic, and muscular form, his almost perfectly chiselled features, his beautiful blond, wavy hair, and his outstanding intelligence. Two years ago, he had asked her out for a walk along the lake, and she had found him to be charming but superficial and very much in love with himself. He was also a member of the Hitler Youth, which she despised and feared. Apparently, his father had become an important figure in the SS in recent years. At that time, nobody knew she was Jewish. He had asked her out again. She had refused, being more abrupt than she had intended to be.

Recently she had told Matthias (the only person) that she was a Jew. He reacted somewhat surprised, then shrugged his shoulders and said: "It makes no difference to the way I feel about you, Judith, but we have to be careful."

That was the first time they kissed. As luck would have it, Frau Krieger had just come out onto the yard and had observed them and the kiss on the bench under the oak tree beside the lake in the evening sunshine. She had smiled.

Hinrich Richter was a different kettle of fish altogether. In his Abitur, he had an average grade of 1,0 – over ninety per cent in all subjects. However, art was not his strongest skill set. Although he was good at sketching, he knew a lot more about art than he could practise competently at a high level. Judith was certain that it would be most irksome for him to see that others were better than him; he no doubt took satisfaction in the knowledge that he was going to make a lot of money dealing with art in general. Through his father, he had bragged about what treasures the SS had captured in Austria and the Sudetenland. He had delighted openly more than once that Papa had brought such treasures into the house and Mama was absolutely delighted to wear such beautiful pearls (although stolen). Judith was frightened of him, for she knew, if Hinrich could be believed, that up to now, he had done well in the Hitler Youth Organisation and saw his future in the SS or in the safer option, with the Gestapo. Hinrich had told her quite candidly that 'it was important to have direct power over people in order to achieve one's aims, with the least possible risk to oneself'.

Hinrich was sketching, with charcoal, a somewhat clumsy copy from Rembrandt's *The Jewish Bride*, a print of which he had before him. Charcoal was the appropriate medium for Jews, so he thought. He was going to use this. He had announced at the start of their session that although the theme of the painting was repulsive, van Gogh had said of this painting: "One must have died many times to paint like this." And that van Gogh, the mad, Dutch, perverted artist, had, in October 1885, spent many hours and days in the Rijksmuseum, Amsterdam, gazing at the painting in wonderment. Later, he had committed suicide, which was a good thing as far as Hinrich was concerned; only the strong must prevail. *The law of nature*, he concluded smugly.

Everybody seemed to stir uneasily, their chairs scratching against the surface of the pinewood floor, as he made this pronouncement. No one dared to contradict him. He continued his lecture by describing the tenderness of the two figures, their loving devotion, and their inward gaze on what they were together and perhaps what the future may bring.

After that, Hinrich continued his sketching, and gradually it became apparent that the man was not resting his hand on the young woman's heart in gentle affection and she touching it with her own hand with unconscious love. No! Judith looked across again. The hand Hinrich had sketched was squeezing a much fuller bosom and the young woman's face was showing pain. The man's face had been changed to look like Hinrich and was showing pleasure. The young woman's face (and bosom) were Judith's.

Hinrich, seeing Judith's shocked expression, smiled, and said: "My farewell Jewish present for you, my dear *Jew-dith!* Are you coming to the end-of-school party down at the lake this evening? Please do. There will be plenty of pork steaks and sausages for you to enjoy, *Jew-dith!*"

Judith paled and shrank back under the force of Hinrich's attack.

"He knows, he knows!" she exclaimed to herself, sinking down miserably into her chair, her mind filled with the humiliations, beatings and murders the Jews in Germany had had to endure. Why did her father want to stay so long in this nightmare of a country? It could not be just his work at the university.

"Shut up, Richter, you poisonous snake!" shouted Matthias instantly, placing himself between the two of them, with Judith behind him.

"You be careful, stumpy little farmer boy in your silly short trousers, or I might just deal you out the thrashing you deserve."

"You arrogant Nazi piece of dirt!" cried Matthias and lunged towards Hinrich in red-faced fury.

"*That's enough!*"

Judith looked across and saw Herr Ganther moving surprisingly quickly between the two would-be fighters. He pivoted and then held Matthias from behind, locking both arms. Matthias began to struggle and was driving them both towards a pale-faced Hinrich, who was beginning to realise what he had set off. They were all standing by the big window in the full glare of the sun, Matthias sweating heavily, with Hinrich giving off a fearful smell. The room seemed to grow smaller around them. Hinrich, realising he wasn't cutting a good figure by backing off, took up his piece of charcoal and dabbed Matthias deftly on both cheeks. Matthias roared with anger and, freeing himself with a wild wrench, threw himself at Hinrich, the two of them rolling on the floor exchanging blows, although Hinrich was scratching and biting rather than punching.

Hinrich's easel came crashing down on top of them both, with Herr Ganther screaming at the top of his voice for them to stop. There was a sudden lull, when only the snorting and gasping of the two combatants was audible, and Judith called out, half imploring, half commanding: "Matthias, please *stop!*"

Matthias, suddenly motionless, seemed momentarily lost in thought. Then, he let go of Hinrich and with one huge, strong shrug, shook off Hinrich's hold on himself. He stood glaring over Hinrich. For a full minute, there was silence in this house of God, until Herr Ganther spoke with a firm, yet somewhat quivery voice: "Now then, you two, enough is enough. I want you both to shake hands and put this incident behind you. Otherwise, I shall see myself forced to inform both your parents, for fear you should continue with this stupid, distasteful fight later on."

"He started it, Herr Ganther, and I have got a splinter in my behind, my trousers are ruined!" blurted out Hinrich, causing the others to laugh with astonishment at his childishness.

Herr Ganther soldiered on regardless. "This evening, you have the end-of-school celebrations down at the lake with the rest of your class. So, shake hands and leave in peace. Shame on you both; this is a spiritual place," said Herr Ganther calmly, now completely composed again. "Shame on you both."

Matthias hesitated and somewhat shamefacedly then stuck out his hand.

Hinrich half-heartedly gave it a weak shake and, looking down on Matthias, announced: "I really don't know what all the fuss is about, Herr Ganther; most disturbing, I must say."

Judith groaned and, glancing across again at Hinrich's fallen easel, noticed that he had removed the offensive drawing. There was nothing more to be said.

"Come on, Matthias, let's go. Thank you for everything, Herr Ganther," she said quietly.

"Yes, it would be better if you left now. You can pick up your work tomorrow. I will tidy up the rest. Hinrich will help me, will you not, Hinrich…"

Hinrich smarted, thought about it, and nodded his agreement. Some minutes later, just as Matthias and Judith were leaving the room and standing behind Herr Ganther, he called out: "See you down at the lake, *Jew-dith*, and I'll save a couple of nice pork sausages for you. I'm sure you will like them, their form especially."

Matthias made to turn back, but Judith held him tight and so they struggled their way out of the door and into the hot sunshine, holding on to each other tightly.

2

10TH NOVEMBER 1942 – THE TRAIN FOR THE WOUNDED

IT IS DARK. ALL I *can hear is incessant moaning. I see darkness – am I blind? I cannot move. There is an evil black weight pressing and pushing down on me, in on me. The smell of it! The moaning is becoming louder, rising to a panicky waver, subsiding again to a whimper. My right leg is sending flashes of electricity that hurt and jag so that I feel my splitting mind slipping away again. Hard to breathe. The gagging stench of it. The bile of panic rises to my craw.*

Think.

My eyes. Are they stuck together? Perhaps I have not lost my sight. I try to bat-blink them open. Through a slit, I see the outline of a chin, through a chink, a hand. A leg is half covering Martin's face, who is staring straight at me. We two are nose to nose.

The pain is coming from my right leg; the knee, I think. Is this moaning coming from me? Try to stop it – start it again. Yes, it is.

Oh, God!

I hear voices: "Achtung! There is somebody still alive in this heap, get him out and see if he's worth saving."

Pain flash. Darkness.

I see Judith riding on her bike, smiling towards me. The sun is shining on her ebony-black hair floating over her shoulders. White blouse, dark-blue skirt, little white socks on brown legs, black shoes. Gliding round the curve of the shimmering lake, she dismounts, takes me by the hand and leads me to a glade within quivering lakeside trees; the flowers of blue, yellow, and red sway slightly, as do I. I feel the warmth of the sun on my shoulders but, strangely, I'm still cold. Come, let us lie together, she says, and her funny English accent resonates in my mind. She kisses my eyes.

Jerk by jerk, I watch as Martin's face moves away from me, as do more and more of the bloody torsos, heads and legs sliding now to the left and to the right.

Ah!

The sky is blue with puffy clouds hardly moving, but now I am! And it is so cold!

"So, Kamarad, welcome back from the dead! Into the operating tent with him and let's get that bloody leg off."

Darkness.

Now I am floating forwards on a stretcher. My knee hurts, hurts, hurts and my head is unbearable, but onwards I float past the mounds of my slaughtered comrades. Will I ever be able to play soccer again for Friedrichshafen FC? It's so cold I can't stop shivering; my whole body quakes.

Darkness.

11

On the table in the tent, the surgeon, in a blood-red-and-black-stained apron, impatiently awaits – saw in hand – the cutting open of what is left of my combat trousers and the cleaning of my wound. The disinfectant powder stings like bloody hell.

Now I am awake!

Through the tent opening, I see a stack of legs; long ones, short ones, an irreverent tepee of frozen discarded limbs waiting to run away to anywhere at all. Next to this desolate row, there are oil drums with arms sticking out, hands frozen in waves to their former owners, or to anyone who will take pity.

"Bandage it up; I'm leaving," I croak. "It's my leg and it has got me from Friedrichshafen to here. We're a stone's throw from Moscow, they say."

"More like a hundred kilometres, and winter has called. If you can keep the wound clean, you might have a chance; it's not quite as bad as it looks," replies the surgeon, who looks unblinkingly straight at me. He is a big, and very weary, man waiting to move on to his next patient, but patient enough to try to complete his task professionally. I feel respect for him.

"That's good," I say.

"I'll get them to clean the wound and sew it up, and bandage your head. With the concussion you have, the only place you're going is to convalescence camp, which is still behind the lines, and that's an order, in case you have any other ideas."

"No, I haven't," is all I can manage to whisper.

"Glad to hear it," he replies dryly. "Blood and iron, Herr Leutnant Krieger, blood and iron. Your blood and Russian iron with a slight dose of steel. That is what we wished for and that is what we have received, is that not true?" He looks at me quizzically and says: "And may the Lord make us truly thankful."

"Amen," I reply with more sarcasm than I intended. You can never be too vigilant.

"Bring him to transport, Müller. Next!"

Now I like him.

We are surrounded by pine trees. There are four first aid tents, and behind them, rows of our dead soldiers are laid out. I see Martin staring at the sky and say goodbye – no prayer; God is dead, as is my friend. Further back, before the green wall of the forest begins, is an improvised graveyard with row upon row of wooden crosses fashioned from sawn-off tree limbs.

The dead men lie out in the open; the frozen ground is now too hard to dig a grave. In the distance, I hear the hungry crows cawing. They, like the trees and the clouds, don't care.

The wind suddenly whips around us, sending flurries of powdery snow to sprinkle the dead and freeze the living.

"If you don't mind wearing a dead man's clothes, you can get yourself a good winter coat; if you're lucky, you will find one over there in the green tent," says Müller.

"I'll help you hobble over there; we will wait until the transporter for the wounded comes to take you to the convalescent station behind the lines," he adds sardonically.

Music to my ears, I too am sceptical that this is still possible.

***

THE TRAIN FOR THE WOUNDED was made up of twenty empty wagons, many of which were low-loaders for tanks and artillery. It was returning from the numerous depots and weapon dumps it served resupplying the fighting units at the front lines. The last four wagons were converted carriages, modified for the wounded and their nurses. As Matthias walked alongside the train, he looked up into the first of these carriages. He saw strange net bundles hanging from the ceiling, containing torsos of men without arms and legs, dangling, slightly swaying in their and his horror.

His designated wagon was a newly converted one, made also for those men who could not sit but only lie, facing the wooden roof. Some of these were accompanied by stands holding liquids that contained, in hanging bottles, life-saving supplements supplied intravenously. Many of the men had legs; others didn't; some could possibly walk but not see; and a few didn't have a face at all. All of these soldiers lay silently, as if contemplating, whatever you contemplate when you are decimated.

The smell of fresh pinewood immediately took Matthias back home to the surveying of their part of the forest with his father. His father patiently choosing trees that were suitable for their building business and, thereafter, the lengths of wood being fashioned for roofs and windows in one of his father's workshops. His father's particular perseverance ensuring every step of the work was fulfilled with the appropriate care and skill. He would pick out a suitable tree and stroke it along its bark with his big strong hands and say, "This one will do very nicely." He would mark it with JK painted in red: Joseph Krieger. Matthias was the designated holder of the paintbrush and pot. Occasionally, he was allowed to paint his father's initials on a chosen tree. The colliding visions of past and present bewildered him.

"They have been drugged."

Gingerly, Matthias tilted his head to his fellow traveller who had spoken, apparently to him. He was sitting opposite at the window, which showed the Russian countryside slipping slowly past; it was gradually becoming whiter and whiter. Matthias estimated that it must be mid-November.

"My name is Warner, Major Warner. Would you like a cigarette? They are real ones; Russian, no less," he said with a touch of irony.

"I would if I could, but I can't. Thanks anyway. I'm Leutnant Matthias Krieger."

"I see. The head injury, no doubt; is it that bad?" the major asked with a quizzical grimace.

"Only when I breathe, and my knee is not too good either." Matthias groaned despite himself.

Warner only had half of a left arm, cut off just below the elbow, but he managed to light his cigarette with his right hand as if he'd been doing so all his life, smiling at the same time.

"Fortunately," he said, "I no longer have any pain. I have transmuted into one of our super *menschen* that Nietzsche foresaw, and Hitler loves to dream about realising for our master race. He's such a bad, sad dreamer is our Uncle Adolf."

Matthias turned and observed the major closely as he lolled against the window. He had red hair, which put him as an outsider straight off the bat. He was rather small and slender with a determined chin jutting out below his long nose and green eyes. His open sarcasm and caustic comments about Hitler and other German greats, both dead and alive, had shocked and amused Matthias since the beginning of their slow journey. He wanted to laugh out loud, but at the same time, he felt a trickle of fear in his gut – for his new companion and also for himself.

As he looked up, he saw a pair of eyes and ears looming over the wooden bench behind Warner's head.

"Steady now, that's the vodka talking, and benches have ears, especially the two big ones behind you," he said in a half whisper, staring down at Warner's feet, between which was a bottle of vodka.

"*Fuck off, Willibald!*" Warner shouted so loudly that even their half-dead comrades lying opposite seemed to stir.

Willi's head disappeared immediately.

"You have not seen or experienced enough. No, not yet, but on this route, perhaps." Matthias felt his steady eyes appraising him.

"This route, not enough! *Verdammt*! I've been in this shitty war since it started three years ago and fighting all the way, all the time, in three different countries! Do you know how many comrades I have seen die? Look at these brave, ruined men around you! How can you say something so demeaning and degrading?"

Matthias had paused to catch his breath, astonished at his own fury, but before he could continue, Warner answered in a steady tone: "Herr Leutnant, I apologise for not saying what I wanted to impart in a more appropriate manner. My intention was not to question your valour or that of those around us. Let us leave this be and try to enjoy the rest of the day and our company, as best we can. Agreed?"

"Well, I'm... yes, of course, dammit again, Warner, err... Herr Major, please do be more careful, watch what you are saying!" faltered Matthias.

"Oh, I do, Matthias, this I do."

The noise of the connecting door being opened caused them both to look up. Matthias observed that this long, wide Russian carriage had been divided into two sections: theirs, for officers such as himself and Major Warner, and the other for the lower ranks. It was from this area that Nurse Pavel entered and walked towards them with a slight swing of her very nice hips.

"Herr Major Warner, have you been upsetting people again? I heard you shouting from next door! Please do not upset my patients."

"Lovely, gentle, and patient Nurse Pavel, I apologise to you too. For one kiss from your sweet red lips, I will remain silent as long as you wish."

"You will behave yourself, or you will feel the wrath of my tongue upon your big, fat, red head!"

"Now, is that the way to address one of the Führer's most decorated front-line majors of the magnificent German Wehrmacht?"

"Josef, enough is enough. *Liebling, sei still.*"

Warner blew Nurse Pavel a kiss, reached for his vodka bottle, took a long slug from it, and replaced it under his seat so that it wouldn't roll away. He then reached for his cap, which was out of sight, hidden under a blanket on the rack above his head, and settled into the corner with his head half against the window, cap over one eye, the other one eying Pavel.

"Such lovely, delicious thighs and buttocks; I have never seen the like!"

"Herr Major Warner, be quiet at last!" yipped Pavel, obviously outraged and pleased at the same time.

"All is good," replied Warner and settled down again. Seemingly for good this time.

Nurse Pavel continued on her way, working quietly and efficiently, helping her patients in tandem with Nurse Wagner, who had just joined her.

Matthias suddenly felt an overwhelming heaviness, though, at the same time, his headache was thankfully diminishing. He went through his masochistic counter-sleep list: that their train must be a sitting duck for enemy planes; although, until now, they had had almost complete air superiority, so there was one worry less, hopefully. However, they had experienced the resupply difficulties first-hand at the front, adding to the misery of fighting on muddy, now-frozen terrain, with bogged-down armoured vehicles and ill-equipped comrades. General Winter was gradually taking over command – and he wasn't on their side.

On the other hand, they were metre for metre, kilometre for kilometre, crawling and bleeding their way day by day in every way, towards Moscow. *If we capture Moscow, we'll have won the war with Russia. Or will we have?* pondered Matthias; then again, Napoleon did not. What did the major mean by, "You have not seen or experienced enough. No, not yet, but on this route, perhaps?" Had he not looked into Martin's dead eyes every night since – and more? What more was there to see or not to see? That was the question.

English Abitur; he had got a good grade in English before he ran away to join the army, thanks to Judith for both. Lovely, gentle, and clever Judith. What had she thought of him, running away and leaving her in danger?

He was woken by the train jolting and jerking to a standstill. His head was now thumping away as if the blood inside was trying to fight its way out. At the same time, his knee had stiffened and, moving his leg, he felt a jag of additional agony in his head again.

"Aha, I spy with my little eye, the romantic heroes of our Fatherland striving upwards to yet again achieve the national purity of our great Nordic forebears." The bitter words of irony Warner slowly enunciated forced Matthias to follow his gaze out of the window.

They had stopped, as was so often the case on this single-line railway, to let a supply train pass through in the other direction. The side track they were on looked over towards a village and directly onto a field. There a bulldozer had excavated a pit. At the edge of the pit, people stood, or rather turned and twisted anxiously, shivering, and behind them were more women, children, and men, mostly elderly.

Behind the first row at the pit edge stood a line of soldiers dressed in black uniforms. The SS. They commanded the people in front of them to fall to their knees and pistol-shot them in the back of the head. It was shockingly simple. The snow by the pit was red. From a distance, SS black. The bodies fell into the pit and the next row was moved up for execution. On the opposite side of the trench, three SS men machined-gunned anyone in the pit who showed remaining signs of life.

"Help me get this window open, damn you!" With his one good arm, Warner frantically tried to pull the sash down. Matthias leapt towards it and together they pulled it free.

One pretty little girl broke away from the line that was awaiting its turn; her young mother immediately started to run after her and was quickly felled by a shot in the back. The officer then took the little girl into the sights of his pistol. The crack of the shot and the child's forwards dive were simultaneous. The officer clapped his hands on both knees and laughed out loud: "How about that, a twofer!"

"You cowardly swine! Sons of whores! The filth of filth!" screamed Warner.

The officer turned towards their train and, at the same time, summoned the three machine gunners to join him. Matthias now stood next to the major; he watched and waited as they strode, snow-crunching, towards them. They then lined up in front of their window four guns, three of which were automatics, pointed upwards at them.

"Such outrageous impertinence, such insolence. We are doing necessary work here clearing the land of this Jewish filth!"

The executions had stopped.

The silence was iron-like. In the distance, a line of silent mountains, witnesses to all this. Beyond the village, a river gleamed in the reflection of the pearl-grey sky and the snow-white fields. For the first time, Matthias felt no pain and, surprisingly, no fear. He noticed, or rather sensed, that Major Warner was now holding his pistol by his side.

Between river and village, Matthias saw small figures in white, creeping and running in turn, from tree to tree, cover to cover. He turned to inform Warner. But he was venomously addressing the man in the black uniform.

"Listen, you SS travesty, you are not doing a man's work because you are not a man, like all the rest of the SS: you are a pervert."

"If I were you, Major, I would shut up; and to make sure you do, I will do the job myself!" replied the Sturmbannführer, slowly raising his pistol.

Plunk!

Matthias heard a sound like that of a pumpkin being hit by a hammer, and the side of the SS major's head turned crimson, followed by the *thud, thud* of many bullets hitting bodies. As he fell to the right, the three SS privates obediently followed him to the ground, blood spurting from them in all directions.

Domino dead.

Matthias looked across to the field, his attention caught by the sound of women and children screaming. The crowd at the pit dispersed; they were running back to the village away from the gunfire, the old and infirm making their way as best they could.

"Partisans! My God, partisans; look!" the major shouted again and again. "Look, look!"

The partisans had the SS pit squad surrounded and were concentrating their fire on one of the two SS groups on either side of the pit. The first group on the far side disintegrated almost immediately.

The four surviving soldiers strove to defend themselves against a well-executed, encircling action. Matthias watched, fascinated, as the villagers threw themselves to the ground, and the SS were cut down by partisan rapid-fire. Some of them lay twitching next to the trench they had excavated, now for themselves, as they were then finished off in the same fashion the Nazis had done to the villagers.

Simultaneously, the train lurched forwards, and Matthias got a closer look at one of the fighters; bizarrely, he was wearing a captured SS helmet with a yellow band around it bearing the Star of David. He raised his weapon and drew a bead on them both.

Warner screamed in Russian: "Мы все калеки, это эсэсовские убийцы. Мы не имеем к ним никакого отношения!"

"Нет."

"No!" The command from one of the partisan executioners at the pit rang loud and clear over and above the crying women and the shrill cries of the children.

Suddenly, the sun came out. The whole scene painted in a watery, yellow light: the pit of the murdered, the dead SS soldiers, the dirty, blood-red snow and the silver river, which wound its way through the fields towards the grey and white mountains.

In the distance, Matthias watched as an old man raised his crutch to beat it down on a wounded SS soldier lying on the ground, arm raised in pitiful surrender. The fighter who had them in his sights lowered his weapon and nodded his head grimly as the sun caught the Star of David on his yellow bandana half covering a dirty-white swastika on his captured German helmet.

The men who had shot down their would-be SS killers appeared on the left side of their window as they moved onwards. Matthias wished the train to move faster before they changed their minds and added all of them to the pit. The partisans stared at the Germans as they passed them by. Matthias felt a tingling in his anus. Fear's welcome-back sign. One of them spat on the ground. Then they were gone.

Matthias fell back onto his seat, as did Major Warner, and they stared at each other. Matthias lifted his head and observed the wooden ceiling and the weak orangey light bulb that never went off. The yellow sunlight from outside mixed with the pale luminous rays from above caused a surreal setting for his exhaustion, despondence, and relief.

The smell of the wounded pungently returned after the shock of the inrush of freezing air from the now-closed window. From the nurses' compartment next door, Matthias was suddenly conscious of their sobbing and their loud gulps as they struggled to catch breath.

After a while, the train set up a steady rocking momentum, which failed to comfort.

"If I may, Herr Major, I would now like a cigarette and a slug of your Russian vodka." Matthias sighed.

Warner leant over, clicked open his cigarette case, and offered him one, all the while staring steadily at him with those unblinking, examining green eyes of his.

"Here."

After returning his silver cigarette case to his top pocket, he produced a silver lighter, the second element of a matching pair, this time from his side pocket.

"Please light it yourself, Matthias."

Almost in the same movement, he leant down and up again, flourishing the bottle of vodka.

"Drink."

Which he did, and then took a deep, deep pull of the Russian cigarette. Matthias felt his head starting to spin and to throb again.

"You speak Russian, Major, and I can't smoke this."

"Yes, I studied the language and spent some years in Russia. My English is up to scratch too. Hey, don't stub it out; give it to me."

Which he did. The major took a long drag and leant back to enjoy it, while Matthias observed his tight, well-formed lips – for the next minute, no smoke seemed to emerge. He had never met such a poised, tough, elegant, educated man in all his life.

"Why did they let us go? Herr Major, why?"

Once again, under his gaze, Matthias felt himself being measured and appraised. He feared, all of a sudden, that he was too light for this heavyweight character-class assessment from the man sitting opposite him.

"Perhaps the partisans saw that we were both against the SS, broken as we are. We are not all barbarians, and we are most fortunate to still be alive."

They both sat in silence digesting what he had just said. After a while, the major declared: "Now you have seen with your own eyes! Always keep them open and close your mind, in order to survive, that's what we soldiers must do. Now you know what you and I are fighting for, dear Matthias, and what they, the SS, do behind the front after we soldiers move forwards. *Na ja*, in my case: have been fighting for." He nodded laconically and slowly moved his stump arm up and down.

Warner took a deep drag and continued: "Not only the SS. Many regular German soldiers have been involved in these atrocities, which Field Marshal von Reichenau in his general order to the 6th Army deemed necessary 'to free the German people for once and for all'. Yes, my fighting days are over, thank God. But you, *mein Lieber*, you will doubtless have to fight on. Oh, yes, they will grant you a few days of respite at the rehab centre. Then back to the front in a new unit for you! As far as I have been informed, the Infanterie-Division which you once belonged to—"

"What do you mean 'once belonged to'?"

"—has been decimated, rubbed out. You will return for the simple reason that we haven't any more reserves to spare on this front and we are suffering. You see for yourself, perhaps, the number of supply trains moving forwards is insufficient. Our advance is losing momentum in the fight for whatever it is we are fighting for."

"I thought we were fighting communism and stopping the tide of the Bolshevik Revolution," replied Matthias and simultaneously felt the hollowness of what he had spoken to this serious-minded man.

"Be that as it may, we are fighting to own more land, to breed on like cattle, and to destroy the people who get in our way, be they German, French or Russian. Then, of course, there are the Jews. The National Socialists want to eradicate them – all of them."

"Yes, I've experienced that kind of hatred in my hometown," growled Matthias.

"And where is that?"

"Friedrichshafen on Lake Constance."

"So, you are a Swabian! I thought I recognised your accent. How old are you, Matthias?"

"Yes, I have lost a lot of my dialect, though the accent still seems to come through. I'll be twenty-one in December. I joined the Wehrmacht in the summer of 1938, and I'll tell you why, if I may."

"Please continue."

"We had all just passed our university entrance exams at grammar school and were out to celebrate. Some celebration! I was at the lake with a girl called Judith, an English Jewess. I mention this because it is relevant. A boy out of our class, Hinrich, was jealous, and he was furious with Judith when he saw us together. We fought over her, and he lost. Hinrich doesn't like losing, I can tell you that. Hinrich was in the Hitler Jugend. His father was, and doubtless still is, a bigwig in the SS, not only in Friedrichshafen but within the party itself. He was often in Berlin; they say he also met Himmler. Some of his political opponents disappeared and ended up dead in Berlin-Plötzensee and, as you perhaps know, Dachau is just down the road from us. My father, who has a small farm which he supplements with a building business, refused to join the party. The disadvantages of this gradually became more and more apparent. After our fight, Hinrich shouted out he would make sure that the Jewess and I would suffer badly. When I got home and my parents saw I had been fighting, I knew I had to explain to them what had happened and of Hinrich's threats. The situation was serious. My father said I was in grave danger and that I must flee and should join the army immediately. The same evening, I got a train to Ulm, where my auntie lives, and, on the following day, signed up. I stayed with my aunt until I joined my unit."

"And your pretty little English Jewess, what became of her?" The major's firm tone was gentle, enquiring, devoid of its standard sarcasm.

"I don't know," moaned Matthias.

"So, you left her behind."

"Yes."

"So, what do you think the SS would do to a Jewess and her family when Dachau is just down the road, and they are angry with them?"

"I hope and pray for the best."

"You do that, Matthias, you do that. What the heck was a Jewish, English family doing in Friedrichshafen in 1938, for Heaven's sake?"

"Her father was a visiting professor at Freiburg University. He took long weekends and travelled back and forth to Friedrichshafen."

"There may be hope that they got back to England safely; the Swiss border is but a stone's throw away, is it not, Matthias?"

"Yes, that was what I was hoping they would do if they realised the gravity of the situation. They are rather unworldly, and they always see the best in people."

"Well, at that time, Great Britain and Germany were not at war. So, young man, in retrospect, what would you have done differently, if anything, if I may ask?"

"You may. I should have escorted Judith back to her home and explained the situation to her parents and I should have urged my father to have warned Mr Lareine too, Judith's father."

"What else?"

"I must and will find her and make it up to her. I will survive."

"You might find the former to be even more difficult than the latter, my dear Matthias."

"Yes, she has a heck of a temperament!"

"Hell knows no fury… *Na gut*, one thing at a time. One day at a time. Come, let us rest awhile – we will need our strength for tomorrow. And by the way, Dachau is for political and religious German prisoners, also for their torture, of course, and – of late – for murdering Russian prisoners. With that in mind we were, at our last stop just now, most fortunate. So, so, a member of the Hitler Jugend was passionate about an English Jewess. What a conundrum! *Sola veritas una veritas est.* The only truth is one truth."

With that, Warner swung his feet up onto the bench, laid his head on his bundled winter coat and closed his eyes. Observing him, in spite of the agony of today's incidents,

Matthias felt as if a sack of lead had been removed from his shoulders. No doubt the grim events of today would return tomorrow to be fought down as a drowning man struggles to keep his head above water. Bewildered, Matthias asked himself how he was to deal with this in this never-ending war. But just for now, on this island of sudden tranquillity, his heart felt gentler than it had in many a year. Matthias Krieger was still alive! He swore to himself and the God he no longer believed in that he was going to survive this war and then find Judith.

He closed his eyes and started to drift; for the first time in a long time, he didn't see the day's latest horrors or Martin's bloody, lifeless eyes staring at him, but Judith laughing at his bumbling English pronunciation as she kissed him quickly before leaving their farmhouse to cycle to her next student and his later adversary, Hinrich Richter. Hinrich was not only in their class, but also in their art study group. Yes, the art group, Judith getting into trouble with her passion for expressionism, Hinrich sketching away for all he was worth and he, Matthias, with his sculptures.

She stopped some twenty yards away and shouted out: "Remember your Milton for the exam: 'Come, knit hands, and beat the ground in a light fantastic round!'"

She banged heftily on the handlebars, threw her head back, shook her hair out, stamped down on a pedal and, with a shout of joyous laughter, rode weaving off down into the sunset away from Matthias's family's lakeside dwelling.

3

20TH JANUARY 1942 – JUDITH LAREINE, AUXILIARY NURSE

JUDITH LAREINE STOOD IN FRONT of the mirror with a large pair of scissors in her right hand, observing the brown lights in her otherwise long, deep-black, shining hair that she was so fond of. She began cutting just below ear level, tears streaming down her face.

"This is what they do to Jewish women over there!" Judith raised her voice to a scream: "And this is what they would do to Jewish women over here in Lichfield, England!" She continued, sobbing and heaving violently, now hacking more than cutting. In one jagged thought of realisation, she saw the culmination of all the German frustration, anger, and wounded pride she had sometimes experienced in Friedrichshafen. The arrogance, the overwhelming self-pity and hatred was venting itself in bombs and death. Here! How could she ever have fallen in love in that country? She continued to hack. Her screams seemed to bounce off the walls and ceiling, filling her ears with white noise.

Behind her, she heard, through her pain and fear, the door to her bedroom burst open and her mother striding up to her, saying: "What on earth are you doing, my dear, why this noise? Stop cutting your lovely hair off like that! Stop! *Stop!*"

Judith suddenly felt her mother's long, elegant arms enveloping her. She struggled briefly against them so that she could continue her outburst. Her mother's hold was much stronger than she anticipated. She suddenly felt her strength leave her, sagged and leant into her mother's embrace.

"They bombed Birmingham last night. The noise! The noise! *The noise!* I thought it would never stop, I felt as if I were going mad! All they do is bomb and burn, bomb and burn! Everywhere and everyone! Oh, Mother, when will this ever stop?"

"When we have beaten them. That is the logic of war, and we will win – we are winning, although a lot of people do not realise it yet. Hitler recently declared war on the USA, the day after Pearl Harbour, which was a huge mistake, and his advance on Moscow has stalled, so they say. Your father and I think that the Royal Navy together with the Americans will eventually prevail in the Atlantic. So come, calm yourself, my dear, my sweet."

She held her daughter in a tight embrace and let her sob until her shaking slowly shuddered to a standstill. The two women stood silently now in the centre of Judith's bedroom rocking gently to and fro.

Judith let her mother lead her to the floral, cushioned stool that stood before her dresser. As she sat, she let her mother slowly clip, brush, and tidy her now short hair back into shape.

Her slim, gracious mother gently turned Judith's head by moving her chin with the tips of her fingers, before continuing the grooming and snipping, softly humming a lullaby that Judith recognised from her childhood.

"That's better," said Mrs Lareine as Judith's sobbing subsided. In the mirror, her daughter looked up and regarded herself critically, then moved on to dry her tears.

At her feet lay clouds of black hair.

Suddenly, Judith heard her mother say: "Tibbles is coming. What do you want here, *you?* Do you want Judith to stroke and spoil you?"

The small ginger cat jumped lithely up onto her lap as if sensing her distress and arched his neck and head so as to be stroked and scratched, thus taking centre stage.

"Render unto Caesar that which is Caesar's." Judith giggled and stroked the family pet softly, humming the Jewish lullaby she had just heard, now to the cat. Together, she and her mother continued humming in unison with the cat purring its contentment.

In her room was a simple bed with a night table on either side; to the left a reading lamp, on the right a small pile of books. The wallpaper, with an eggshell-blue background patterned with the flowers of the spring depicting crocus, snowdrops and lily of the valley, provided a backdrop to a contrasting display of three paintings in the style of the German artist Gabriele Münter: the first showed the fenced driveway leading to the Kriegers' house and farm buildings at the lake, depicted in the classical expressionist blue and greens so typical of Münter; the second, a riverside scene with the church spire of Eriskirch in the background; the third, a winter scene of the Kriegers' modest lakeside property, with Swiss mountains silent and white in the distance.

In the corner near the window, next to a walnut cupboard, an easel and a table with various painting utensils; the picture on the easel depicted Lake Constance in the evening with the shoreline bending its way around on the Swiss side. The water of the silver lake silent and still. The little boats were remote and lonely.

"Would you believe it!" she heard her mother exclaim. "Short hair suits you, Judith! As is often the case with beautiful women, hair long or hair short, they always manage to look extraordinary. Now you are ready to get ready for work again; the night shift calls Nurse Lareine!"

"Thank you, Mother, for everything," replied Judith. She turned, stood up and kissed her mother on the cheek and hugged her briefly again. Mrs Lareine smiled with pleasure and hugged her back.

"'Twas nowt," she replied gruffly, imitating the local Lichfield accent she occasionally heard.

"Look at him; his majesty is leaving us." Judith pointed at Tibbles, who, with a swaying bottom and an almost vertical tail, anus showing, headed majestically towards the door, ignoring them completely. "And it's Auxiliary Nurse Lareine, Mum."

"Yes, I know, and it's fine work that you are doing in the burns unit; I don't know how you do it."

"Fighting fire with the fire of love, as you and Father say."

"Exactly. Now then, how is Tom doing?" asked Mrs Lareine as she eyed her peculiar daughter quizzically.

"His chest burns are as good as healed; the scarring is awful, of course. We went for a walk in the park yesterday, and he expects to be flying his beloved Spitfires again soon."

"…and to God the things that are God's," replied Mrs Lareine as she picked up comb and scissors. "You know, we have some time before you have to get ready; let's follow Tibbles into the front room and sit by the fire for a while. I shall play."

In the front room, which looked onto the quiet of Wordsworth Close, through the bay window, Judith could see snowflakes gently spinning down. Tibbles now lay stretched out on the hearth rug, basking in front of the fire, observing them indifferently. At the other end of the room, a large window showed a view on to the garden, which had been formerly made up of two lawns separated by a pathway leading down to flower beds. Now it was all an intensely cultivated vegetable patch, consisting of cabbage, sprouts, turnips, and potatoes.

"Light the candles on the menorah, Judith."

"Oh, Mother, really!" exclaimed Judith.

"Judith, I respect your rather negative attitude towards the Jewish religion; please, just humour me. I need some comfort too. As you know, it is the one Matthias made for us."

"I'm sorry. Of course. It does bring back some nice memories, even if they are German ones."

"Well then."

With that, using the shamash, Judith set about lighting from left to right the candles of the small, elegant, oaken menorah that was standing on a little table in front of the street window. The fire burned colours of orange and red.

There was no other lighting in this room. The nine menorah candles flickered and danced on the window and walls.

Judith settled on the sofa opposite the long walnut bookcase, her elegant, stockinged legs tucked under her, watching her mother as Mrs Lareine deftly took the cello out of its case, which stood against the corner wall next to the thick, red, velvet window curtain. The deep-brown and vibrant tones of the cello filled the room as the serious, flowing music seemed to echo of will and determination. Judith gazed at her mother, who was intent and immersed in her playing, and saw the strands of grey in the long auburn hair and the new creases of worry in her delicate face.

Then she and Tibbles both closed their eyes and sat and listened. Mrs Lareine did not look up until some seconds later, when the last notes had stopped reverberating.

"Johann Sebastian Bach. There! I needed that!" said Mrs Lareine, exhaling a big sigh.

"Yes, it was so lovely, Mother, thank you. We both needed that. I hope you feel better now, as I do. Unfortunately, it is time for me to get ready, or I'll miss the bus."

"Pop your head round the door to say goodbye before you go and say hello to Tom if you see him."

"Mum, fraternising with the male of the species is looked down upon at the hospital."

"Nothing ever stopped you from kissing a nice handsome chap, Judith. In fact, I could do with a wee bit of that myself, come to think of it!"

"Mother! Father will be home tonight!"

"He'll have to do, I suppose," quipped Mother Lareine, winking at Judith.

"You are impossible, dear Mater, one minute light the menorah, the next kissing men!"

"Both are rather nice, I would say; now hop it or you will be late."

"*Jawohl, Mutter*! And give Father my love."

"I will, and watch it, you – and if you are looking for your uniform, it is in the airing cupboard."

Judith was already out of the room – but her laughing could be heard throughout the house.

Once again, Judith stood before a mirror in her bedroom. This time, one of three-quarter length. She straightened her blue-and-white-striped uniform and donned the white apron. Above her breast, she straightened her Civil Defence badge, which she had earned for good work and faithful service.

Satisfied that her startling blue eyes had the look of a woman who meant business and not one of a young girl preening herself, she turned sideways to check the fit again. Suddenly, a quiver of inner anguish bubbled up from within, causing her to sob and quiver again. Last night, one particular sequence of German bombing seemed to go on forever; she thought it would never stop. She started again to imagine what these bombs would do to the people below.

"No!" she said, straightening her CD badge. "No time for crying."

Satisfied that all was ship-shape on her, inside and out, she went down to the hall cupboard and put on her big warm Civil Defence service coat of grey and blue, calling out as she opened the front door: "I'll see you in the morning, Mother, I've got my winter boots on."

A muffled 'Bye!' and 'Take care, dear' echoed through the ground floor of their modest detached house. As she stepped out, she immediately caught her breath in the icy-cold air, the snow catching in her long eyelashes and settling on her bonnet and coat.

"Oh, how lovely!"

As she stepped off the doorstep with further vegetable patches to the left and right of the garden path, she stared up at the snow as it silently swirled and curled around her. Tonight, she wouldn't walk – too much snow and ice – but she could still enjoy the spinning snowflakes and the quietude of the winter night on Brownsfield Road. She could already see the Midland Red bus half trundling, half slithering with its slit-eyed headlamps and dimmed interior lighting, reminding her of the monster in a horror film she had watched with Tom at the pictures. Tom had been allowed out of hospital on the condition he'd take it easy. But he didn't. Nor did she. They ended up kissing and cuddling in the back seats of the cinema with Tom's hand not only caressing her breasts but finding its way up the inside of her skirt until reaching her garter, which excited her intensely. Just at that moment, a huge, slimy, black monster had slithered across the big screen, and she had grabbed Tom's hand in fright and delight, which put an end to further explorations on both sides.

"We must be careful, little Scottish lover. One step at a time."

"Ay, you're right, no doubt, but you are awfully lovely, my sweet, my darlin' Judith," he had replied in his thick Glaswegian accent. Tom had sighed, leant back, then lit up a Player's and whooshed the smoke out and up onto the projector's light beam, causing a quiet chaos of exploding smoke and light.

The red bus arrived, coughing and snorting, causing her to start and shake off her reverie.

"Hop on, sweetheart; we haven't got all night, darling!" sang out the red-faced conductor, who was certainly way over seventy and obviously enjoying every minute of his new-found usefulness.

"You're a sweetheart yourself," replied Judith as she made her swaying way to a seat and noticed that the elderly man was blushing and smiling at the same time as the bus chugged off. The musty, rattling, shuddering old bus smelt of damp clothing and old leather in contrast to the sharp, clean cold of outside. After rubbing a see-through spot on the fogged-up window, Judith looked out at the snow driving past the window, settled back in the worn-out seat, and smiled at her reflection. Her thoughts once again returned to Tom and how they had had a beer together six weeks ago. It had been at the local arts centre, where Shaw's *Pygmalion* had been put on. She had looked down the row and recognised Captain Nailon, one of her patients, who should have been in hospital, in bed. He was watching the performance intently. He had a good profile, she mused. A fine head of hair and a lovely nose on a good, but somewhat pale, face. Altogether, a handsome chap, a bit on the small side, but most pilots were. Matthias had been slightly smaller than her as well. No, she had not wanted to think of him; the whole thing was too difficult. It had been almost four years now. She had sadly gulped down a shaft of pain and turned her attention back to the play. Sheila Livingston had played the part of Eliza Doolittle, and very well too.

She remembered sitting there thinking that all the actors were good, and the crowd was obviously enjoying the play too. A good-natured lightness and hilarity were in the air. The plush red furnishing of the theatre had added to the convivial feeling of enjoyment and relaxation. She, settling back and setting her thoughts about bloody stupid men aside and turning her attention to Eliza's screeching cockney accent, which truly had made her toes curl.

In the intermission, she had found herself standing in the bar, two rows behind Captain Nailon; he too was trying to order a drink. Pushy men (and some women) were constantly elbowing her aside. So, she had shoved her way towards Nailon and tapped him on his right shoulder and said: "Captain Nailon, could you please get me half a pint of Guinness?"

Nailon turned round and his face was a picture worth framing: surprise, consternation, and guilt about having been caught outside the hospital when he should have been in bed.

"Gladly, Nurse Lareine," he said, recovering quickly.

"Auxiliary Nurse, actually. I'll be sitting over there near the door."

"Until then, fair maid." Tom grinned.

She had observed him as he pushed deftly past a man with a big stomach who was blethering on about the weather and how awful it was. He made it to the bar, turned around and saw that she was still watching him over her shoulder as she was making her way to the empty seats near the entrance. He waved to her. She remembered blushing and feeling that, somehow, she had been caught out.

"Hold on," she had said, annoyed at her own reaction. "He's the one who is supposed to be in bed and not to be here!" Judith smiled to herself at the memory and rubbed her spot on the window, which had misted over again. She mused on dreamily: so, she had sat down on one of the scruffy, worn, red chairs next to the bar door and watched Tom navigate his way towards her, carrying two half-pints of beer. She remembered, too, the bar becoming noisier and noisier all the time and that a pall of blue cigarette smoke hung over them all. The hum of conversation, interspersed with laughter, seemed to lift the ceiling.

"One half-pint of a drink full of character for a lady who possesses the same qualities."

"You mean I am of barley, hops, and water, Captain Nailon?" she had tried to reply sternly whilst forcing herself not to laugh.

"Call me Tom. No, I meant Guinness is a dark, beautiful drink full of strength and character. Unfortunately, without the hypnotic, startling blue eyes that you could fall into and never see the light of day again. However, that would be, no doubt, asking too much from a half-pint of beer."

She had gasped at the sheer force of the compliment; she had felt her cheeks burning. She hadn't known whether to laugh, which would have encouraged him in his forwardness, or to keep face and not let him notice the effect he was having on her. In the end, she had burst and snorted with laughter, causing her to spill her drink over his neat RAF uniform trousers.

"Hell's bells!" Tom had roared as he instantly leapt up and furiously tried to sweep the beer off his uniform, and she couldn't stop laughing at the absurdity of the situation. "Worse things have happened at sea. Auxiliary Nurse Lareine, who is very good at her work, and I thank for her dedication in looking after myself and my fellow comrades. Cheers."

Without stopping to take so much as a breath, he had continued onwards: "So, what do you think of the play, the acting and the direction? You do realise it is based on the Greek saga of King Pygmalion wishing a statue he had made of an extraordinarily beautiful woman to come to life? The goddess Aphrodite granted his wish, and they had two children and lived happily ever after."

Judith had felt as if she was sitting in the eye of a storm, her brain racing with the images that Tom was creating for her. Sitting now in the bus, gazing out at the driving snow, she grinned at her reflection as she remembered her reply.

"Well, no, actually. How does your warm bitter taste?"

***

"THE RAW SURFACE OF A third-degree burn must be covered by a skin graft."

Doctor Timothy Brown (everyone called him Doctor Tim behind his back) paused, looked up from his notes and across the table at his Intensive Care Team for the Lichfield Burns Unit. To his right sat Matron Jill Henderson, and on his left Nurse Greenwood and Nurse Cunningham, and opposite them Nurses Gregory and Randalls. Judith Lareine sat at the end of the table. She was responsible for writing up the minutes of the meeting at Doctor Tim's direction.

"To sum up, McIndoe was using saline baths at 105 degrees Fahrenheit, the advantage being that the patient could be completely immersed. The treatment could be accompanied by the employment of a Bunyan bag, an oiled-silk envelope encasing the limb. This procedure has been endorsed by *The Lancet* so we are on firm ground and can move on with using it for our patients. Well, I've written to McIndoe and Gilles and was also on the blower more than once to Rosenheim. Our Matron Jill Henderson spoke to Matron Huddlestone to check procedures. It seems we are doing the best we can! Well done, everybody. Now back to work; let's get that saline bath up and running for Lieutenant Goodman. Before you go, patient Captain Tom Nailon, the little Scots feller, he's to go back to his squadron after the weekend. He's just about fit enough and certainly tough enough. I wouldn't like to get in front of his Spitfire's cross hairs! Auxiliary Nurse Lareine, have you got all this in this meeting's protocol?"

"Yes, Doctor Brown."

"Good, then read it back to us, so everybody knows what's what, thus avoiding unnecessary griping and whining," said Doctor Tim with his cheeky grin.

Judith read back the procedures that the team had agreed upon quietly and diligently.

"Okay, everybody, agreed?"

Doctor Tim was commanding rather than asking. His open, friendly style, coupled with his highly professional capabilities and driving work ethic, created loyalty and self-confidence in his team, whose individuals he trusted, and from whom he sought opinions – be they fellow doctors, nurses or even auxiliaries. As a result, the patient treatment and care were as good as Judith privately thought it should be: very, very high.

In the middle of the conference room, which also served for the storage of medical supplies, stood the conference table. The shelves on three sides of this large room were thankfully full (for now) of what they needed to serve their patients. In the corner were kept tea-making facilities: a kettle, a teapot and cups and saucers, which were now all on the conference table. The professional atmosphere that prevailed countered the sterile, white walls and the harsh, bright lighting. All the windows were blacked out. The combined smell of cloth, packaging and cleaning fluids coupled with the body warmth of the seven adults present lent the room the unmistakable atmosphere of a hospital at work. Suddenly the door swung open, and Doctor Weston came into the room with a quizzical expression on his friendly, moon-shaped face. He frowned slightly, which creased his forehead, which in turn set in motion the waggling of his head of frizzy hair. Judith noticed that he encountered a room of smiling welcome. How nice.

"Doctor Brown, my apologies for interrupting. I have to operate shortly; could Nurse Greenwood assist the rest of my team?"

"Yes, certainly, if that's okay with you, Matron?"

"Yes, Doctor Brown."

"Thanks, Doctor Brown, and you too, Matron – come, come, Nurse Greenwood; time is of the essence, dear lady."

Without further ado, Doctor Weston gallantly held the door open for little Nurse Greenwood to leave the room, saying: "There is no rush, no need to rush at all," all the while tapping his right foot impatiently on the floor.

"Yes, Doctor," squeaked little Nurse Greenwood, who scurried past him, smiling that her skill and patience were required by Weston and his team. As soon as the door closed, the room broke out into joyous laughter.

"Alright, you lot, calm down. Good: you yourself, Matron, Nurse Cunningham and Nurse Lareine, you will come with me; we've Lieutenant Goodman to attend to. The good man needs our best treatment, ha, ha; did you get the pun, ladies?"

"Yes, Doctor Brown," said Matron again and raised her left eyebrow at Cunningham at this minimal display of deference. Judith felt laughter bubbling, and she snorted and held her right hand to cover her mouth.

"Wasn't that funny; good of you to laugh though, Judith! Laughter is the best medicine, but Robert Goodman needs more than a smile, so let's get in there and help this fellow."

With that, Doctor Tim bustled out of the conference room and turned right along the brightly lit yellow-walled corridor and through the door of the treatment room, leaving the three women tripping along in his wake. Judith, slightly behind the group, smiled to herself again.

***

"TOM, DO YOU KNOW WHAT the Jewish name is for Thomas?"

"No, Judith, I don't know that, but I have the feeling you are going to tell me, lassie."

The day following Tom Nailon's discharge from the hospital, he had asked her to go for a late-afternoon walk in Lichfield Park.

"Thomas comes from the Hebrew word 'taom', meaning 'twin'. It came into English via the New Testament of the Bible, where St Thomas was one of the twelve apostles of Jesus. Origin: the Hebrew word 'taom' led to the Aramaic name 'Taoma'."

Judith had been surprised and pleased at Tom's

unannounced visit to the Lareine residence in Wordsworth Close. He had insisted upon not only seeing her yet again but also 'going for a stroll', as he called it – no matter what the weather. He was due back to his fighter squadron at Uxbridge the next day.

Great Britain needed every single pilot, for the country was in danger of slowly but surely starving to death. In the grim and unyielding war of the Atlantic Ocean, the German U-boats were sinking supply ships from the USA faster than the government could replace them.

Fortunately, the sun had come out and the wind had dropped. They had slowly proceeded alongside Stowe Pool arm in arm without conversing, enjoying each other, the sun, the bright blue of the glistening sky and the brilliant white of the swathes of untouched snow stretching beyond the cathedral to Beacon Park, occasionally greeting fellow walkers who drifted past them. The air was sharp and clean, and both of them felt reinvigorated after the nights in the 'smelly hospital' as Tom called it, much to Judith's annoyance.

"It's not smelly; it is to keep you alive and clean, you dirty beast!" she said in exasperation at what she called 'his Scottish bloody-minded stubbornness'.

"No offence meant, Judith, I'm just glad to be outside in the fresh air again, alive and with you. I always want to be with you. I think about you in the morning, I think about you in the afternoon, and in the night, especially when my burnt chest hurts. Then I feel better. I always feel better when I'm with you and I always want to be with you. Now and until the end of my days. Do you want that? Would you, could you, take me for your husband, my fair Jewess?"

They had now arrived at the cathedral. Judith and Tom

looked up in silent admiration at this impressive edifice to God. Judith stood motionless, thinking once again if she could imagine being the wife of this hard-headed, challenging little Scotsman. She took a cold-blooded assessment: two thirds of her felt she could marry this man; perhaps more would come later – and who knows how long they had to live? Things were bad, very bad.

"Thank you, Tom. That was lovely. I do love being with you too, and yes, thank you. I want to be your wife." She ran her slender fingers through his brown wavy hair and kissed him on the forehead. Judith paused, she felt the surge of conflicting emotions: of pleasure and concern.

"But, well, how are we going to tell our parents? I'm Jewish and you are Catholic. What will your dear parents in Mertoun Place, Edinburgh, have to say to that? They are very nice, but I've only met them once. Will they like me when they find out I'm of Semite origin? What shall I tell my parents? They are tolerant but also practising believers. I couldn't bear to hurt them. Oh, Tom!"

Judith studied Tom's face carefully, ready to weigh and measure his answer.

"You are right; this is important. Now then: true believers are, like both our parents, tolerant. Ergo, in our future extended family, everyone will have to put up with two diverse ways of believing in one God. Apart from that, between you, me, and the gatepost, I think the Jewish religion has got its nose out in front. All that nonsense about the miracles Jesus supposedly performed was just a bit of overdone marketing by the Bible scribes, methinks. Jesus tried to teach us to believe in ourselves and to treat others as we would want to be treated. As Abraham Lincoln put it, we should listen to 'The Better Angels of our Nature'. Perhaps the death of Jesus by crucifixion, which was normally reserved for the lowest of the low, shows us that we can rise up and try to be better people on the ashes of our former selves. So, my private Catholic religion gives me hope and comfort – and to blazes with what the Church bosses think about mixed marriages. We'll do what we bloody well want to!"

"Strike a light, Taoma! You don't fly half throttle, do you, my darling, my beamish boy!" Judith laughed out loud.

Judith danced round Tom with her eyes locked into his, the fingertips of her outstretched arm resting lightly on his shoulder, switching arms and direction as she danced around him, humming lightly a mazel tov melody. Her feet crunching in the snow.

"Tom, you are blushing! Am I embarrassing you?"

"You delight me beyond what I can say. You are my light, my life and my wife-to-be. Come, let us walk back to Wordsworth Close; your father returned yesterday from Birmingham. We will inform them of our wonderful news, then this evening I'll call my parents in Edinburgh on the phone and tell them, too!"

"Oh, Tom!"

Arm in arm, they made their way back along Stowe Pool, and now and then, Judith broke away and conducted her wedding dance, tripping around a beaming Tom. Her head thrown back, laughing, so that passers-by smiled, stopped, and looked fondly on. In turn, Tom moved away and danced a gentle Highland jig around his raven-haired, blue-eyed love. On the horizon, the sun was no longer visible; inky-black storm clouds driven by an icy east wind scudded towards them, whipping the snow off the trees, lending them the appearance of huge black crosses. Judith felt the shuddering cold of premonition. Quivering, she broke off their dancing and linked up with Tom and hurried them on towards home.

***

TWO DAYS LATER, TOM WAS twenty-five thousand feet up in the sky at minus twenty-five degrees Celsius. He glanced down at the two-squadron formation of the new Avro Lancasters; he had never seen such huge planes before. They had a crew of seven and a range of up to 1660 miles and could carry a fourteen-thousand-pound payload of bombs, all meant for the U-boat pens of Dieppe today.

The U-boats were sinking so many cargo ships that Britain was struggling for her life. Destroy the U-boats; win the war. Thirty-two Avros all in all but, even so, he doubted if they could crack the pens' roofs. Hearsay had it that these were made up of about six yards of reinforced concrete. What the heck! Whose idea was this? The Lancasters were bumbling along at about twenty-four thousand feet, their max – or near enough to dammit – average speed 270 miles per hour. *Fast for them, too slow for us Spitfires*, thought Tom.

He impatiently looked around himself yet again. He was flight leader of the Red group at the very front of a finger formation of four, four groups of which made up the fighter squadron of sixteen Spitfires escorting the bombers.

His wingman was AA, Alexsander Abraham, a Polish Jew who had saved his bacon more than once in the past and, on a couple of occasions, Tom, his. Tom and AA flew tight and fought honourably but mercilessly, granting no quarter, and expecting none. Tom had not solved this seemingly moral contradiction; he concluded his thoughts on this matter with 'kill or be killed', which suited his Scottish ferocity nicely and left his mind clear. There wasn't much leeway in the battle of the skies.

The heavens today were clear and so enormously open that he felt he would have preferred to drift on forever in this ocean of cloudless air and space. The late-afternoon winter sun high on his starboard wing. The sea below a silvery-blue of glistening gentle ripples, little waves scurrying towards the snow-covered French coast, creating a restful pattern of harmony. Three small, brave, fishing boats, risking everything to feed England, lay upon the water as if painted there. This peaceful scene jarring with a Royal Navy corvette continuously circling, like an anxious parent watchful for lurking sharks.

Tom felt his chest tighten and he coughed into his mask, forcing down the tight, painful urge to be sick. His chest and lungs still hadn't recovered fully. He inhaled the leather stench of his mask and gagged again. Resisting the temptation to force back his cockpit window and blow out his mind and lungs with the gale-force icy air, he wrenched his mind back immediately and scanned the skies yet again, on the watch for the Butcher Birds, the Focke-Wulf Fw 190-D-9s, which operated out of the airfield near Dieppe, who were notorious for their savagery, even by German military standards. The fact was that the Butcher Birds were faster, heavier-armed, arguably more manoeuvrable, and could fly higher than the Spits. The best way to combat them was through teamwork, which the German pilots also had down pat; they'd been fighting and killing their prey since the Spanish Civil War.

"Here, Squadron Leader Thomas: Butcher Birds at nine o'clock, estimated altitude thirty-five thousand feet, splitting into two groups; one for us and one for the Avros! Red and Blue Flight intercept them directly, Green and Yellow put yourselves between them and the Avros! Go! Keep cool and keep killing!"

"Tough bastard," said Tom.

He saw that the situation was such that the Butcher Birds were attacking from a superior height and had the sun behind them; they had all the advantages. *That's good flying*, thought Tom; using their superior altitude advantage, they had flown above them undetected and wheeled around to come at them from behind and out of the sun.

Tom spoke into his intercom: "Okay, Red-Boys: tactic loop and a roll, get straight at them and keep it tight! On my count... Go!"

The incoming Birds were caught unawares; the tightly, perfectly synchronised action (the product of many hours of rigorous training) allowed the Spitfires to face them straight on. Simultaneously, Tom let loose his canons and Brownings, causing the Spitfire to shudder and rock and roll, whilst keeping his steely sight on the 190F roaring straight at him until it disintegrated before his eyes. Tilting slightly to his left, he caught the 190's wingman with a short burst, followed by a long one so that the 190's engine literally blew up. The German pilot struggled to slide his canopy back in order to bail out. Tom was forced downwards to avoid his first opponent's blazing plane, all this happening at 370 miles per hour with his Merlin engine screaming and rattling in protest. His downwards glance showed a huge Avro Lancaster being viciously attacked by two Butcher

Birds. The tail segment of the Avro suddenly came adrift from the rest of the fuselage, taking the trapped rear tail gunner with it in a slow-moving downwards spiral; the other crew members were bailing out. Simultaneously, one Butcher was firing at and killing the hapless men as they drifted down in their parachutes. Tom felt the fire of his Scottish blood inflame his senses. He flipped his plane over and came up under the killer Focke-Wulf, firing until his opponent's port wing abruptly sheared off, sending the fighter down in a violent spin. Flying debris was smashing into his screen and simultaneously he felt the deadly thuds and hammer-like thumps of being on the receiving end of canon fire ripping into his plane. It came from his starboard side. *Nothing any good comes from the right*, thought Tom in a flash of nonsense. His Spit was going down! He had to bail out!

Now they were nearing the French coast, he had a chance. Tom clambered and balanced, ready to jump out of his coughing and snorting, dying plane. His last conscious moment was of raging pain and his mother's face, as a long, hard burst of canon fire forced his wretched body to weirdly dance like a rag doll suspended in mid-air and then fall – tumbling ever so slowly head over foot, down, down, down into the deep blue sea.

Alexsander Abraham, Tom's wingman, was onto Tom's Butcher just a microsecond too late. Tom's furious twisting and turning in the melee of fighters was impossible to follow closely enough. AA's line of tracer-bullets stitched along the length of Tom's killer, and smoke belched out of the German's engine; nevertheless, the pilot skilfully eased his plane down towards the fields of France – almost colliding with a monstrous, sinking Lancaster of fire and red, on its way down billowing flames as crew members tried to jump out – they and their parachutes likewise ablaze. Dante's *Inferno* flashed into Alexsander Abraham's mind, and then he thought of death, but not his. Alexsander Abraham followed his twisting and turning enemy down, firing intermittently, trying to finish off his target whilst making sure he stayed down. Alexsander Abraham was not acting rationally; actually, he was disobeying orders. He should be up there fighting, protecting the crews of the Avro Lancasters and ensuring the success of the mission. Alexsander Abraham's mind turned again to the enemy whose plane was suddenly landing safely in a field after executing an extremely steep and final descent in another direction. The German pilot had jumped out, and he turned, laughed, and waved at Alexsander Abraham. He made a run for the nearby trees. AA realised he was over-shooting. The German thought he was safe. He could think again! AA pulled off the tightest loop he had ever managed until then and since, shook his head violently clear, lined the enemy pilot up in his cross hairs just before he reached the trees and watched as the tracers sped towards him, causing a long line of little big puffs of exploding earth and snow until they reached the killer and ripped him open from crotch to head.

"An eye for an eye, a tooth for a tooth," murmured Alexsander Abraham to himself.

The shock waves of the exploding Lancaster, as it hit the ground, bounced his plane around like a little boat in a stormy sea; the smell of kerosene and burning materials caused him to retch and cough. On this lovely winter, sunshiny day, with a sea of azure blue below, Alexsander

Abraham turned and climbed back up into the raging battle, passing downy chutes of warriors floating towards the white fields of France. The taste of blood between his teeth, his iron eyes fixed to kill or be killed.

4

11TH NOVEMBER 1942 –
HINRICH RICHTER

HINRICH RICHTER WAS SITTING OUTSIDE the Five Seasons, enjoying the sun whilst smoking a Gitane and thinking about Ida. What a beauty! Perhaps not the brightest lamp in France; at Chez Philippe, she had listened attentively to him talking about the things only he knew, and she had asked simple, naïve questions. He could tell that she was in awe of him. *Wait until she finds out who I really am*, he mused happily, salivating. He was going to enjoy fucking her, in all three holes. In the dungeon. In the castle on the torturing table. Nobody would know apart from Frank, and when he, Hinrich Richter, was slaked, he would let him have a little poke or two afterwards. Just to keep him quiet. She would comply; they all did, and they kept quiet afterwards.

Fear was such a fine psychological instrument. He was proud of his intellectual prowess; only recently, his father, who was in the SS at Dachau working for Obergruppenführer Theodor Eicke in tandem with Obergruppenführer Pohl, had asked him for a complete economic analysis of the net worth of a Jew whilst alive and when dead. Lovely money! Jews always meant money. *We rob them, burn them and even sell their ashes.*

But first, he was also going to fuck her in the torture chamber and, at the start, put that long-bladed steel dagger of his just a little bit in her cunt just to show who was boss. The employment of cold steel in battle, ha!

Beautiful Ida reminded him of that lovely Jewess Judith Lareine, which reminded him yet again of the beating Matthias Krieger had handed out to him at the lakeside end-of-school celebration in Friedrichshafen back in '38. His mother had given him hell for coming home beaten and bloody.

"You let yourself get beaten by the son of a local small-time farmer who is in your class! You are a head taller than him, and all because of a filthy English Jewess! You, like your father here who works only as an accounting assistant and plays soldiers in his stupid SS playgroup, are truly a pathetic creature! Go to your room and stay there. No supper tonight! What am I going to say to the other women at the Ladies' Protestant Church Society? Why do I have to bear this cross of indignity?! *Why?* You stupid fools, go, get out of my sight, the both of you!"

For this reason, too, Hinrich had not forgotten the humiliation he had suffered by the lakeside all because of this little English Jewess. After Germany had won the war, he would pay her a visit; he knew where she lived, Wordsworth Close, Lichfield, England. The same applied to the little farmer boy in Eriskirch, back home on the lake. "Matthias Krieger," he said to himself out loud, "too bad for you if you survive the war; you will not survive me."

Contemplating his revenge and savouring the sight of beautiful, wholesome Ida walking towards him, Hinrich was getting a hard-on already. Just thinking how he was going to take out his rage and revenge on Ida caused his blood to flow all in one direction: away from his brain. He watched her approach along the quayside; by God, what a woman, and how she moved, and she was smiling! So she should.

He straightened his perfectly aligned tie, then the ashtray, and aligned this with his cup of coffee and then moved an empty cognac glass to the edge of the table. He sat upright, put his shoulders back and crossed his long legs nonchalantly. He looked at her again, looking glorious in the sunshine, wind in her hair. He tilted his head ever so slightly so it would catch the sun and show his fine profile.

Yolande Acier, otherwise known to a certain German as 'Ida', was walking along the harbour front with the gulls crying to her left and the fishing boats rocking gently at their berths just beneath her, the fishermen mending their nets sitting, smoking, and the murmur of their conversation occasionally drifting up to her in the late-afternoon Sunday sun. The birds were wheeling and diving down at silver shadows off the point of Roscanvel. They glided, twisted, and screeched in the orange sunlight as they plummeted down to capture their prey. A wind ripple along the water generated rows of small waves and the silver shadows were gone, with the gulls screeching outrageously at their loss.

This was the town of Brest she loved, with the warm late-autumn sun shining on her auburn hair. As she walked, she seemed to sway gently in harmony with the sea breeze coming in from the west; her slightly loose-fitting mauve dress swayed along with her and her long, flowing, auburn hair. The men passing by nearly always looked again, admiring the brown legs, the slight outline of her fine thighs, her full red lips, and the very fine cheekbones. No make-up, but long sleeves and lace gloves to hide her working hands and her muscular arms.

She was on her way to meet the most handsome, brown-eyed man she had ever met. He was tall and broad-shouldered with an athlete's figure, lovely dark-blond wavy hair, and the most beautiful nose she had ever seen on a man who could also move with such grace and elegance.

He spoke excellent French. Germans learning French reminded her of the German family who had stayed with them one summer holiday as workers in the vineyard. They were polite and amiable, and their twelve-year-old son was the same age as she. He caught her attention through his love of nature and the countryside; what that short-trousered boy didn't know about flowers and trees, birds, and insects! He described and named them to her, haltingly asking all the while for their various names in French, which she didn't always know. In the evening, he would sketch some of the birds and flowers they had seen during the day, and she helped him name them correctly in French and German with the help of a big dictionary the family had brought with them. During this activity, outside on the porch, his mother would usually sew, and his father often read a book and smoked his pipe. They were polite, but rather stiff, she thought, friendly in their own way.

One afternoon, Gerd was standing in the shade beneath a chestnut tree. He looked so calm and tranquil that she stole up to him and kissed his cheek. He immediately turned bright red with pleasure and instead of kissing her back as she had hoped, he knelt down before her, knees next to his ears, to show her a pretty little flower neither of them had ever seen before.

"Look," he said, "it is lovely like you."

Smiling at the memory, she continued her walk.

As she looked up, she saw the Château de Brest, the old fort where the Germans and, even worse, the Gestapo had their headquarters. Yolande felt a wave of chilling doubt pass through her, for she had seen that lusting glint in his eyes and realised he was not the type to give up easily – was used to getting what he wanted. Should she, could she, go through with this? Even if she didn't keep this date, he would probably come looking for her. Normally she would have been flattered, for they would have made a fine pair. But for the fact that she thought Hinrich Richter was as vile as he was dangerous. He was Gestapo. He was filth. This she had felt more than ascertained through any particular facet of his behaviour or what he had said last Friday night when he had moved in on her at Chez Philippe – the popular bar on the town square. The cold, calculating, arrogance at the back of his charming patter.

The damned thing was that she had just spoken to her Resistance comrade, Catherine, at the bar, giving her the okay for the evacuation of the two British airmen or, better, one rosbif and a Pole they called AA. They were to be picked up by a British submarine tonight, Sunday, off Camaret-sur-Mer at 7.15pm. Meet 6.30pm. Quai de l'Est. Although dark at this time, even so, this would be risky. Why this change in procedure? More she did not know and didn't want to know.

To help, Rosa, their commander, had ordered that the French ladies who worked in the German soldiers' canteen should spread the rumour of a TB outbreak that was spreading rapidly throughout the city. Tuberculosis! The Germans were even more health-conscious than the French, so that should dampen their enthusiasm, she thought.

At the bar, Catherine had just bought some cigarettes as Yolande was ordering her drink and they had half turned and casually greeted each other, Yolande saying, "Change of plan: 6.30pm, Quai de l'Est."

Catherine raised her left eyebrow and then wandered off to talk to some people near the exit.

That was it.

Turning back, she looked up at the big mirror behind the bar, through the noise, the smoke and the laughing, and identified the Gestapo man looking straight at her. Instead of automatically looking away in fear, she smiled at him, and he grinned back. She then faced the room and him and raised her glass and smiled again, this time a shade more primly. It worked. This beautiful, dangerous man walked up to her, gliding past the smokers and drinkers as if he were on a dance floor.

And now she had a date with him at the Five Seasons café on the harbour front. What she didn't do for France! The land she loved. All that secret training with the Resistance from endless self-defence to first aid – and now this!

She had given Hinrich a false first name – 'Ida'. No more – even that was risky, but he seemed genuinely attracted to her as a woman and not as a suspect. She wanted to keep it that way, string him out, give him titbits of herself here and there and milk him for information.

What about sex? She would cross that bridge when she came to it.

Merde! What she didn't do for France! *Merde!*

Also, there was some protection in the fact that messing about with French women was very much frowned upon by the Kriminalrat, the head of the Gestapo in the port of Brest. Nobody wanted a posting to the Russian Front away from sleepy, trouble-free Brest.

Yolande didn't come into town much; she preferred to stay on the family vineyard and keep her head down. Moreover, she knew her beauty made her interesting, so she made herself scarce and when in town, toned her appearance very much down by wearing a headscarf, trousers, and old boots, like many of the other farm women on market day. Giving her shoulders a slight stoop gave that often-seen impression of beaten-down passivity. But not today.

She focused her very sharp brain; she was almost at the café putting her shoulders back and her fine breasts forth – in this manner she was armed and ready to fight for her country.

"What a dick!" exclaimed Yolande to the pavement and looked up and gave Hinrich her most radiant smile. "So nice to see you again, Hinrich; you cut such a fine figure of a man here before the café."

"Yes, of course, Ida, you too are looking most lovely today. Please sit down. What would you like to drink?"

"If you don't mind, a small glass of red wine."

"Naturally, you may have one. Waiter!" Hinrich called, snapping his fingers imperiously. The waiter came immediately, rubbing his hands anxiously, knowing full well who he was dealing with.

"A small glass of wine, red, for the lady, and another double cognac for me. No staring at us! You may go." He swivelled back to Yolande. "And I have a small gift for you, Ida; it is nothing really."

"How thoughtful you are, Hinrich," said Yolande, unwrapping the small, carefully wrapped package, which contained a bar of expensive Swiss chocolate. "And generous as well."

"You exaggerate, my dear; exquisite chocolate for a profoundly beautiful lady! As William Shakespeare put it: 'Beauty itself doth of itself persuade the eyes of men without an orator.' From his work *The Rape of Lucrece*. I find that most apt, this title," said Hinrich, downing his double cognac, which had been quickly delivered by the frightened waiter. "Yes, my eyes are persuaded well enough," said Hinrich, staring fixedly at Yolande's fine décolletage. "My dear, delightful Ida, let us take a stroll up to the château; as you know, I do some work there when I am not entertaining lovely women."

"Oh, I bet you say that to all the girls, Hinrich. How come you know your English literature so well?" replied Yolande, her stomach turning, the wine making her head feel light and cloudy. She suddenly felt cold.

"Oh, I had supplementary tutorial lessons with a pretty little English Jewess back in Friedrichshafen. Unfortunately, she later caused me a lot of trouble. That was one score I have not been able to settle. But who knows what the future may bring us both, Ida?"

Yolande tried to suppress a shiver as she made to look around, observing everyday life continuing on a Sunday afternoon in Brest. Couples out walking, the occasional cyclist puffing past, and out in the bay she could see two little sailing boats fluttering in the wind. The crying of the gulls now seemed like a harsh warning. As she shivered again, she felt Hinrich's pleasure in the power he had over her to generate this sort of abject behaviour. Time to act.

"My dear Ida, the air is cooling rapidly, and it is already approaching evening. Come, finish your wine and take my arm and we will walk briskly to the château. I absolutely insist."

"Yes, of course, allow me to put on my headscarf," she said firmly, taking inward control of herself. Scarf on, head down.

As she arose, she reached out and touched the chequered tablecloth with her gloved fingertips; she felt she had to say goodbye to the life she had known until now. She sensed, with dread, nothing would be the same after this meeting.

"Let's go." She linked her arm under Hinrich's, and they set off at a brisk pace.

The Château de Brest was a few hundred metres further along the waterfront, and they walked in silence, both sensing that the framework of their connection had shifted from one of casual conversation to one of purpose.

Yolande suddenly realised that Hinrich was straining forwards like a dog on a leash that had picked up the scent of something to be had and devoured. He suddenly slowed the pace and said: "I will show you my place of work, and afterwards, we can dine at Louis's, if you would care to, *chère* Ida."

"That would be nice," replied Yolande brightly as she felt a surge of hope expel her dark thoughts. Almost immediately she was plunged back into fear. She knew: this man was dangerous, Gestapo dangerous.

They turned into the keep of the château. To the right was a small office guarding the entrance. Hinrich waved his hand, keeping Yolande on his blind side so that the sentries in the office couldn't see who he had with him.

"He's at it again, the dirty devil. I wouldn't mind a bit of that myself," said the one sentry to his fellow guard.

"Yeah, you should be so lucky. Regarding Kriminalkommissar Richter: keep your head down and your mouth shut!"

Crossing the courtyard, Hinrich led the way to a wide stone stairway down into the gloom.

"My place of work is in the dungeon; fear not, I have thoroughly modernised everything." His voice echoed around again and again. Down into the foreboding darkness they went. She winced as Hinrich tightened his grip on her arm and called out to Frank, who was at his desk in a small office to the left of a massive oaken door.

"You can come in later, Frank, when I've – pardon – we have finished."

"*Jawohl*, Herr Kriminalkommissar Richter!" replied Frank enthusiastically.

Yolande couldn't see Frank's face, but she could sense him judging her figure. She was filled with a moment of dread realisation: she was going to be raped, probably repeatedly.

"After you, Ida."

Hinrich half snorted with laughter, and she felt the not-so-gentle shove that caused her to stumble down the stone steps into the chamber. She gave out a gasp. High up on the stone walls opposite were chains and manacles, and leading down from them were dark-red and black streaks, which cried out to her in the silence of this terrible cavern with its rounded vault of black rock. The air was damp and clammy. She shivered and felt herself starting to tremble throughout her whole body, which she forced herself to stop. At the far end of the room was a desk with a table lamp, a telephone, and a chair, behind which stood two filing cabinets. About three metres before her was a slab of stone mounted on a plinth, along the edges of which were two runnels to run off the blood that stained this tableau and was caught in two buckets on either side of the table. At the head of the table was a tray with evil-looking instruments that could be used for only one thing: to cause pain. Behind this, in the back wall, was a fire in which two pokers were fixed by iron holders, ready for use.

Yolande heard herself shriek in fear. She turned instinctively to get out of the room and was confronted with a long, wicked-looking stiletto that was pointed straight at her throat.

"If you try to resist in any way whatsoever, no matter how small, I will cut off your left breast and feed it to my dog. Do you understand, Ida? If you behave yourself, I will let you live, and I may even invite you out on a date again." Hinrich was laughing and grunting with delight as he continued: "Now get on the table and spread your legs, you dirty little French bitch!"

The insult clicked in Yolande's three-step Resistance training. Yves had insulted her time and again to toughen her up and endlessly repeated his mantra: "First: if captured, they will try to make you small. Stay focused and look for a way out. Second: use whatever is in the room to make this possible. Make a weapon of anything at hand from a book to a chair – anything. Third: strike in order to disable, preferably to kill." This they had practised time and again. She still had the bruises to prove it.

She forced herself to switch mentally from defensive to offensive modus, and although she felt an inner dichotomy of emotion, a part of her wanted to give in to this awful pressure – against this struggled her urge to strike back, thankfully supplemented by her rigorous training. She focused on this.

Until now, she had played the part of a slightly simple country girl. She sensed Hinrich was sure of this; he was also overconfident (he was also soft). A drastic mistake in war. Frank had been told to wait outside, which was good.

With the knife to her back, she stepped over to the blood-stained stone table and as she stepped up to swing her leg over it, she felt a vice-like grip on her crotch with a hard thumb pressing against her anus. She twisted around and lay down on the stone surface, thus freeing herself and obeying at the same time.

"Very clever," said Hinrich. "Now spread your legs, bitch."

This she did. Hinrich took the stiletto dagger and moved it slowly up between her legs, rubbing her breast with his free hand as he did so. She felt the sting of it at the tip of her vagina. Hinrich left the dagger there whilst he dropped his trousers.

"Open your mouth, French whore! Now suck this!" This she did, taking his swollen penis into her mouth and sucking hard as she did so.

"Ah, you know what's good for you, Ida," he groaned, holding her head with both hands. As he moved to put his free hand back on the dagger, Yolande instantaneously punched his arm away and bit down viciously again and again, twisting on her side as she did so until she was forced to let go by the rain of punches Hinrich was hammering down on her face.

Hinrich screamed and desperately tried to stem the flow of blood, looked down and vomited and soiled himself all at the same time. Frank, who had been waiting impatiently outside the slightly open door for his turn, came rushing in, saw Hinrich on the floor clutching his groin, strode over to Yolande and bent down and screamed in her face: "I'll make you pay for this!"

Yolande spat out the rest of Hinrich's blood in his face, reached between her legs and rammed the dagger into his fat Gestapo neck. She instantly felt his hot blood on her right hand. Frank turned, looked at her in disbelief, sank to his knees and bled all the more.

Yolande sprang down from the table, skittering and sliding across the bloody, filthy cobbles between the two men, and grabbed her bag, which was by the door. Stumbling up the three stone steps and through the open door, she managed to stop shaking and quivering so as to take the headscarf out of her handbag but fumbled as the shakes returned, trying to tie a knot under her chin. All the while, Hinrich's screams were echoing around the stone corridor, which led up to the courtyard and the guards at the entrance.

"God, God, please let me tie this knot. I must not be seen!" She repeated this time and again until, at last, the knot was tied. Hinrich's screams had subsided to a murmur. She stopped and held her breath; from above, silence, no movement. She tried to wipe the blood off her face with a small handkerchief, with little success.

She said to herself: "It's dark outside; keep moving, keep

moving. They'll be used to women coming up from the dungeon scared out of their wits, no need to act that part."

Reaching the courtyard, she immediately took in the beautiful sea air and breathed out long and slowly. She walked quickly across the seemingly vast space of the castle forecourt. To her right was a set of double doors that led to the main part of the castle itself. She finally reached the exit where the two guards now stood. She walked straight past them saying '*Bon nuit*' in a shaky voice she didn't need to put on.

The two SS guards replied in unison: "*Bon nuit*, ducky, that was a quickie; well fucked yet again!"

They both laughed uproariously and lit up their cigarettes, half choking whilst stamping at their humour and the ridiculousness of the situation.

"What to do? Where to go?" Then 'meet 6.30pm, Quai de l'Est' popped into her consciousness and she automatically turned to the right and was gone.

Striving desperately to think clearly, she wondered what time it was. She reckoned it was a forty-minute walk to Quai de l'Est, which was in more of a commercial area. What was a damn fishing boat doing there to smuggle out two British airmen? This whole thing was a mess!

Under a street lamp, she checked her watch; 5.45pm. She now realised she had to get out of France and onto that British submarine. If she didn't, the Gestapo would eventually find her and her family, which meant certain death for all.

She hurried on and on. She could almost hear her pounding heart. She wanted to cry so badly. At the Jardin de l'Académie de Marine, she stopped at the fountain pool and washed her mouth out. Gurgling and spitting out the vileness loudly and repeatedly, she washed her face and wiped her hand on her soiled and blood-stained dress.

In the half-light, she saw blood inside the battered stocking of her right leg. She felt darkness flow up from the ground and began to lose her balance. She desperately wanted to lie down on the ground. The sea breeze of the evening was refreshing and comforting; her Brest, her France! She sank to her knees and was about to lay herself down on the grass when fear jolted her back to reality.

"Keep going, you little fool. Do you want to die? Dear God, please give me the strength to save the lives of my family and, if it pleases you, my own too." She forced herself to her feet and staggered onwards, her right foot squelching with the blood in her stocking.

Coming out of the Jardin de l'Académie, she passed an old man taking his dog for a walk along the quayside. He took a quick look at her, saw her desperate plight, and raised his hat. She bustled onwards. Otherwise, there was nobody about; everyone was having their evening Sunday meal, particularly the Germans, always at 6.30pm. Apart from that, who wanted to go out and contract TB?

All of a sudden, she heard the wail of a siren and the roar of heavy vehicles. She pressed herself against a tree and watched as the fire engine rushed past followed by two troop carriers. To the south of the city, she saw the red glow of fire – coincidence or planning? She wouldn't put it past Rosa to plan some diversionary tactic like this. But she didn't know. Still, the fewer Germans around this part of town, the better.

What time was it? She looked at her watch; she could just make out the dial: 6.20pm! Suddenly, she felt hot tears running down her face and began to run. She wanted to take off her high-heeled shoes but was afraid of leaving a bloody footprint trail to the boat. Both of her sides began to hurt, and she felt the bruises on her face where Hinrich had pummelled her to force her to release him from her mouth.

As she staggered down the last fifty metres towards the fishing boat, the wall next to her seemed to move in and out, and the ground beneath her feet was starting to give way. Yves was there. The two strangers behind him were probably the airmen. In the background, the boat's engine was grumbling quietly.

Yves said harshly, "What the devil are you doing here?"

"I was tortured by the Gestapo; they know absolutely nothing about us. The men were after sex only. I think I killed them both. My escape hasn't been realised yet."

The skinny but tough-looking man behind Yves said nothing but came towards her as she felt herself give way ever so gently. He caught her in his arms just as she was falling. Yolande felt everything turn grey, then absolutely black.

He surprised her awake by speaking French.

"You are safe now. Yes, I speak French. I am from Lublin."

She heard Yves say: "They know alright. The risk is too great for the mission; you stay here, and we will hide you," said Yves roughly.

Yolande glanced up at the other airman, who lit a match over her.

Alexsander Abraham realised that she was losing blood and began ripping off Yolande's bloody stocking and stemming the blood from the knife wound on her right thigh. He took off his jacket, pullover, and shirt, then, taking his shirt and a penknife from his trouser pocket he calmly cut off the right sleeve and then the left. He first formed a pad then bound it tightly around her wound, taking great care not to touch the intimate parts of her body.

"She fought for us too; she comes with us too," he said.

"No!" retorted Yves angrily. "I tell you it is too risky, and there is no room on the submarine."

"Well, they'll have to make room. Either she comes with me and John, or I stay here! You should know I have shot down twenty-four German fighters and bombers. I am of value. Do you want to deprive us all of this value? Apart from that, how are you going to move her from here? Do you want to drag her through the streets?"

"Damn! Look, the fishing boat is ready to cast off! Get going! I'll inform her family," replied Yves over his shoulder as he moved away.

AA knelt down again, brushed back the bloody hair from Yolande's brow and grazed her forehead with his lips. She felt herself being gathered carefully up, and, swaying slightly, they moved together with John towards the boat.

"And take good care of her; she is magnifique!"

***

IT HAD BEEN TWELVE WEEKS since Ida had almost bitten his dick off. Hinrich had been lucky. In his 'office', he had been able to crawl to the telephone on his desk and call for help. The first two weeks were pain, pain, pain. The second two weeks he had been depressed – he had been defeated and de-manned. Since then, he couldn't give a fuck. He was alive and Frank was dead. He had been lucky. In future, no more risk!

The 'Higher Ups' had organised a specialist urologist surgeon to operate on him so at least he could now piss standing up, but perhaps he would never be able to fuck a girl again – too bad, but he never really liked them anyway. He liked power, money, and adulation much better.

For some reason he could not quite divine, his anger at his recent defeat was directed more at the English girl, Judith Lareine, than Ida. His wounding at her hands had been in battle, so to speak, and he actually halfway admired her for putting up such a courageous fight. But to be humiliated at the lakeside in front of his class – even if it was four years ago – still nagged. And as the best academic scholar in the class – almost – to be beaten by the little Jewess who had pipped him at the post was simply intolerable! And to be handed out a thrashing by a stumpy little famer's boy was more than he could abide, for the simple reason that he would never be able to admit to himself he had been in love with Judith Lareine. Not only was she stunningly beautiful, as was his mother, but also, unlike his mother, she was gentle and kind, tolerant and wise, with a lilting laugh and a sense of humour that was foreign to him but forced him to hoot despite himself.

She had rejected him; she had been the cause of his humiliation and she, together with little farmer boy Matthias Krieger, would pay and pay in blood as he had done just now. That was why he was in this damned hospital. *They will pay! I know where they live!* thought Hinrich. He seethed silently, momentarily forgetting his discomfort. Looking at the mirror on the far side of the room, he shouted: "I will have my revenge, no matter what!"

Although his commanding officer had bought his story of an interrogation gone wrong and thus keeping a lid on the whole affair, he had made sure that Hinrich was transferred to a private hospital in Rennes. He also knew that Hinrich had influence; his father was on good terms with SS-Obergruppenführer Eicke, a man he wanted no trouble from. The SS hated the Gestapo and vice versa.

The 'Higher Ups' had also made it absolutely clear that he was to leave the Gestapo. Which was fine with him; everybody was laughing at him behind his back and calling him Little-Bit-Dick – very bloody funny! He had been shamed! To hell with these civil servant arseholes! He had written to his father asking for a post together with him at Dachau in the SS. At first, he had considered signing on with Oskar Dirlewanger and his SS henchmen, whose ruthless perverseness he found rather attractive. Unfortunately, Dirlewanger also did some actual fighting and had been wounded a number of times. So, he, Hinrich Richter, had been hurt enough already fighting for his country. He would work with Daddy.

That was the place to be – Dachau! Together with Obergruppenführer Pohl, his father had been planning and realising – with the statistics he, Hinrich Richter, had provided – the extension and replication of the concentration camp based on the Dachau model in the east, specialising mainly, but not only, in Jews. Nobody lived out there apart from a few peasants and no one there gave a fuck anyway about how many Jews were murdered.

The beauty of it was the economic aspect, after the deduction of all costs and estimating an average life of nine months per prisoner, there remained a median profit of 1630 Reichsmarks. Not only that, one camp or another could make even more money out of the bones and ashes –

depending on how efficiently they worked. *Bones were ground up for fertiliser and marketed to German agriculturalists.*

Daddy had certainly moved up in the world; he was now a colonel in the SS! Back home, his mummy was delighted and never spared a moment to make sure everyone knew about his meteoric rise in society. They were planning to move to Berlin – in the Tiergartenstrasse, no less. Just as satisfying, his father had begun to collect beautiful artworks of great value, confiscated from Jewish families, of course. Hinrich preferred Goya's works, particularly the series *The Disasters of War* – with their intense depictions of torture and savagery. He also realised that Pablo Picasso, so despised by the Nazis, was the most valuable artist of the era. *Collect these paintings from rich Jews!* This should be possible; he was certain to make the grade of at least first Leutnant. After all, let's be honest, he surmised further: the SS was made up of the dregs of society – most of them had been no-goods before the war, had absolutely no manners nor social *savoir faire*, and they were anxious to please nasty perverts. The dregs of society.

He should go far, and he had something to look forward to after the war had been won. *There is more than one way to skin a cat*, he surmised happily.

5

28TH APRIL 1944 – MR AND MRS LAREINE

THE BLACKBIRD STOPPED, PICKED, AND pecked, nodding away between the blades of emerald-green grass on the path between the rows of potatoes, which were coming along nicely. So green thanks to the rain this morning and the hot June sun this afternoon. He hopped further along and plucked and pulled again at the base of a potato plant whose leaves were starting to wither. He really was suitably named; what a lovely black coat he had with that startling yellow beak, almost orange, with ringed eyes of the same colour – and what a peaceful, gentle little manner. *Off he goes!* With a single movement, the bird stretched his wings and was gone.

The flowers she had planted between the potatoes and runner beans, the lettuces, and tomatoes (if she was lucky), seemed to be reaching up to the sun, which had sent the bees filling the air with humming and a rising fragrance that washed over her and through the kitchen door and into the house.

The vegetable gardens at the front and back of the house were important, very important, but no longer so very desperately so. The tide had turned. The Battle of the Atlantic, as Churchill termed it, seemed to have turned in favour of Britain. Herbert said that the Americans were building more supply ships faster than the Nazis could sink them and the Royal Navy was sinking more U-boats faster than the enemy could replace them. The invasion of France could be any day now; that meant a lot of young men were going to die.

"May God be with them," murmured Rachel Lareine to herself.

Rachel Lareine noticed the difference in the shops: she could now, occasionally, buy the items she wanted with her ration card. They were not going to starve. Food! What was she going to give her guests tomorrow afternoon? They would have to speak German, of course; their English was too broken to enable easy conversation. On the other hand, Yolande didn't speak any German at all and was very uncomfortable at the mention of the language or in the company of the people who spoke it.

The poor dear had gone through a terrible ordeal at the hands of the Gestapo in Brest. Alexsander had looked after her since. How he had managed to keep in touch with her after she arrived in England on the submarine was anybody's guess. Then he asked Herbert and her if they would let Yolande live with them as an official refugee. He was a decorated warrior, dealing with the authorities. How could they refuse? They had room enough, so they approved. Herbert had exerted his influence too.

Strange how Yolande kept Alexsander at a distance, even though it was plain to the onlooker that she was attracted to him. They had arrived at the Lareines' front door one Monday afternoon, both of them tired out.

The moment Judith saw Yolande on the doorstep, she embraced her, and they both burst into tears. Yolande's face was then still an awful sight. Gawky Alexsander, standing in the background, not knowing what to do with himself; it was seeing him again, the bearer of ill tidings of Tom's death two years ago, and poor Yolande's broken face and nose, that had hit Judith so hard.

Tom's death. Alexsander had been very brave. He had come round to the house, had sat in the living room with them and told them that Tom had been killed in action whilst fighting to save his comrades' lives. Judith stood up, went over to Alexsander and kissed him on the cheek and then ran out of the room.

Rachel saw her the next day at dinnertime. She ate nothing at all and obviously had not slept and then her beautiful, pale, gentle, kind daughter said: "Mother, Father, I shall never marry, ever!"

"This bloody, bloody war!" cursed Rachel loudly. At this, the sparrows in the garden rose as one and sped away.

Nevertheless, she had devised a plan together with a reluctant Judith: work and art. She had encouraged Judith to fulfil her wish to become a qualified nurse specialising in burns. That meant a lot of hard, exhausting (both physically and mentally) shift work. Furthermore, Judith had, thankfully, continued painting, so she took her shopping for some very fine paint colours and other materials at a specialist art shop in Birmingham. Judith's work was becoming better all the time. She seemed to be truly inspired by the work of Gabriele Münter. Her paintings of Lake Constance, the

Swiss mountains and the quaint harbours and the people there were wonderful – abstract but approachable, strong yet delicate, exquisite even.

Yolande. When she came to them, she was so disturbed that she would hardly speak, although she, Herbert and Judith spoke French quite well – in fact, Judith was most fluent in the language. Physically, Yolande would remain disfigured for the rest of her life. Her left cheekbone had been broken in the fight with the Gestapo. Such a beautiful face! How could they want to humiliate and destroy such loveliness?

Rachel had read about the successful treatment of shell-shocked soldiers after the First World War. Louisa Pesel, head of the Winchester Cathedral Broderers, had let them work on embroidering and sewing cushions, and the results had been most gratifying. The men tended to become calmer and steadier – such was the soothing effect of having to work minutely and creatively with their hands. So she suggested to Yolande that they sew and embroider together a picture or emblem of their homes. Rachel did one of her vegetable gardens, Yolande of vines growing in their vineyard near Brest.

In the morning, they would work in the vegetable garden together. Yolande came from a farming family, so that was a plus. She was responsible for the veggies in the front garden up to halfway around the side of the house, and Rachel for the other half around to the back garden. They would confer together on various points of procedure, if necessary. In the afternoon they would embroider, she in the front room and Yolande in her bedroom.

The result was most heartening and, gradually, Yolande began to talk to them more and more about her home, her parents and her brothers. Less so about her work with and for the Resistance.

Apart from that, Rachel ensured, gradually but firmly, that they transferred from speaking French to English, with Yolande making good progress.

Most encouragingly, she had formed what seemed to be a strong and deep friendship with Judith. Her English was now so good that she was working as an auxiliary nurse at the hospital with Judith, who was now fully qualified.

On the other hand, although her eyes moistened whenever Alexsander appeared, she kept him at a distance and was even curt, if not sharp, with him. Alexsander bore this patiently and, as always, was quite attentive in caring for her needs, making them all laugh with his quaint English and even quainter French! He was still flying dangerous missions; just of late, night missions escorting the bombers over Germany. He was flying Mosquitos. Rachel suspected that Yolande didn't want to go through what Judith had been through and, after two years, to a certain extent, was still enduring the nightmare of the SS torture chamber.

The blackbird was back again, looking so lovely in his shiny black coat and handsome beak, hopping along, stopping, looking quickly and carefully around before he pecked at something on the ground. The humming of the bees seemed louder than before, as did the singing of the birds in the bushes.

From a distance, she heard the high lilt of children's voices playing and the clack of bat hitting ball. She sighed, lit a cigarette, and leant against the kitchen doorway gazing, thinking, her elegant, shapely frame silhouetted against the light.

"I have some apples left over, so I'll make an apple cake. Germans like cake and coffee in the afternoon. I can ask Mary next door if she can lend me some flour and eggs to supplement what I have, and we do have some coffee beans left over; that should do the trick. If they stay longer, it's egg and cress sandwiches with a cup of tea for us all."

THREE HOURS LATER, RACHEL LAREINE, together with her husband Herbert, was listening intently to one of their guests, Herr Morgenthaler. She was impressed with the intensity with which he spoke.

"I was on the Underground heading for Alexanderplatz, Berlin when I felt the need to sneeze. I dived into my pocket for my handkerchief and with it I jerked out the yellow Star of David, which, as you all know, by law we had to always wear when in public.

"It fell at the feet of a most imposing German army officer. The penalty for Jews not wearing the yellow star ranges, as you may or may not know, Herr and Frau Lareine, from a very heavy fine to torture and/or death.

"There were many onlookers, and the atmosphere changed from disinterested commuter boredom to one of electrifying intensity; everybody stared at the sternly erect army officer. The carriage seemed to rock louder and louder. My brow erupted in beads of sweat, and I was hot and very, very bothered.

"The officer picked it up, bowed in my direction and said, with a broad smile, 'I think this belongs to you.'

"I always remember hearing a child's voice asking: 'Mama, why is the soldier giving out yellow stars? I want one too.'

"Everyone in this circle of onlookers smiled and

laughed; still, I got out at the next stop, even though it wasn't Alexanderplatz."

"That was a most unusual occurrence, Herr Morgenthaler!" exclaimed Professor Herbert Lareine. Herbert was a big man measuring 1.90 metres, broad-shouldered, wearing glasses with thick lenses. He was, as host and through his strong, gentle, personality, the natural leader of this modest, intimate group.

They were sitting in the lounge of the Lareines' house, Rachel, with her husband, Herbert, in the armchairs on either side of the unlit fire. Their guests, Herr and Frau Morgenthaler and young Siggi Bernstein, sat on the big sofa opposite the fire. Everyone had a small drinks table before them, with their coffee and empty cake plates on it.

Rachel noticed that Herr Morgenthaler's business suit was frayed but still wearable. On his head, a kippah. Next to him, his wife, Sura, in a simple dark-blue dress complemented by a headband of the same colour. They were both in their forties. Herr Morgenthaler nodded his head slowly at the memory of the incident he had just related. His wife smiled tightly and clutched her hands together, leaning forwards slightly.

"We lost nearly everything," she said quietly. "Our car, our beautiful house, our freedom – our money and jewels we managed to hide early on. We even had to give up our pets – by law! And we don't quite know when we will be reunited with our two children. They came over in 1938 with the Kindertransport. We live in a very small room now, and they in a camp."

"We have our lives, Sura, we have our lives. We used everything to arrive in this country, and we can visit the children and shall reunite with them soon. Let me continue telling them, Sura, about our people back home in Germany and how we got to England." Herr Morgenthaler continued: "As I was hastening along the platform towards the stairs, not really knowing where I was going, I felt a hand touch my elbow.

"'Shalom, my friend, fear not; I, too, am Jewish.'

"My first reaction was, 'Just leave me alone! I don't know you; I don't want to know you. I do not converse with strangers on the U-Bahn, and if you really are Jewish, what in the name of Yahweh do you want from me?'

"'You live dangerously and perhaps foolishly. Let us converse over a cup of coffee,' he said. 'Like you, I am not wearing my star, but I keep it in a designated pocket with nothing else in it. Look, you see, it cannot possibly fall out. Come, we must talk to one another; I know a little coffee shop.'

"We found the café. It was one of these little places that serves snacks and drinks to passers-by and commuters. It was a construction of wood, on three sides small windows of glass panes: inside, simple wooden tables and chairs. There was a small counter before an open doorway that led to a kitchen, and behind the counter was the tiniest woman outside of a circus I have ever seen, who seemed to be in charge.

"She didn't say a word all the time we were there. She was obviously Jewish. Her eyes followed us until we took our seats. I felt her dark eyes beneath her jet-black hair appraising me. She looked at my companion and nodded slightly and disappeared back into the kitchen.

"The windowpanes needed cleaning. If you were standing outside, you could have hardly seen in, which I knew, because before I went in, I tried. I like to know what I'm getting into before I go to strange places with strange people.

"He led me to a corner table, and he ordered coffee, or whatever they served that was supposed to be coffee. This tough-looking little man in his black leather jacket sitting opposite me had dark curly hair and a very dark complexion; he could shave as often as he wanted, and he would always look unshaven. With his green eyes and a hooked nose – a classic Jewish profile – how on earth he could travel round Berlin without wearing his star and not get stopped by the police? It made me wonder if he could be trusted. Was he bait? Was this a trap?

"'Relax, my friend,' he said, 'I was brought up a Christian but, unfortunately, my grandparents are Jewish on both sides of the family, so I'm screwed just like all the other Jews in this shitty city – well, almost.'

"I said to him: 'I must say, I cannot approve of your choice of words, Herr…?'

"'Johann Hoffnung will suffice for now. What's your name?'

"'Morgenthaler, if you must know!'

"'I do and I don't, Herr Morgenthaler, but I admire brave people like you, and I like to help them to, shall we say, extricate themselves from the unfortunate circumstances in which they find themselves.'

"'If they have enough money!' I shot back.

"'That helps the world go round and also to get you from one place to another where it is easier to stay alive; England, let's say.'

"I looked around the café; the floor could have done with cleaning and the table in front of me needed wiping. The dim half-light made everything seem somewhat surreal. We were alone.

"'How do you mean "stay alive"? England?' I said. 'I am German! Things are very difficult here, no doubt, but at some time or other the war will be over, and we can get back to leading our lives.'

"'Listen!' he shouted. 'Stop being so prim and naïve! They want to kill all of us; they are killing us now,' he told me, very carefully enunciating every word as if he were talking to a child.

"'That they despise and hate us, I agree, and we all know what the Gestapo does. This filth!'

"'What is, or rather, what was your profession, Herr Morgenthaler?'

"I thought it was about time to tell this little man who he had in front of him.

"'I am a highly qualified civil servant and was a member of the administration of the Berlin City Council up to when I was forced out of my position by the "Law for the Restoration of the Professional Civil Service" – not to mention "The Nuremberg Race Laws"!'

"'And since then, things have progressively deteriorated; they must have passed hundreds of laws and decrees limiting our freedom,' replied Johann quietly. He leant back and lit a most disgustingly smelly little cigarette; we were surrounded by heavy blue smoke in this little grey room.

"'Herr Morgenthaler: I've owned this café since the 11th of May 1933. I'm a sociable man and I like to engage with people and gather news – intelligence, if you like – for the future, our future. Let me tell you a story.

"'Ten years ago,' said Johann Hoffnung, 'A tall, thin young man came bursting through the door and, without ordering anything, sat down at the table next to mine and burst into tears. He looked a mess, his tie askew, his jacket dirty, his blond bushy hair all a-straggle. He had obviously been up all night.

"'My dear young fellow, what is wrong, can I help you in any way?' I enquired.

"'I need a beer,' he replied, 'not coffee!'

"I ordered us two beers and moved to his table.

"'Listen!' he croaked. 'Yesterday evening, my girlfriend and I were cycling down Unter den Linden. It was such a lovely May evening, but it was already dark when we heard the loud moaning, groaning, and screaming of a crowd, so we cycled over to see what was going on. There was a mob gathered on the Opernplatz standing around an enormous bonfire. When Jana and I got nearer, we could see that young men in Sturmabteilung uniforms, apparently students, were throwing books onto the fire. The fire was a fire of books! The brownshirts were nearly all drunk. I picked up some of the books that landed near my feet; they ranged from Albert Einstein and Heinrich Heine to Thomas Mann, Jack London to Ernest Hemingway! Jana and I tried to hold onto the books we had picked up when a big drunken SA student thug and his equally horrible friend stood in front of us and ordered us to throw the books we were holding back onto the fire. I refused and then the big fellow slapped me across the face both forehand and backhand. They were just about to start in on Jana, so I threw my books onto the fire, grabbed Jana's books out of her hands and threw them on too.

"'The cinders of the fire were swirling and crackling into the night sky, dancing and pirouetting to this grotesque event. The burning pages turned by themselves. The inebriated, swaying crowd was becoming more and more restless and singing Nazi marching songs, which caused the two brutes to turn towards the fire, swaying drunkenly – so I dragged Jana away and we cycled on further down Unter den Linden, the so-called artery of German culture, until we stopped to catch our breath at the Military Museum. Jana immediately shouted at me.

"'Why did you throw our books onto the fire?'

"'Because they would have beaten us up! Regardless of the fact that you are a woman!'

"'So what?! Don't you realise what's going on? Heinrich Heine once said where they burn books, they will soon burn people.'

"'Come now, Jana, it won't come to that, surely. I mean, I was only trying to protect you.'

"'Protect yourself, Peter!' she shouted at me and cycled off into the night, skirts and hair blowing in the wind. I haven't seen her since.'

"'Although it was only 8.30 in the morning, Peter took a long, deep draught of his beer and sighed and shuddered as he put his glass down.'

"Hoffnung told me he said to him, 'Your girlfriend was right, Peter, Heine was too; where they burn books, they will soon burn people.'

"That was the first story Johann Hoffnung related to me," said Herr Morgenthaler and looked around the room, sighed, and relapsed deeply into his own thoughts.

It seemed to Rachel that Morgenthaler had more to impart, and she glanced across at her husband who, reacting to her prompt, said: "Horrifying! But please do continue, Herr Morgenthaler," his customary pleasant, deep, voice shaking slightly.

"This I will do," replied Morgenthaler.

"Would you wait a moment? I'll just open the windows onto the back garden, or, rather, the vegetable patch; we all need some fresh air in here," exclaimed Rachel, gently laughing and somewhat embarrassed at interrupting the tense atmosphere.

As she did so, the early summer birdsong from the garden filled the room, accompanied by the faint sound of the children playing again. Everybody moved in their seats and shuffled their feet. The general feeling was of wonder and surprise with being confronted with this natural daily occurrence from outside and the depiction of malevolent violence from within. They then almost collectively breathed the fresh air in and relaxed somewhat.

Herr Morgenthaler was not to be deterred; it was apparent to all that he was relating what he saw from the picture bank of his memory.

He continued: "So, somewhat taken aback, I looked across at Johann Hoffnung and asked him, 'How can you be so sure, Herr Hoffnung, that we will burn?'

"'It is already taking place as we speak,' he replied, looking me straight in the eye.

"'Listen, Hoffnung,' I told him, 'the Nazis may beat us, deport us to concentration camps, even kill some of us, but until now, in the main, we are sent back home to our families. We just have to hold tight and hope for the best.'"

Rachel was becoming increasingly agitated. She looked across to Herr Morgenthaler and said, "Was this not a most unusual conversation to be having with a complete stranger, Herr Morgenthaler?"

"Indeed, Frau Lareine, indeed. However, Johann

Hoffnung had, despite his appearance, an aura about him that inspired trust. This observation may seem melodramatic to all of you in this room, but it was so."

Morgenthaler adjusted his tie and looked at his wife, who was still clenching her hands together intensely. She nodded her head slightly for him to continue. He leant forwards and resumed his account in his subdued tone.

"Hoffnung then said to me: 'Let me relate to you about the second fire.'

"I replied, 'You mean the 10th of November 1938, the Reichskristallnacht – the Night of the Broken Glass.'

"'I do indeed,' he replied and continued, 'I was sitting here one morning when a well-dressed man sat down at my table and asked me for a light for his cigar,' said Hoffnung.

"'What was a well-dressed man doing in a dirty place like this?' I said rather loudly. I'm afraid I was rather rude to him."

Siggi, who was sitting to the right of Frau Morgenthaler, guffawed loudly.

Ignoring Siggi's outburst, she looked disapprovingly at her husband as he shifted a little away from her on the sofa and gazed at the pale-green wallpaper with a classical fleur-de-lys motif. He noted the print of El Greco's 'Jesus Throwing Out the Moneylenders in the Temple'. In a Jewish household! He sighed and continued…

"Hoffnung blew a stream of his vile, blue smoke at me and snapped: 'In these times, many people come here to speak with me. The well-dressed man wore a tailored suit of fine material, English style, complete with a bowler hat and a yellow Star of David as a pinhole. He was quite small, had a round face and was portly; he even held an umbrella by his side. I'll be damned if he didn't remind me of Winston Churchill! After dusting down a chair with his handkerchief, he sat down slowly and sighed. He said nothing – he was sitting where you are sitting now – he stared straight ahead at the open kitchen door. My mother had not come in yet.'

"'I'd like a cup of your best coffee, please. Last night they burnt down our beautiful synagogue in the Fasanenstrasse.'

"'Whilst speaking, a tear trickled down his pink cheek from his left eye, and then another, followed by one from his right eye. He was crying. I got up to make coffee for the both of us.

"'Coming up.'

"'As I stood up, in passing him by, I laid my hand lightly upon his right shoulder. He at once touched my hand with his, he crying silently, me waiting, listening, imagining. Outside, the sound of the traffic passing by, indifferent to our sorrow. The moment passed, my visitor sat up even more upright, and I hurried on towards the kitchen to make the chicory coffee. When I returned, he was sitting dry-eyed and smiling.

"'Explain to me what happened?' I asked.'"

***

"LOOK, THERE'S ANOTHER PAIR," SAID Judith.

She and Yolande stopped their bikes at the side of the forest trail, holding on to the handlebars. Both women, feet on the ground, were staring skywards observing the two kites circling lazily and giving out their typical high-pitched call as they sought their prey from above in the fields and meadows below. They had just finished their picnic and were ready to start homeward again, leaving Beaudesert behind them. Both women wore shorts of blue and black with white tucked-in blouses, barefoot in their sandals. Judith's hair was gathered in a ponytail. Yolande had kept her auburn hair cut short, very short, since she had arrived in England.

"Oh, yes! I wish I could drift above in the sky like that," replied Yolande wistfully.

"All the way to Brest, eh?"

"Yes, that would be nice. Judith?"

"Yes, Yolande."

"These men we treat with the terrible burns, what becomes of them?"

"They usually are moved on to convalescent homes, where they are helped to return to everyday life."

"But a lot of them will not be able to do that."

"I know, Yolande, I'm sure the government will care for them in special facilities. They fought for us, didn't they?"

"Yes, they did, Judith. Judith? You know I was very *triste* – how does one say?"

"Sad, Yolande, melancholic. Yes, you were, very."

"Well, when I see these brave men, I realise how lucky I have been. I have fought the enemy, I have been wounded, and I bear the scars, but I am still alive! I can see and smell, work and pray and laugh with you here in this beautiful English countryside. *En outre*, I mean – furthermore, we shall win – how do you say? – this fucking war."

"Well, that's one way of putting it, Yolande." Judith laughed, grinning from ear to ear.

"And another thing, Judith," said Yolande, laying her bike on the wayside again. "I have been thinking."

"Yes, Yolande, I'm definitely all ears," said Judith, laying her bike next to hers.

"Alexsander is coming off night flights with his Mosquito, which he seems to love more than me, and will be in future teaching other crazy Englishmen to fly the damn things. So now he is safe, I will take him as my lover, for always. That crazy Polish man will have to marry me and come to live with me on our vineyard in Brest. I want to have his children."

"Gosh, you don't hang about, do you, Yolande? I'm so glad you are feeling so much better now and in the past few weeks. That's super news about Alexsander. Does he know what he is in for yet?"

"Not yet; I shall tell him soon."

Judith laughed and then turned away from her friend, her shoulders starting to shake. She was crying. Yolande embraced and held her tightly.

"I'm sorry, Judith, I'm so sorry."

"First Matthias left me without saying why, and almost immediately after that, Father said we should return to England at once! Then, Tom, I asked Tom not to go back to his squadron so soon. He wasn't really fit. He could have stayed with me a few more days – this is all so terrible. It splits me in two again and again."

"I know, *ma petite*, my lovely friend, I understand."

She let Judith cry until she could no more. Above, the kites were emitting their lost and lonely cries echoing across the English countryside.

In the silence of the hot June sun, they mounted their bikes again. After a mile or so, Judith turned and said: "There will be Germans at home when we get there. You know that, don't you?"

"Yes, but they are innocents and have been damaged by evil people, just as we have been."

"Your English is becoming very good, Yolande, very good."

***

RACHEL WAS JUST ABOUT TO ask Herr Morgenthaler to resume his account when the sound of women's voices coming from the hallway caused him to pause. He looked up in irritation – his mind's eye was obviously still deeply immersed in the visions of his experience in the small café next to a U-Bahn station in Berlin two years ago.

Herbert Lareine leant across and said, with a smile: "Just a moment, Herr Morgenthaler. I am, as I'm sure we all are, most affected by your gripping narrative. Before you continue, I suggest we welcome the young people into our circle."

Herr Morgenthaler looked up, pursed his lips, and nodded.

The door to the living room opened wide and in walked two of the most beautiful young women he had ever seen. One of them, who Frau Lareine introduced as Yolande, had a misshapen cheekbone, which did not detract from her attractiveness nor her self-confidence in the way she gripped his hand firmly when they shook. The other one, the daughter, Judith, was superbly radiant and spoke very good German. Yolande, apparently, spoke none. Herbert announced that Judith would translate for Yolande from German into French and asked everyone to kindly speak slowly and clearly.

Rachel could not help but notice that Siggi had perked up markedly and greeted the two young women, enthusiastically viewing the abundance of beauty and shapely brown legs. And also, that Frau Morgenthaler was smiling and was visibly more relaxed – sensing the atmosphere was losing some of the tension her husband had generated. Last but not least, she saw that Judith had been crying.

Judith and Yolande sat on the small couch underneath the open windows to the back garden. They both smiled across at Siggi, who immediately blushed bright red, causing everyone in the room to laugh.

Rachel looked across at Herbert, nodded at him as a prompt, and he then said: "Excuse me, Herr Morgenthaler, but I just want to use this opportunity to explain a little bit about ourselves so you can understand our connection with Germany and how Yolande came to live with us as a part of it. In 1931, I had a position as a professor of physics and mathematics at the University of Freiburg in southwest Germany. Rachel and I decided to live in Friedrichshafen on Lake Constance; as you well may know, it is beautiful there and one could relax wonderfully, and we always did enjoy boating.

"However, I was in Freiburg for two reasons, firstly to work with Professor Doctor Georg von Hevesy, who was researching the various aspects of nuclear medicine. I was also asked by the British Government to see – 'on the side', as it were – if this research could have any application in other areas, such as the military. Secondly, Friedrichshafen was known for its military industry nearby at the Dornier plant at Manzell. Also, it was home to an extensive research and development centre. Sadly, Professor von Hevesy was a

Jew and in 1934, one year after Hitler had bullied his way to power, he was forced out of the university, so I continued working together with his successor, Professor Doctor Walter Noddack."

He paused to let Judith catch up. In the background, one could hear the modulated tone of Judith translating from German to French, occasionally halting while she struggled to find a word or phrase, though Yolande would gesticulate for her to continue anyway.

Lareine continued, "I commuted to Freiburg Mondays to Thursdays. Fridays, I would cycle around and past the Dornier works on the lake. Occasionally dropping in for a beer where some of the workers used to go. I used to play the part of the naïve and somewhat dotty and harmless professor and ascertain which men in the bar were dissatisfied with their work, and who would talk all the more about what they were making if supplied with enough beer and schnapps by a stupid, tipsy, English tourist. In winter, I would say I was here for the skiing in nearby Austria or Switzerland; both countries were on the lake.

"In 1938, things became too politically difficult. I was a secret Jew in Germany, and also, our daughter became involved, against her will, with some very nasty young Nazis. My government agreed to recall me, and, under diplomatic immunity, we left Friedrichshafen in the summer of 1938 quickly and quietly. I then resumed my post at Birmingham University. I work together with Randall, Booth, and Sayers. Rachel and I, we both come from the Midlands, and I grew up in Great Haywood, my wife in Lichfield. We enjoy rural life very much. Yolande fought in the French Resistance against the Gestapo, escaped to England, and now she is, most pleasingly, with us and works as a nurse with Judith, who you see sitting next to her."

Herr Morgenthaler bowed politely in the direction of the two young ladies, and his wife smiled broadly at them.

Rachel was just about to ask Herr Morgenthaler to continue his narrative, when Siggi beat her to it.

"I'm a country boy too," interrupted Siggi, "I come from Marktoberdorf, Bavaria, with a fabulous view of our beautiful mountains. I used to sing in our synagogue and play football for the town. One day when I was playing, some of the regional SA thugs stood on the sidelines and started catcalling, 'Jew boy out, Jew boy out!' I went rocketing down the right wing past them, dribbled through many defenders and set up Ronnie, our centre forward, who banged the ball into the back of the net. Man! Did he have a shot on him! I then turned around and gave those SA twats the finger. They were furious and helpless, for the rest of the crowd was laughing and cheering and let the gang of brownshirts know in no uncertain terms that they were to shut up and get out, which they did.

"That evening, I sang in the synagogue again at the evening service. The next morning, I was on the football pitch doing some training, just loosening up. I have very powerful, muscular legs, you know, and they need looking after," said Siggi, looking meaningfully across at Judith and Yolande.

"Well, they certainly carried you to safety, Siggi." Judith laughed and translated for Yolande, who raised her left eyebrow and looked at Siggi as if he was a silly child. Judith paled and Rachel looked across at her, surmising that talking about football had reminded her daughter of Matthias back in Germany, who had also been a passionate player of the game, and who she had so very much loved – and he her. *Where is Matthias now?* she wondered. *Is he deceased like Tom?*

Herr Morgenthaler sighed heavily and looked straight ahead. His wife touched her hair and looked fondly at Siggi, enjoying his youthful exuberance, despite everything.

Herbert glanced at Rachel, who beamed and nodded at him.

"Well, young Siegfried, please continue."

"Thank you, Frau Lareine," replied Siggi gratefully. "Well, I was doing some ball juggling – I can keep the ball in the air for almost seventy-five touches without it falling on the ground."

Again, Siggi glanced at the two girls who, one after the other, nodded politely, smiled, and waited for him to continue.

"Anyway, I was still doing my exercises when I heard a voice calling me: 'Siggi, Siggi!'

"I turned around and it was Father Baumgarten, the local Catholic priest, who was running towards me as fast as he could in his black cassock. Behind him, I could see my wonderful Bavarian mountains. It was windy and quite cold; there was already snow on the peaks. I remember his hair was almost standing up. He arrived panting, his hands on his knees, gasping.

"'Siggi, you must leave,' he gasped, 'the word is out. The SA is after you and wants to do you over and then have you transported off to Dachau! My boy, you must go home and pack at once! Come, I have my car here – I'll drive you home.'

"I just had time to say goodbye to my parents and my sisters. I begged Father Baumgarten to drive me to see my lovely fiancée Rebecca, so I could say goodbye. He refused point-blank and said that if I wanted to live, I had to run, and I've been running since – until I arrived here. How is a long story, and perhaps I will relate this another time," said Siggi sadly.

He threw his head back, shook his dark blond curly hair and began to sing. His voice was clean and becoming. The song was a sad Jewish lament, but after two verses, Siggi stopped and spoke: "That was 'Mai Ko Mashme Lon', about a poor student who is cold and hungry and fears the coming winter. You English say 'now is the winter of our discontent,' do you not?"

"Yes, Siggi, we do," Rachel remarked gently.

"Well, I do not know what has become of Rebecca and my family or hers; I fear the worst but hope for the best."

The room seemed to sigh and hope with Siggi. Frau Morgenthaler gently laid her hand on the side of his face, and Siggi leant into the palm of it.

Judith looked across at Siggi and enquired: "But, Siggi, a Catholic priest helps a Jew, how come?"

"The Catholics in Germany are, in the main, more tolerant of us. Not so with many Protestants; Martin Luther hated the Jews ferociously. What can you expect from a Northerner?"

It seemed to Rachel that everyone in the room was digesting what they had just heard. For a minute or so, coming from the open windows behind the two young women, there were the everyday sounds of the birds singing and of the children who were still at play. In the distance, the faint snatch of a woman's voice.

"It pains me to ask, but may I continue to relate to you all of my conversation with the strange man whose name was Johann Hoffnung in this odd café next to the U-Bahn station?"

Rachel, with a sense of foreboding, knew that they had to hear what their guest had to say.

"Pray, do so, Herr Morgenthaler," she said and added, "Please, you have been most patient, but as you have heard and will no doubt hear, we have all here – German, English and French – had devilish dealings with the Nazis!"

"Of course," replied Morgenthaler. "Of course, my dear lady, of course."

Morgenthaler drew breath and continued his saga.

"As I was saying. This Herr Hoffnung was relating to me the incident of a Jew who was dressed as an English gentleman and who walked into his café and started crying. Hoffnung had asked the stranger what the matter was.

"The gentleman visitor had replied: 'My name is Isak Levi. Yesterday, I was strolling along the Kurfürstendamm when I saw smoke rising into the sky, lots of smoke. And it was coming from the direction of the Fasanenstrasse, where our beautiful synagogue is situated. I immediately crossed the road and went down the Fasanenstrasse, where a crowd of SA brownshirts were watching and laughing whilst the synagogue burnt! The fire brigade had just arrived and were occupied unravelling their hoses and going about the business when they were set upon by the brownshirts. One fireman, the captain probably, protested, and he was beaten to the ground and kicked. Anyway, we all stood around and watched this magnificent building burn and burn. After a while, the crowd, not only made up of SA thugs but also people like you and me – well, perhaps not quite so exotic in appearance as we two – but many seemingly average everyday Berliners – grew restless. They wanted more action, and somebody cried that there were Jews living in the house opposite! With that, people started hammering on the door, demanding that the residents come out, and finally, they broke the house door down using a fireman's axe, with the firemen looking helplessly on.

"'A cheer went up as the door went down and they dragged a man out into the street and started beating him. I will always remember hearing a voice crying out: "This is disgraceful, leave that poor man alone, you brutes!" At that moment, the police van arrived, and the policemen forced their way through and rescued the poor devil by bundling him into the van and driving off. I returned to the scene this morning; the synagogue was completely burnt out.'

"Hoffnung told me that Levi paused, looked at the table for a long time and frowned as if he saw something he didn't like and finally spoke.

"'We are in great danger, my friend, great danger.'

"Levi finished his coffee, rapped on the table with the knuckles of his right hand, replaced his bowler hat on his head at a slightly dashing angle, straightened his Star of David and looked at Hoffnung and said: 'Goodbye, fellow traveller, keep well.'

"'That I will do. And if you are ever in need of aid, this is the place to come. I, or my mother, are always here.'

"He then picked up his umbrella, swung it purposefully and strode across the room and through the front door as if into battle.

"Hoffnung swept the cigarette ash off the café table with the edge of his hand, exhaled another stream of his blue smoke, and said: 'And I haven't seen him since that day.'

"He looked at me askance and added, without a trace of sarcasm, 'So, Herr Morgenthaler, do you still think we Jews can make it through? That conversation took place years ago. Look at the beatings and killings they are allowed to commit against us Jews. They use our own institutions to execute their myriad of laws and decrees against us.'

"'But the British have started to bomb us regularly. Göring said that would never happen. So, there is a chance for us, is there not?'

"Hoffnung looked at me for a long time and at last spoke. 'Let me tell you a story.' And he did. Shall I continue?"

Morgenthaler looked around the room, his gaze resting on the cello in the corner of the room behind Herbert Lareine. Rachel looked around her; apart from the everyday sounds from outside, the room remained silent. Nobody said anything. It was becoming uncomfortably warm. Siggi took off his pullover and sat there in his shirt sleeves, gazing down on the pullover as he held it tight between his hands.

"Please continue, Herr Morgenthaler, don't stop," she answered.

"Good. I will tell you – in part, not everything – how we came to be with you today in this pleasant sitting room enjoying your company and hospitality, so I will continue.

"Johann Hoffnung then lit up yet another of his blue-smoking cigarettes and began again.

"'Last week, a young mother came into our little café with a babe in arms and asked if we could warm the milk bottle for her child with some hot water. My mother came out from the kitchen and said yes, she would make a bottle. I asked her to sit down. She was slim – in fact, too thin – attractive with brown hair kept in the fashion of the day, also her clothes, which, in spite of being clean and well-kept, had a slight shabbiness about them. But then who am I to judge other people's appearance? The young mother looked distraught. Even after she fed the baby and it was sleeping soundly, she still looked worried and unhappy.

"'I am a Jewess,' she said; her voice was shaking – tremulous. 'I don't wear the star; these days, it is less dangerous on the streets than if you do in this terrible city.'

"'We, too, are Jews,' Hoffnung told her. 'Here you are safe. What has happened? Why do you wander the streets?'

"'I thought so; I could tell when I walked in here that I was safe. You know, according to the new laws, we are not allowed to keep anything of value; we had to give up our homes and live together with other families in tiny apartments.'

"'Yes, of course.'

"'Well, my husband protested against moving. He was overheard and then our neighbour betrayed him to the authorities. The Gestapo came by and picked him up. For days I heard nothing! Then I went down to the Gestapo Headquarters in the Burgstrasse. I was so frightened. I asked about my husband. They wouldn't tell me anything. About two weeks later, a letter arrived. It was a government fee demanding payment for the cost of executing my husband by hanging.'

"'How very savage, how terrible,' replied Hoffnung.

"She didn't say anything. Hoffnung's mother came in from the kitchen and, seeing her plight, gently took the baby off her, cooing and humming a lullaby. She didn't resist. The baby slept. She sat there clutching her elbows, rocking to and fro for minutes. She resumed.

"'There is more: I live, together with all these people, in the Quitzowstrasse, near the Moabit freight train station. Early this morning, when it had just become lighter, I was awakened by a strange shuffling sound from outside and the occasional cry of a baby. At first, I thought it was a train. I looked out of the window and saw a long procession of people, families with their old and young walking towards the railway freight station – at five o'clock in the morning! I put on my coat and went down to see more. From behind a wall, on platform seventeen, I could see people getting into cattle wagons that made up the train. Some soldiers were there to make sure everybody got on. Everything was done in a quiet and orderly manner. I overheard one old man who was showing an officer a letter he had received, telling him to be at this address at this time.'

"'Has there been a mistake?' he asked politely.

"'Are you a Jew?' asked the soldier back.

"'Yes.'

"'Well done; you are at the right place at the right time.'

"'But—'

"'No but! Shut up and get into the wagon, or I will strike you with this pistol!'

"'No need! No need!'

"'The old man hastened back to his family, who were in the process of climbing aboard. When everybody was in these cattle wagons, the atmosphere became decidedly more unsettled; the children were crying, people were speaking agitatedly and asking the soldiers where they were going to go. The soldiers replied by sliding the wagon doors shut. One of them called out: "Up the chimney!" 'And he laughed as the train slowly chugged its way out of the station.

"'None of the soldiers who were left behind said anything. They seemed uncomfortable and hurriedly piled into an army lorry and left immediately. I saw one of the station guards coming towards me; he was making his way home after finishing his shift. I stepped out from behind the wall as he came closer. The sun was rising, and it was clear that it was going to be a nice day again. I was cold. What I had just seen had shocked me to the bone.

"'I asked the old station guard, "Excuse me, but where was that train going that just left the station?"

"'I don't know, and I don't want to know, but they always come back empty, and they always smell like hell.'

"'The man walked on without pause. I then realised that our street could be the next on the list.'

"She looked at Hoffnung and waited. He said, 'So, there is just you and the baby now?'

"'Yes.'

"Hoffnung paused for what seemed a long time; he had finished his last story. Everything seemed very quiet. Then he looked across at me and posed the same question he had asked the young mother: 'Herr Morgenthaler, is there just you and your wife?'

"'Yes, why?' I asked him.

"'They are killing us, all of us, mostly in Poland and the east, where there are many millions of Jews. That train was on its way to Auschwitz. When they arrive, they will be gassed with rat poison and burnt in ovens. The fitter ones will be worked to death or complete exhaustion and then gassed and burnt.'

"For a moment, I simply couldn't comprehend what he had just said. Can you?"

Morgenthaler looked around the room. His wife had bowed her head and was reciting what seemed to be a prayer under her breath. Nobody said anything. The murmur of Judith's translation came to an end and there was then complete silence in this room of allies. Yolande's late reaction of disbelief evolving into dismay seemed to add to the anguish emanating from the air itself.

"*C'est horrible!*"

Rachel got up and signalled to Herbert to swap chairs. She went over to the corner behind the chair that Herbert had occupied and picked up her cello and the little stool that stood next to it. She placed this in front of the empty fireplace and arranged her dress so that she could play comfortably.

She said softly, "Avinu Malkeinu. It's a lament, Yolande."

And she began to play. The first tender, gentle, sad, middle tones – reminiscent of a mother sobbing, remonstrating, and despairing. The music then became tighter and higher like the voice of a child who doesn't understand the pain they must endure. And then the rich resonant tones from deep within the wood of the instrument – of the father echoing all of the indignities, thefts, and murders they have had to live through over the centuries, and now, yet again. The sadness of the music echoed and resounded throughout this room of tears.

Rachel stood up abruptly, placed her cello in Herbert's hands and announced: "I must make those sandwiches and some tea for us all." She hurried out into the kitchen, opened the door onto the garden, breathed in the fresh air and struggled to light a cigarette.

"Here, let me take that off you." She let Judith take the cello bow so gently out of her shaking hand. She and

Yolande must have also grasped the opportunity to get out of the living room and had followed her into the kitchen.

"Let me light the cigarette for you," said Yolande, and took the cigarette from her, lit it with a match from the box that was always on the kitchen windowsill, and took a deep drag herself then gave it to Rachel.

"Look, he's back again."

"Who is back again, Mother?"

"My little friend with the beak of gold, the blackbird. Do you see him?"

"Yes, Mother."

"*Oui, Rachel, je peux le voir. Il est très joli.*"

"Yes, you are right, he is lovely."

The three women stood in the doorway peering out into the golden evening sunlight; the setting sun shone through a distant copse silhouetting the single, lonely trees. Rachel was still shivering somewhat with the two girls linked on either side of her arm in arm.

***

RETURNING TO THE LIVING ROOM with the two young women, Rachel was just in time to hear Herr Morgenthaler announce: "My dear friends, we have refreshed ourselves with those delicious, although unusual, sandwiches and tea. Now, I suggest that I impose myself on you all again and relate my final account of my sojourn in this 'Haven Café'. I think it is important and relevant to us Jews, so if you would permit me to continue to the end?"

Herr Morgenthaler looked across to Herbert, who glanced at Rachel to see if she could take any more. Rachel paused, then said quietly and clearly: "Of course, Herr Morgenthaler, we are all together in this, please continue."

Judith announced quite clearly that she wanted to hear all he had got to say. The others solemnly nodded their approval.

Siggi said, "Our enemies have been trying to kill us all for the past 2500 years. We here are proof that we will continue on."

"It gets better," announced Herr Morgenthaler. "Dear friends, it indeed gets better as it gets worse. I shall explain through my continuation. So, back to the café: Hoffnung pushed the ashtray towards me and stretched his legs, folded his arms, and brought them down on the table with a crash.

"'Morgenthaler, if you want to live, if you want your wife to live, go home, if you can call it that, and bring her here. I will then bring you all to safety.'

"'There are others?' I asked.

"'Yes, there are others,' came a voice from the kitchen, and out stepped a nice-looking young woman and, behind her, the little lady who was Johann's mother, cradling a sleeping baby.

"'My name is Rivkah. You can trust Johann; you can more than trust him.'

"'Morgenthaler, where do you live?'

"'In der Reichenbergerstrasse in an apartment with four other families.'

"'Go home to your wife and come here this evening at eight o'clock. Remember the curfew – and don't wear your stars! Bring all your hidden jewels and gold; you will be paying for your journey to England, and also for Rivkah and her baby. You will travel by train to Paris and then onwards to the French coast. Our workshop will make all necessary documents of excellent quality. Your money and jewels will serve as bribes for the three officials involved – all the way to England. And, Morgenthaler: do not dress like a Jew!'

"And so it came to pass, my dear friends. We met at the Haven Café and proceeded deep into the nearby wide-reaching Weißensee Cemetery. There at the furthest point was an entry, covered with branches and foliage, to an underground labyrinth. It was in this cemetery that the gravediggers were busy burying our Jewish friends who had committed suicide. They were busy from morning to late in the evening. They also hid Tora Rolls there. Praise be to Yahweh. We shall live on and on! On that rainy night, with the trees bending in the cold, harsh, wind, my wife and I met not only Rivkah and baby but also Isak Levi, who really did look a little bit like Winston Churchill. My wife and I, also Isak, gave Johann Hoffnung many jewels and much gold. He said to me, 'It is for a good cause, Morgenthaler. Tell our story to our people over there; but know this: the goyim in England are not interested. They let Chełmno, Belzec, Treblinka, Majdanek, and Auschwitz-Birkenau continue to exist. The goyim in England, Morgenthaler, they bomb the women and children here in Berlin, but they let Auschwitz live on.'"

6

26TH JUNE 1944 – HERR AND FRAU KRIEGER

SEPP KRIEGER STOOD AT THE lakeside and felt the ground shake and tremble. He looked up and across into the night sky, watching as Friedrichshafen was being crucified on a cross of raging night fire. He knelt down to minimise the effect of the blast waves that were raging towards him, then he lay down on his belly. He had to.

At about 2am, he had been awakened by the town's various fire sirens that had shrieked out their symphony of warning. He knew what was coming: death and destruction to the quiet little town at the side of the lovely Lake Constance. The town that produced weapons for this bloody war with slave labour. There was talk of them building a new super weapon they called the V2 rocket, which was supposed to, at the last minute, win the war for them all.

The many coloured flares that descended slowly over the town had a beauty of their own: of red, white, blue, and orange illuminating the town, laying her naked and bare for the second flight of deadly bombers, and the third and the fourth, until Sepp gave up counting; it was non-stop. The air reverberated from the ever-increasing pressure of the blast waves three kilometres away, forcing him to block his ears and hug the shuddering ground, craning his neck, and watching as the town was converted into a single, raging, hellish fire of at least a couple of kilometres in breadth and depth. His own breath was blocked and interrupted by the enormous shock waves that pushed him down to the ground. The RAF wasn't just going after the factories of Maybach, Dornier, and Zeppelin but also, it would seem, the whole town itself, where friends of theirs lived.

To his left, he heard the bomber's four-engine roar as it came lumbering across from the Swiss side of the lake directly down towards him and his home. In the night sky, the flames from the wing of its right-side engines belched red and orange. It was going down. Behind the plane, a row of deep rumbling explosions followed by huge fountains of water came towards him. It was getting rid of its bombs! Sepp was then rolling across the ground towards his house. The water hit him like a heavy wall, over and over again and again. His last conscious thought was of Anne.

Anne Krieger didn't want to die under the rubble of her own home. The shock waves from Friedrichshafen forced her to compromise. She pressed herself up against the front door of their small house, which she hoped and prayed would withstand the violence of these howling winds of fire. The Bernstein family had not emerged from beneath the boathouse. They would have to decide for themselves! Looking to her left through the window, she could see an illuminated Sepp lying down on the ground, hear the sirens howling, the thunder of the attack and the huge aeroplane belching fire, simultaneously dropping its bombs into the lake, and coming down inexorably towards her. Sepp disappeared in the cacophony of explosions and huge fountains of water.

As Anne started to race towards the motionless form of her husband, the aeroplane thundered across their roof, showering it with sparks and pieces of debris. Its flight ended a couple of kilometres behind the house in a huge explosion and a ball of fire. As Anne turned her head, she saw the Bernstein family holding hands in a row: the mother, the father and the three little girls standing outside next to the front door, illuminated in a light of orange aircraft fire behind them and the brilliant white flashes of dying Friedrichshafen before them. They stood momentarily as if frozen, then they too threw themselves to the ground.

Anne fought onwards on her hands and knees towards her prostrate husband, crying as she went.

"Sepp, get up! Get up, for heaven's sake!"

Her knees were soaking wet from the water that had washed over from the explosions, and she kept kneeling on her nightdress, which brought her to a sudden halt, making her angry and frustrated as she pulled at it until she screamed a scream she barely heard in the thunder of this hell.

As she reached her husband, Sepp Krieger opened his eyes and smiled at her.

"I got a bit of a shock there, you know."

Anne buried her wet face in his soaking shirt and cried. The two of them crawled back to where the Bernstein family lay huddled together, shivering, seeking warmth midst this night of fire. She steered them to a shallow depression well away from the house, towards the boundary of their property. She had had Sepp make this hollow especially for this purpose. With Swabian efficiency and foresight after the first two bombings, she realised they all needed a well-disguised refuge away from the house and the trees and flying debris. In the hollow was a big chest that contained all they needed to survive the night(s): clothing, blankets, food, water and three thermos flasks with soup that would be eaten the next day if unneeded the night before. Tarpaulins to lie on under the two canopy-like constructions without side walls. One for Anne and Sepp; the other, bigger one for the Bernsteins. Over the canopies was a pile of carefully chosen long tree trunks that Sepp supposedly needed for his construction and supply business. Around the hollow, a discreet little grassy mound that prevented water from getting in and which funnelled it off to the left-hand side.

***

SEPP KRIEGER LOOKED ACROSS AT his former schoolfriend, Wilhelm Tischler, who stood at the edge of the lake and surveyed the destruction before him. The expanse of flattened and ruined reeds at this southernmost tip of Eriskirch saddened him, as did the sight of the dead swans and bloated fish that floated on the oily surface. These were only the outward signs of the destruction that had been caused to this gentle, otherwise peaceful, wild habitat. He had grown up here and all this 'thing', as he called the wartime destruction of his *Heimat* and home, sickened him. As did the sight of the still-smoking ruins with their many dead citizens of devastated Friedrichshafen in the mid-distance. Apparently, the underground armament production tunnels dug out by the slaves from Dachau and Dora-Mittelbau had not been affected.

Wilhelm was a very big man, almost two metres tall, broad-shouldered with a big belly, and brown hair, which was becoming thinner and thinner due to the stress and responsibility of being an army quartermaster in charge of the region of Friedrichshafen Depot and beyond, or so he said. In reality, he was just getting older, thought Sepp, as he stood beside him. They made a contrast, Sepp thirty centimetres smaller than Wilhelm but with stocky broad shoulders and muscular due to his constant physical work, contrasting to Wilhelm's flab from too much good living.

Sepp had a moonlike face, which was also reddish due to the occasional schnapps too many that he distilled from the apples in the large orchard he cultivated in a part of the woods he owned. This was situated conveniently to the rear of his property. It was fenced in, with his two Alsatians to keep guard. Also, his ears stuck out prominently, which had earned him the nickname of 'Twobig', which was short for 'Two Big Ears'. Sepp had taken this all in his usual stoic manner, but any schoolboy who had misused his nickname in a mocking tone often found himself very quickly to be in trouble.

He had gone to school at the same time as Wilhelm; they had not been together in the same class, but in the same year. Both average students achieving average marks. Both excelling later in their own way – Sepp could do and make anything with his hands, particularly with wood. He discovered, to his own surprise, that he was also able to develop the skills for running a business efficiently. His father had been a fisherman cum farmer and a builder of boats. Sepp followed in his footsteps but quickly realised that there was no money in fish and, therefore, little demand for boats. He diversified into the housing industry, building, and installing frameworks for roofs. He also made kitchen cupboards and furniture of wood. Since the war had started, he had specialised in repairing the horse-drawn wagons and carts that the army, the Wehrmacht, still employed to a very large degree.

Hardly a way to conduct modern warfare, Sepp often thought.

His son, Matthias, who was somewhere on the Russian Front, had excelled in carpentry, making beautiful pieces of furniture and also sculptures in stone. The last piece was of that English girl, Lareine, who had been the cause of so much trouble with the Richters. The statue of Judith Lareine, which stood unfinished on Matthias's workbench, was beautiful in its delicacy and firmness that seemed to reflect a certain resolve in the girl's character. Judith had visited them in order to sit as a model. Apart from the fact that she was a foreigner, he and Anne had found her not only to be lovely but also respectful and polite. Furthermore, the young girl was, like their son, a gifted artist and had sat outside their farmhouse in all kinds of weather painting scenes of their property and of the lake.

Then came that fateful incident where his son had had a fight with the Richters' son, Hinrich, down at the lake in '38 when they were celebrating the end of school and good exam results. Hinrich Richter lost that fight, Judith being the cause of it. The Richters were then, as now, Nazis, and Father Richter an influential man in the SS. Fearing reprisals, he had told Matthias to flee. He and his son decided that the army was the safest bet, for the fury of the SS knew no limits, and now he was on the Russian Front. Still! Hadn't he done enough after being wounded? But they had sent him back to fight again and again.

Army Quartermaster Wilhelm Tischler was an excellent organiser and understood the labyrinthine workings of the army supply system down to the last 'T'. This was all he cared about, making sure his boys got all the things they needed, from blankets to any kind of meat, and making certain that his own needs were catered to at the same time, food, schnapps, and women. He was visiting 'his old schoolfriend', as he called Sepp, to obtain some of the first two. For the latter, he relied on his 'natural attraction', as he called it. Sepp reckoned that his attractiveness lay in the fact that he was able to supply the ladies with anything from food to nylons with charm and in a manner that respected their dignity. He was a good man; he was also a tough, intelligent soldier. This Sepp knew from first-hand experience. They had both fought side by side for their country on the Russian Front and then in France in the First World War. In spite of this, Sepp viewed Wilhelm with caution and calibrated his behaviour in catering for Tischler's army and personal requirements in an outgoing business-like manner. Not too friendly, not too bold, with the right touch of banter for former 'schoolfriends'.

Tischler turned and walked towards the log-covered hollow of the family's air-raid shelter. He bent down, trying, as far as his big belly would allow, to peer in and under the logs.

"Odd," he said more to himself than to Sepp. Sepp said nothing.

"Two tarpaulins on the ground, one very much bigger than the other. Why is that, I wonder?"

He straightened up and looked directly at Sepp.

Sepp stretched expansively, yawned, and replied with genuine tiredness, "Well, you know me, Wilhelm, I like my comfort, and the ground can get wet, so we cover it up as much as possible. And would you look at this place! It is really too big to run almost on my own. If I didn't have the two Ukrainian slaves who come afternoons, I would be in trouble," he said, stretching his right arm out describing a semi-circle of his property.

"No doubt, Sepp, no doubt. You should know that I was at a supply and maintenance meeting in Ulm yesterday. We need more of everything. So, unfortunately, you are going to have to give me those pigs of yours in the sty next to the boathouse."

"As long as you leave us the boar to mate with a female and one young one, Wilhelm; you will want more in the future, no doubt."

"Quite right, and thirty sacks of potatoes from your field over yonder and the same number of greens as last time."

"That was a lot last time, Wilhelm."

"I left you more than enough to feed just two people, Sepp." Wilhelm looked at Sepp questioningly. "Now, Sepp, you're not selling your stuff on the black market, are you? That's illegal and at our coordination meeting last week, your family friend, SS Obergruppenführer Hannes Richter, decreed that the punishment for said offence would be death by hanging. Which means we would probably have to hang all of you lot, and that would be a shame for all concerned. The army and the SS are trying to coordinate our supply lines; things are desperate, the fronts are crumbling – and I never said that," said Tischler, quietly.

They were now standing at the fence of the pig area looking across to the sty, where twelve pigs were finally starting to settle after the trauma of the air raid two days previously. Under the floorboards of the sty was the entrance to the tunnel that led to the living area underneath the house itself and the boathouse where the Bernsteins hid day and night. The barn for repairing carts stood next to it.

"I wouldn't dream of taking such a risk, but the army doesn't pay market prices, and I am an honest businessman. It does not seem fair," Sepp said deliberately, and looked questioningly at Tischler.

"Fair!" Tischler snorted. "Fair! What the devil are you talking about, man?"

"Wilhelm, how nice to see you again, in spite of the fact you have come to plunder and lay waste to us yet again." Frau Krieger leant into Wilhelm, kissed him on the side of his jowly right cheek and gave him an affectionate hug. She had observed the two men from the kitchen window and wanted to get them away from the pigsty and boathouse as quickly and discreetly as possible.

"Now, you two old friends, no quarrelling. Sepp! How many times have I told you not to make Wilhelm's task even more difficult? He has to do his duty. Now come into the house, both of you. I have a wee glass of schnapps for us ready and waiting."

Anne Krieger was a tall, slim woman with a delicate but tired-looking face, with long, greying, auburn hair. She was Swabian born and bred, and although retaining her accent, she seldom lapsed into the thick local dialect.

She was tough, intelligent, and well-read. Anne dressed in the traditional *Hausfrau* manner, which she regarded as a disguise and also practical for her work around their property. She was determined to preserve her sense of civility and decorum in this time of 'obscenity', as she called it. She and Sepp measured their convictions with deeds. Dangerous deeds. If they were caught hiding a Jewish family, they would die a certain death. Doubtless Obersturmbannführher Hannes Richter would see to that with the greatest of pleasure.

"Schnapps! Excellent, dear Anne, excellent!" replied Tischler, his joviality magically returning.

"Come into the house, the both of you, I have also some dried pork crackling to go with the schnapps."

Passing the boathouse, Sepp watched as Tischler moved towards the big doors at the entrance.

"Let me have a look to see how much progress you have made building your new boat, Sepp."

"Ach, I never seem to have enough time; I'm too busy getting enough rations together to supply the Wehrmacht," replied Sepp with gentle irony.

Tischler hauled open one of the big double doors releasing a small flock of birds that fluttered noisily past him and looked in to observe the wooden boat resting on two very large and solid trestles. On the right-hand side, a hoist on rails ran out into the yard. The soldier walked slowly around the big vessel, running his hand admiringly over the side of the hull.

"Oak?" he asked, kicking at the wood shavings that were piled up on the floor around the hull.

"Yes, the hull is; the cabin is made of ash."

"That's a lot of shavings for an almost-finished boat, Sepp. You're not trying to hide something, are you now? You don't seem to have done anything since last year; most unlike you, this disorder, most un-Swabian-like."

"It is virtually impossible to get the wood – the army takes, I mean, needs everything. That is just the way of it."

Sepp glanced across at Anne who was struggling to hide her inner anxiety. She had warned the Bernsteins, who were hiding in the secret cellars below, by dropping a stone down the hidden air duct between the boathouse and the kitchen.

"Now, you two, enough of what we can't have and more about what we do have, namely a glass or two of schnapps. Come now, Wilhelm. You too, Sepp."

Wilhelm Tischler was not a man to be easily diverted.

"What about the barn, Sepp?" Striding to the rear, Tischler opened the connecting door to the barn.

Sepp breathed a sigh of relief and almost ran to stay apace with Tischler's huge steps, saying: "There is money to be made in these repairs, Willie."

"Good money for good work is fair enough," grunted Tischler grudgingly.

He cast a critical eye around the workshop, which consisted of two supply wagons in various states of repair and wagon wheels that were being respoked.

He stamped on the bare ground of the workshop, spat on it, and said: "What a damned stupid way to run a war. The Americans and British use petrol-driven lorries. Let's get that drink."

***

116

SEPP, ANNE, AND WILHELM WERE standing in the driveway next to Wilhelm's *Kübelwagen*. It was late afternoon, and the sun was gradually moving on its downward path, reflecting on the calm waters of the lake and illuminating the distant alps in pink and white. The air smelt fresh again, and the birds were chirping and chattering in the nearby bushes. A general feeling of serenity and harmony was settling into the early evening.

After saying their goodbyes, Wilhelm was about to step into his *Kübelwagen* when he turned and said, "Sepp, know this: SS Obersturmbannführer Richter announced that he was going to examine some of their new suppliers personally and he made sure that the Krieger family was on his list. He'll be around on Friday according to the itinerary we jointly agreed upon. So, if I were you, I would definitely recommend that you prepare yourselves for another, shall we say, looting raid." He paused and muttered, "All of you," looking at them both, half smiling, part grimacing. "Take care, old friend; goodbye, Anne, and thanks for the hospitality. You deliver the produce tomorrow at our depot and no cheating!"

Despite his bulky figure, Tischler swung himself lithely into his vehicle and drove off towards the entrance, stretching his right arm in a mock Hitler salute as he did so.

Sepp waved back and turned to Anne.

"What did he mean by 'all of you', Sepp?" asked Anne urgently with a quaver of fear in her voice.

"We have work to do, Anne," said Sepp grimly. "A lot of work. Let's go inside, now!"

Seated at the kitchen table, Sepp looked across to Anne, who had folded her arms and had that mulish, stubborn look on her face that he knew all too well.

"Look, Anne, as I've said repeatedly, we've done our duty as neighbours and as Christians. What is the point in risking who knows what sort of death for us all: you, me, and the Bernsteins with their three daughters?"

"Oh, so you want to throw them to the wolves, is that it, Sepp?"

"Steady on, Anne, that's unfair! No! I could sail them across the lake tonight to Switzerland in the dinghy."

"Yes, well, that's one possibility, and then you set them out on the shore and just say goodbye and good luck? Where do they go from there in the middle of the night with three little girls? You know, too, that the Swiss government is changing its policies towards refugees all the time."

He sighed, looked across and said: "We can only do so much, dear wife."

"Yes, that is true, husband. If we are going to move them to Switzerland, then this must be planned with more care and time than we presently have at our disposal."

Sepp groaned, looked down at his brown, meaty hands with his banana-like fingers and sighed deeply, letting out his pent-up breath slowly and evenly. There was no other sound in this cosy little farmhouse kitchen other than a fly buzzing noisily and irritatingly around the blackened and dimmed ceiling light.

"I don't want you to die, Anne, and I don't want those sweet little Bernstein girls to die along with their parents. And last but not least: I don't want to die. I am afraid. It's as simple as that."

"We will not die when we know what to do. Let me sit on your lap and you will kiss my neck, and we'll go to bed, and in the morning, we will know how to do it."

She moved around the table and sat down on him, took his right hand, and placed it on her left breast above her heart. Her breast hardened with his caresses as he nuzzled her neck and massaged her nipple gently. Taking his right hand, she moved it up between her thighs.

"My love."

***

THE WEATHER HAD CHANGED - grey clouds scudded across the sky, bringing rain, and there was a chill in the air; autumn was calling already. The happy little birds were silent; the lakeside devastation of the reed biotope seemed uglier than ever; the water was unsettled as the wind created waves that lapped heavily and despondently against the shore.

Sepp Krieger stood next to his wife in front of the barn and observed Obersturmbannführer Hannes Richter whilst his men searched their property. Richter stood with his back to the grey lake, his legs and arms akimbo, surveying the Krieger property with a critical eye. He was, like his son, a tall, slim man, and when he moved it was also in a lithe and almost graceful manner. In contrast to Hinrich, he was not good-looking, with a long pale face and a beaky, bad-tempered nose, piercing blue eyes behind metal-framed glasses. A former accountant clerk, he had enjoyed his rise in rank and the power that came with it. To accentuate his military appearance, he wore his elegant black SS uniform, complete with stylish riding breeches (Richter had never been near a horse in his life) and the skull and crossbones insignia of the Hussars on his cap.

The power over life and death appealed to his injured sense of self-dignity in a most satisfying manner. He pulled the belt of his black leather coat slightly downwards. They were hiding something! He could smell it; he could sense it!

He took in a breath and shouted: "Obersturmführer Buchmann!"

"Present, before you, Herr Obersturmbannführer!"

"Report!"

"The barn next to the boathouse is in order. It is usually solely for wagon repair and the like. The floor is the earth itself and there is no loft, nor are there any cupboards. The tools are arranged along the walls above the various workbenches. There are two female slaves sheltering from the downpour."

"How disappointing. Throw the women out and back to work, then take a good man with you and examine the fields beyond the house. There seems to be an orchard of some sort way over there. Report immediately to me what you find if anything other than apples."

"*Jawohl*, Herr Obersturmbannführer!"

"The rest of you into the boathouse. Let's rock Krieger's boat and see what drops!"

The six SS soldiers wasted no time in opening the boathouse doors and laying all hands on the boat. They started to rock it from side to side, gaining increasing momentum. With a final concerted push as the vessel reached its steepest angle to the left, they shoved it over the trestles and the boat crashed into the side of the barn, damaging the hull and the partly constructed cabin. The left sides of the trestles were pinned under the hull, and their right sides pointing at a sharp angle into the air.

Sepp and Anne looked on helplessly.

"Clear all the shavings away and let us see what we have," ordered Richter.

After some minutes of diligent sweeping and examining the floorboards on hands and knees, Buchmann reported: "Nothing out of the ordinary to report, Herr Obersturmbannführer! *Achtung!* Here is hollow below, most certainly, and here too." The soldier tapped his machine gun butt along where the length of the boat had been.

"Open it up!" said Richter.

"There is no handle, Herr Obersturmbannführer."

"Tap and see where it starts and finishes, the width of it as well, then shoot through it along the whole length and breadth. Shoot, man!"

The SS soldier began shooting. The thundering hammer bursts of fire reverberated around the building, out through the open doors and across the lake, taking the frightened swans, herons, and a swarm of other birds with them. The peppered section caved in after a few well-aimed stamps from soldiers' boots.

"The cavity is empty, Herr Obersturmbannführer!"

Sepp cried out: "Forgive me, Herr Obersturmbannführer Richter, the cavity was made for the keel of the boats but, since I don't make so many boats anymore, especially the bigger ones, I didn't need it any longer, so I just boarded it over."

Richter ignored him. "Get a man down there and see if there is a hidden door anywhere. Look carefully, mind you!"

After a while, the head of a hot, sweaty soldier in full SS battledress appeared at the top of the ladder that had been set down into the pit.

"Nothing to report, Herr Obersturmbannführer Richter, *alles in Ordnung!*"

Sepp let out an inwards sigh of relief. They had worked hard to cover up this second entrance to the cramped underground living quarters, but nobody was safe yet, not by a long chalk. The rain had set in again, drumming down on the roof in the steely silence that followed the unsuccessful search.

"Obersturmführer Buchmann, to report to Herr Obersturmbannführer Richter. I wish to inform of my findings in the orchard." Buchmann, who had suddenly appeared in the doorway, stood dripping water from head to toe. He seemed agitated and excited.

"Report, man, curse you!"

Sepp noticed with inwards satisfaction that Richter was letting his frustration at the unsuccessful search get the better of him.

"At the far end of the potato field, we discovered an orchard, the fence of which was covered in ivy, behind which was a hedgerow of thorny bushes; it was impossible to see through. We eventually found a hidden gate and forced an entrance. We then discovered, behind a lot of bushes, a pigsty. The pigs were roaming freely around the orchard. The area was guarded by two Alsatians, which we shot."

Sepp groaned; his beloved dogs.

"How many pigs?" shouted Richter excitedly.

"We counted about twenty; there could be more, sir."

Richter turned to Sepp and glared at him, his glasses reflecting the overhead light that had been switched on. In the distance, the thunder rolled across the lake. He gripped the black leather riding crop tighter and lashed out at Sepp.

"I knew you were hiding something! You think you are very clever letting us look in the wrong place!"

"You have ruined my boat and damaged my property," said Sepp, clutching his shoulder, knowing immediately that he had said too much.

"You two, take him outside!" screeched Richter at the nearest SS soldiers – in his hysteria, he sounded more like a girl than a man. "I'm going to teach him a lesson before shooting him!"

Sepp was dragged out onto the grass in the direction of the bomb shelter. He looked across at his beloved lake for the second time this week in this position, knowing full well that it was all over. So, he stood up.

'Anne' was the last word he uttered before Richter lashed out at him with all the fury of a madman. The blows rained down on his head so that he wrapped his arms around it in a helpless gesture to protect himself. Richter, infuriated even more, redoubled his efforts until Sepp sank to his knees in the driving rain. Blood poured from his face, and his arms and back were in tatters. Richter, lungs heaving, continued beating the defenceless man until he fell to the ground. He then aimed his blows at the head again. Sepp felt himself aflame in agony – he wished and wanted it to stop.

"Please, please stop," he murmured followed by a vision of his mother sponging his knee after he had fallen over. Then everything went dark and, in the distance, he felt the thunder of blows overwhelming his consciousness.

"Josef! Josef!" In a blur of movement, Anne had rushed up and flung herself on top of her dying husband to protect him.

"So be it." Richter panted, lungs heaving, and continued his beating, driven on by Anne's screams. His men stood around in a circle, some staring stupidly, others smiling in enjoyment of this spectacle: watching Anne's blood seep onto and mingle into that of her husband's, then thinning and trickling away with the rain.

Once more Richter stopped to gather his breath. He was about to deliver a renewed, vicious attack. He reached back, arching his body like a catapult, raindrops from his coat flew in all directions. He abruptly felt his arm in a painful, crushing, squeezing, grip.

"Now then, Herr Obersturmbannführer Richter, we don't want to kill the goose that lays the golden eggs, do we?"

Richter turned, wincing with pain, to the giant form of Army Quartermaster Wilhelm Tischler. "You are hurting me; I can't feel my whip," he whined.

Army Quartermaster Wilhelm Tischler replied slowly and carefully, tightening and twisting his grip on Richter's upper arm with a massive hand, enunciating every word as if explaining a difficult concept to a recalcitrant child. "I'm sure your very superior Oberstgruppenfüher Bücher would be most upset to learn from my General Baumer that you were the one who slaughtered it. The goose. Just when we all need the food that the Kriegers supply us with, more than ever. Also, is it not so that the SS need every man on the Russian Front?" he asked meaningfully.

"He hid twenty pigs from us," said Richter stupidly. "You are hurting me!"

Tischler finally let his arm go and Richter gasped and shuddered in pain whilst looking around and realising that his goofy little troop of Ukrainian SS thugs were surrounded by a group of very aggressive-looking local soldiers from the Friedrichshafen barracks.

"They all do – hide produce from us. How do you think

they will survive in order to supply us? It is the way things work, and my men are very hungry. I suggest you return to Dachau or Auschwitz, or wherever – and we forget the whole thing."

"Damn you, Krieger!" groaned Richter, holding his aching arm. Abruptly he turned and landed a vicious kick in Sepp's ribs. Sepp emitted a deep, hollow groan of pain.

Anne cried, "Stop, at last, just stop!" She looked across to Tischler and whispered, "You went to school together; you are friends."

Tischler nodded to his battle-hardened men, some of whom knew Sepp and his family personally, and who were due to leave for the Russian Front again. In unison, they raised their rifles and held their weapons 'at the ready', across their chests. He then grabbed Richter's arm yet again, squeezing hard. Richter groaned anew.

"You will not kill my, no, our golden goose, Richter. Please leave."

There was a long pause of almost complete silence, broken only by the rain beating down on them – and Anne's sobs. Looking up from her knees through her bedraggled hair, she watched as Richter turned abruptly and yelled at his men to mount up and they quickly clambered into the army lorry in which they had arrived. He swung himself into his covered *Kübelwagen*, glaring at his opponent.

"You will be hearing from me, Tischler," he growled, "and your superiors from mine."

"You do that, Herr Obersturmbannführer Richter, you do that. Tell them I held your arm and see what they say. And know this: a reliable and constant supply of food has the highest priority at this stage in this miserable war. The

Kriegers have been doing so reliably week for week, month for month, for the last five years."

"We'll see about that," said Richter and nodded to his driver, who let out the vehicle's clutch and skidded off towards the farm's entrance, followed by the grumble and belch of the SS troop carrier which followed it out.

Anne was faintly aware of Tischler turning to his men and saying: "Wunderlich, Schmidt, help these two into the house. Anne, are you still with us?"

Anne forced herself to remain conscious; she could feel the last dregs of her strength rising her within her to meet this last challenge: to give Tischler an answer.

"Yes."

"Is he alive?"

"Yes."

"Good. He's a tough little sod. I'll get your field slaves to look after you. I'll have one of my men call them in, wherever they are."

"They'll be sheltering in the barn, just beyond the pigsty; that is, if it's still standing after this attack."

"Right then, you have the necessary ointments and bandages for your wounds?"

"Yes, but I think Sepp's right forearm may be broken."

"Then put a splint on it," said Tischler, more curtly than he intended.

He stood there gazing across the lake, water dripping from his cap, observing the curtains of rain, driven by the wind from the east, sweeping across its restless surface. One relentless squall after another, again and again, ready to soak them over and over although they were already cold and wet through.

"Let's get out of this damned rain," he grunted and offered Anne his arm, which she took and let herself be guided along the long, arduous way to her house.

***

DAVID BERNSTEIN VERY GRADUALLY LIFTED the wooden lid of the placement's opening. It was no more than a dugout, the top of which was covered with turf and thorny bushes. Hastily dug, but well-disguised in a corner of the wide-reaching orchard. It was almost dark. The rain had stopped the day before – as had the gunfire. They were all cold, wet and hungry. Sarah, his wife, and Alma, Deborah, and Esther had recovered somewhat from the shock of the soldiers firing their guns. Upon clambering out, the girls discovered their dead animal friends, Ricki and Schutzi, their Alsatian protectors and playmates. This wasn't the first time they had all been allowed into the orchard for recuperation – but never like this. The girls ran up to their dead companions and stood over them crying.

"Mama, Papa, can we please bury them? Please."

"When we come back, we will bury them."

"You mean if we are still alive," said Alma, the eldest of the three.

"Be quiet, Alma! Silence, girl!"

At this remonstration, Alma hung her head, tears streaming down her face. David strode over to the desolate little girl, gathered her up in his arms and said: "We are going to see Sepp and Anne, and I'm going to carry you there, my little princess."

"Papa, Papa, will you carry me too?" cried the other two in unison.

"Of course, one after another, but no whinging and no pinching me." With this, he tickled Alma's ribs, and, despite herself, she gave a little burst of laughter and nuzzled her face into David Bernstein's thin white neck. His wife took the hands of the other two, kissed them briefly and followed her husband. Sarah and the children crept behind him until they reached the environs of the Kriegers' house. They took their boots off to avoid leaving a muddy trail from the potato field. There was no complaining, no whining and whinging; their children had grown very old in the last few years, and they knew when to keep their mouths shut.

They washed the dirt off their feet in the cold water of the trough in front of the kitchen door. The squeaking of the pump raised the hackles on David's back. The everyday sound seemed so dangerous as it screeched through the calm evening air of the lakeside. At the same moment, Flecki, the black cat with a white spot on his forehead, wrapped itself around his ankles to welcome him to the house. It seemed so incongruous, this display of cosy, domestic affection.

David knew that the slaves would have made the long walk back to the Friedrichshafen prison camp hours ago. They had to. Their chances of escape were zero. He was troubled that neither Sepp nor Anne had sent word to them. Something had gone wrong. He and Sarah feared the worst.

They entered the house through the kitchen back door. In the silent parlour, they suddenly heard a slight groan. Anne appeared in the doorway. She looked terrible. Her face was lacerated from Richter's whipping. She stood swaying in the doorway.

"Sarah," she said, "Sepp is in bed; could you look to him, please? David, take the girls into the kitchen, give them some soup and bread; you know where to find these things. Go."

The raggedly dressed little girls, aged five, six and eight, with their shorn heads, filthy pullovers and trousers, followed their father into the kitchen, sucking their thumbs. They sat themselves at the table with large, hopeful eyes and growling stomachs. None of them said anything. Thirty years later, when there was a family meeting at Mama's and Papa's house in Tel Aviv, where David still worked as an engineer and Sarah as a doctor at the hospital, their husbands complained, half-jokingly, that their wives never said anything. And often you never knew if they were in the house or not, so silently did they move. So still did they rest in their beds.

First, Sarah took Anne gently by the hand, led her back to her bed and examined her thoroughly. Elvira and Ludmilla had done a good job of tending to her. Her wounds were deep but none of them were mortal. The scars would be there for life. She stroked her forehead and hummed a song her mother had sung to her, and gradually Anne began to relax. After a while, she fell into a deep, exhausted sleep. Just as a child would do.

Sarah then moved to the other side of this big, massive marital bed, to Sepp. He was in worse shape, lying on his stomach, his wounds, also on his arms and the back of his head, still open but covered with goose fat. The women had done well. *Their gratitude for being treated like human beings*, she thought. She examined the provisional splint that they had made and applied to Sepp's probably broken right arm.

This was good, kindly work. She would do nothing, other than take Sepp's pulse, which was rather low.

"We'll have to keep an eye on that, Sepp," she said, stroking his forehead.

"Anne," he whispered, "tell Matthias to come home."

***

ELVIRA AND LUDMILLA WERE ON their long and weary walk back to the camp at Raderach.

As they were reaching the outskirts of Jettenhausen, Ludmilla stopped, sighed heavily, and said: "You know, Elvira, I never thought I would be in a bedroom in this terrible country tending to the wounds of two Germans."

"Yes, some of them seem even human. Just like you and me."

Ludmilla made a sign of the cross. "God help us that the Kriegers are. Now let's get back to the *Lager* before the SS crucify us."

The two women adjusted the slave ID plates that hung around their necks and continued onwards.

7

BERLIN, OCTOBER 1945
– THE RICHTER FAMILY,
TIERGARTENSTRASSE 18

MARTHA RICHTER GAZED OUT OF her bedroom window across the Tiergartenstrasse to the Tiergarten Park beyond with its streams and little lakes, beautiful trees, and lovely flowers. Unfortunately, these days, the scene was marred by the bomb craters, which were unavoidable, of course, when one was at war. The British or American bombers would return soon, no doubt.

The villa she occupied with her family, occupied being the appropriate word, was very much to her liking. Some Jews had taste, you had to give them that – and take it. Ha! It had been most unfortunate, due to bad planning elsewhere, that when they moved in, two years ago, she had bumped into the Jewess who was just moving out. The look this inferior woman had the cheek to give her! Martha was proud of herself; she had shown no emotion whatsoever. She had looked calmly down from this very window as the Jewish family was being loaded onto the back of an army lorry, destination Platform 17 Moabit Station. She had wished them to sleep well in their cattle truck, on the way to Auschwitz town, dear family Heine. Such noisy children, crying all the time. She had never let Hinrich and Birgit cry. Never!

The former owners must have had connections in the highest of places to have been able to stay here so long. Nevertheless, a Jew was a Jew. This lovely villa, with its beautiful furniture and valuable paintings. Hinrich had just simply adored the Monet and the Degas, and there was even a sketch by Rembrandt himself. Hinrich had always been such a beautiful and cultured young man. He took after her, of course. Also prudent regarding wealth. Not long ago, he had removed the paintings and the Rembrandt and had hidden them under their newly acquired boathouse in Friedrichshafen. The silver and crystalware must also be worth a fortune, but was too difficult to move; besides, she wanted to enjoy her valuable possessions day in and day out. However, the gold and silver jewellery of their former owners went with the artwork underneath the floor of the boathouse. They would never have to think about money again! Yes, they had certainly moved up in the world, thanks to Hannes being promoted yet again. Now he was a brigadier general in the SS. He had done some fine work regarding the Final Solution and Eicke had had him promoted. Now Hinrich, who had helped with the economics of the project, was in the SS too, stationed back in the south, in Dachau, not that far from Friedrichshafen, really.

And, it must be said, just across from them was a very well-equipped air-raid shelter called the Tiergarten Flak

Tower. One met such a superior type of person there. After all: this was the Tiergarten, and the bomb shelters underneath the flak tower itself were extensive and well-appointed, with excellent facilities all round. Unfortunately, the flak fire was awfully loud but provided excellent protection.

She, the daughter of a rich landowner in East Prussia, did not like to think about the circumstances of her marriage. To have ended up pregnant and wed to a hook-nosed, bony assistant accountant who spoke German like a Swabian farmhand. An unfortunate semi-erotic incident against a wall at the back of the assembly hall after too much alcohol – all part of her father's campaign to win over these southern yokels for the Nazi party. She despised her husband for what he was: a mean-spirited, barely educated, spineless coward, who had only agreed to marry her after he realised how rich and influential her father really was. Her parents had been of the opinion that it was better to be married to a lower-class nobody than to raise a bastard in the family. However, Hannes had, thanks to her constant and most stringent requirements, revealed that he was highly intelligent in a primitive non-verbal kind of way. He was also highly suited to the SS. It was hardly possible that anyone in that gang of perverts could have a browner nose than Hannes, nor that anybody could be so brutal in trampling down those below him. *And*: he certainly knew how, by hook or by crook, to get people to supply him with intelligence, concepts, and planning options.

Thus, she was proud of his rapid rise to the rank he had now attained. Overall, she was well satisfied, although not sensually. In this marriage, sex played no role for her. Hannes might be successful, but she could not bear the thought of him entering her anymore; he was too creepy, weak, and despicable. She found his subordinate, Major von Fuchs, much more attractive; she would like to feel him on top of her and more.

Enough! She knew she had to get herself ready; Hannes would be back soon, and Birgit from the hospital where she worked as a nurse. She was the bravest one of all – brave but naïve and stupid. Two years younger than Hinrich, and unlike her brother, she was showing less and less respect for 'our glorious cause', as she had sarcastically put it! And the triumph of our 'spiritual will and ancestry' over lesser people and peoples. Birgit read too many unsuitable, troublesome books, and her big mouth could get her into serious trouble one day.

Martha sat down at her vanity table; she was well pleased with her mirror image, as she might well be, she mused – barely a wrinkle! Unlike Berta Schmidt, her friend, who had many crow's feet around the eyes, and her bosom was sagging, too. She stared at her beautiful face with its delicate jawline and the straight balanced nose, the startling blue eyes, the full red lips all in perfect symmetry, such beauty – and she was only forty-three. Martha stood up, shook out her long, blonde hair, and turned to observe her elegant fulsome profile.

"I bet Major von Fuchs would like to get his hands on this, ha! He should be so lucky," she mused whilst lingering in front of the mirror stroking herself until she realised she was becoming more and more aroused. She squeezed her lavish breasts gently one more time with both hands and groaned: "No time for this now!" and left the room.

***

LATER THAT AFTERNOON, MARTHA STOOD at the threshold of the lounge door, with the dining room behind her, and observed her daughter, Birgit, who had been conversing – perhaps quarrelling was the better word for it – with Hannes yet again.

"So, Father, where did those red stains on your black leather military coat come from? Military coat, my foot!" said Birgit abrasively.

"How tiresome," said Hannes quietly. Martha, still watching, sensed that he hoped she would come in soon and put an end to this interrogation. He stretched his long legs out in front of him and settled back into the big Belfort fauteuil and gazed past Birgit, who was unfortunate enough to have inherited his looks and gangly figure. She was standing at the big bay windows with their lovely, delicately engraved patterns.

"I do not like your tone, my dear daughter, but if you must know, these blood stains are due to an unfortunate incident down on a farm back home in Friedrichshafen. I was inspecting Herr Krieger's property in order to secure supplies for our troops. A pig was being slaughtered outside, and I am afraid I got too close. You remember the family; they run a small farm near the lake. Hinrich had some dealings with the son, Matthias."

"Yes, I remember, I was thirteen. He came home black and blue one day, after a lakeside party. There was a lot of talk about it and some Jewish, English girl they were fighting over. We were all terribly upset at the time. But looking back, no doubt Hinrich deserved what he got."

"Perhaps, and Hinrich swears that if he ever meets him at the lakeside again, he will level the score. He is sure that will happen. He is waiting for it to happen! We will see. And now, Birgit, you are nineteen, and you have served your country abroad in Poland and are currently on the home front working at our magnificent Charité Hospital. You have come a long way, in more ways than one."

Martha had to admire the skill in which Hannes had switched the topic of conversation to Birgit herself. However, she could tell by her daughter's expression that she was not to be deterred.

"Father, I have seen blood on SS black leather before, in Poland. The men came back from a so-called mission, time and again. They were shooting and killing Jews and burying them in trenches – men, women, and children! Thousands and thousands of them! Again, and again, and again!"

Birgit was still in her nurse's uniform. Martha reasoned that on returning home, her daughter had seen, once again, the faded blood stains that would not wash out on her father's black leather coat, hanging in the hall wardrobe (she would have got rid of it but Hannes had protested so violently that she had given in – most unusual). She could see that Birgit was determined to have it out with him, about what he did. Now she was wringing her hands in sorrow, her bony, angular face wretched with anguish.

"Father, we are Catholics. Jesus taught us to treat others as we would want them to treat us! And what about little Paul Wagner, who was mentally backward? We watched from our window as the grey bus drew up one day, and little Paul got in and never came back. They gassed him! They gassed him, and I used to babysit and look after him. The head office for organising this programme of killing our neighbours' children and other people who do not fit in

– in other words, the people your Nazi friends do not like – is in this street: Tiergarten 4. They named this euthanasia program the T4 action. We do not love our neighbours but murder them as our enemies! And now we are neighbours with T4!" Birgit was screaming with rage and disgust, tearing at her uniform.

"You should be more careful what you say, dear daughter; be careful."

"Or what? Are you going to put me in a ditch, next to other defenceless women, and blow my brains out? You should be careful! On the U-Bahn I saw a man drop his Star of David onto the floor. It fell at the feet of a big army officer, who picked it up, bowed, and gave it back to him – everybody around laughed and clapped. So, *you* watch out, you fucking *Nazi!*"

"Birgit! That is enough; be silent!" Martha had heard enough. She strode into the room, her long, blonde hair swinging furiously. "Be quiet, I say!"

"And you are no better yourself, dear Mother," replied Birgit, her voice shaking in emotion. She picked up a cushion from the sofa and hugged it, swaying gently to and fro whilst sobbing into it.

Martha felt the atmosphere in her well-appointed lounge with all its finery was full of tension and dread, and the air had become thinner, so that the three of them gasped and struggled to find words.

Birgit continued inexorably onwards: "What do you say, Mother? What about little Paul Wagner?"

Martha welcomed this invitation to speak her mind – she wanted to put Birgit straight for once and for all. She looked her daughter straight in the eye, jutted her chin out and said: "You know full well that the mentally ill, retarded, cripples, and alcoholics who breed like rabbits are of no use to anyone. They cost time and money," she snapped. "Furthermore, that is where the Catholic Church got it wrong and Darwin right. It is a matter of the survival of the fittest. The Führer said we must rid ourselves of a third of our own population to achieve absolute purity. Only then can the German race attain its rightful position as the true master of all races.

"As for the Jews! The Jews! Martin Luther, the founder of the Protestant Church, he hated them; he even wanted to destroy their synagogues. Well, we did it for him! Jews are vermin; they are not even a proper race. They must be disposed of in order that purity prevails. Furthermore, young lady, while we are on the subject of books and knowledge: I suggest that you brush up on your science. Again: Charles Darwin has shown – no, proven – quite specifically, that in nature the fittest survive and dominate. And as the Führer so rightly said, that is us, we Germans, we wonderful Aryans of the north, that rightly should, and will, prevail. Read *Mein Kampf,* written specifically for this purpose. You must widen your mind, girl!" Martha felt her tone becoming harsher and higher.

"Thus, endeth the sermon! So, Mother, not only should we kill anybody who is different from us, like Paul Wagner, but also steal their property, such as this lovely villa. We have become criminals and murderers; not only that, thieves as well. Mother, you are a thief!" she screamed in her mother's face, still clutching the cushion to her breast.

Martha arched back and with a full, cruel swing, slapped her daughter down, again and again, to the floor. The rush of violence and power filled her with pleasure. Birgit sat on the rich Turkish carpet and sobbed uncontrollably.

Her father stood up and murmured: "This is all due to that bloody Catholic priest back in Friedrichshafen, preaching to you that nonsense from Bishop von Galen. You really should consider being more prudent, Birgit. You need not worry about Jews being shot in ditches anymore. We just send a letter telling them to turn up at the railway station at a specific time. We hardly need any soldiers to do that. It is economical, less stressful for our boys and most effective. We now resettle them in the east, you know."

Martha knew that Hannes found these quarrels tiresome and upsetting (apart from that, his pathetic pleading tone made her skin crawl). This had to stop. If it got out about Birgit's views, it would not bode well for his career. On this they both were entirely of the same opinion.

"It is time for the evening meal," she said coolly, and summoned her husband into the dining room.

Looking down at her sobbing daughter, she announced: "And you better change your attitude, young lady, and also learn to keep your big mouth shut."

Birgit moaned and cried wretchedly, "Deutschland, the land of poets and thinkers, the true German Romantics: Goethe, Schiller, the Schlegels, Fichte, Novalis and all the others, they lived or stayed in Jena, creating new worlds of thought with one another, and now it has led to this and to Buchenwald just up the road from where they lived. Buchenwald, the new home for our thinkers and poets!" She continued crying on the floor in a foetal position, weeping and fighting for her breath whilst desperately holding onto her cushion as if it would understand and comfort her.

Martha looked over her shoulder and said: "Get up and shut up."

***

THE SIRENS HAD BEEN WAILING their warnings for almost thirty seconds before Martha could bring herself to react, and then with the utmost of speed.

"Come on!" she cried to Hannes, who was sitting staring moodily at his plate of cheese, bread, and sausage. Knocking her chair back, she half-ran to the hallway and started to struggle with her coat.

"Listen! It is the Americans this time; the engines, you know," he replied, looking up at the ceiling.

"Shut up, you fool, and get Birgit; she is still sulking on the floor in the lounge. Bring her to the Tiergarten Flak Tower and down into the air-raid shelter."

Martha watched in surprise as Hannes, instead of following her command, looked into the lounge and crossed over to Birgit, who seemed to be sleeping. He noticed she was semi-conscious, now stretched out on the carpet, moaning quietly to herself.

"Birgit, move; the bombers are coming. Move, I say!" Hannes, thinking he had not done his duty as a father, shook Birgit's shoulder and said loud and clear: "Move, girl, you don't want to die like this, do you?"

Birgit moaned louder, and whispered, "*Papa, mein Papachen.*"

As a little girl, Birgit had called him 'my little Papa',

and liked to nestle on his lap. He was never quite sure how to react to this sudden display of affection and had usually responded by stroking her head.

This he did now, bending down to her and saying softly, "Come now, Birgit." Doing so, he glimpsed the father he could have become and the man he never was, or ever would be.

"Hannes, enough is enough, you come on, or we will all die here! She will follow soon enough," cried Martha from the hallway. "Come on, damn you, I am going!" Martha moved further through the house, opened the heavy villa front door with a determined swing and clattered down the steps.

Hannes Richter stood up abruptly, embarrassed that his show of affection had kept him behind.

"Of course," he said and hurried out of the door to join his wife.

As Martha and Hannes stumbled down the steps leading to the bomb shelter underneath the Tiergarten Flak Tower, they could hear the distant, rumbling roar of the American Flying Fortresses manoeuvring in for their bombing paths.

In the aftermath of the fight with Birgit and now this tremendous threat to her life, Martha was shivering and shaking all over. She wanted to live! As soon as she entered the dimly lit underground corridor, Hannes left her. Peeling off to the right, he grabbed Berta Schmidt's hand. Berta just happened to be waiting near the entrance to the area reserved for officers and their families and friends. The two of them headed for one of the bedrooms.

Martha was still quivering with fear and excitement when she heard a warm, manly voice in her ear: "Martha,

I'm so glad that you are here, albeit in such unfortunate circumstances."

Martha, on hearing the deep voice of Major von Fuchs, felt herself become wet. In the same instant, in her mind's eye, she saw in a flash of recognition, the destruction of her beautiful new home, of Berlin, of Germany, of themselves.

She turned and said to von Fuchs: "This is the end, my friend."

She took him by the hand and led him towards the officers' sleeping quarters.

***

BIRGIT WAS ROUSED OUT OF her dismal state by the air-raid sirens and the still echoing voice of her mother telling her to get up and get out.

She ran through the many doorways of the villa, down the steps, and into the Tiergartenstrasse itself, still clutching her cushion to her breast. The roar of the B17s was almost secondary as the flak guns belted out their non-stop furious barrage from the flak tower to the enemy above. Looking up as she ran, Birgit saw hell in the heavens. The bombers were no longer in formation but were scattered across the sky. Some of them belching smoke and roaring red flames, harried by a few German fighters, all the while bursts of flak exploding in the atmosphere in colours of orange, yellow, and red. Huge, dying aeroplanes belching fire and greasy, black smoke lumbered awkwardly down to their end. Little men suspended from downy parachutes full of hope amid this purgatory. The shrieking sirens, the cacophony of the flak battery, and now the huge numbing, shaking, earth-trembling explosions of the falling bombs. All this amidst a beautiful late autumn day in 1944 with the trees of the Tiergarten blazing gold. Birgit stood transfixed. She looked up and saw and heard a 500-pound bomb hurtling towards her. She opened her arms as to catch it, as she had done when little Paul Wagner ran to fling himself into her gentle, loving arms.

Martha fancied she heard the echo of a girl's scream as Major Paul Edgar Wilhelm von Fuchs was pounding his penis into her – with both her legs draped over his arms, he was holding her suspended up against the wall.

"Birgit!" she gasped as von Fuchs's hot semen splashed against her left thigh. "Let me go, you fucking donkey!"

He let her down to the ground and, wrenching herself free, barely managing to pull her dress together, she stumbled towards the door. Along the corridor she ran, all the while feeling encumbered, forcing her way past the entrance guards and out into the open, where the air stank of cordite and was still full of settling dust, accompanied by the clanging and ringing of the empty cartridges falling from the guns on the roof of the ack-ack tower above. The row of villas was intact, including their own, in front of which was a huge crater in the middle of the road. In fact, there was, at this point, no longer any road but a row of huge yawning craters, the like of which she had seen in photographs of the inside of extinct volcanoes. This one, however, was still smouldering angrily. She crouched down, looked closely, and brushed some rubble off a dark blue shoe that had once belonged to Birgit. She then removed her entangled panties from her left ankle (which had caused her to trip and stumble on the way to her daughter's grave), bunched them and wiped off the cold von Fuchs semen that had dripped down her leg.

Martha stood up and walked shakily up the steps of her villa. Looking up she said, "And this is mine."

***

SOME MONTHS LATER, HANNES RICHTER was standing at a barricade on the street where he lived. The battle of Berlin was raging. The city had been encircled by the Soviet armies, whose soldiers, many, but not all, had fought, killed, plundered, and raped their way through to the capital of the German Empire. The ninth army, under the command of Busse, had tried to break through the Spree Forest to the southwest of Berlin and link up with the twelfth army and go westwards to surrender to the allies.

They had been destroyed.

Hitler was dead.

Even so, the SS patrolled the streets stringing up anybody they thought might not want to fight the enemy from the nearest lamppost. Usually, they attached a sign to the body saying exactly why. It was expected of every citizen to do his duty and fight against the Soviet invader, which was to stand at the barricades and shoot with an ancient army rifle against tanks and other army vehicles after being bombed and strafed by enemy planes. Hannes Richter had had enough. There had been brutal fighting at Potsdamer Platz, and those caught sneaking away risked being caught by the SS, who were patrolling the back street like a bunch of bloodthirsty guttersnipes.

As it became obvious that they were outgunned and outnumbered, Hannes made a run for it. He was not the only one. He came up against an SS man, who levelled his submachine gun at him and sneered: "Get back to the street blockade, yellow belly, or die here!"

Those were his last words, as a shot rang out from behind Hannes and the killer ran past him shouting, "Keep going or die; come on!"

Hannes ran and eventually arrived at his house without further incident. He burst into the lounge of their villa and screamed as the panic within rose to his throat: "Martha, we must escape; the Russians are just down the road. Come on!"

"Shut up, you idiot! We are not going anywhere. Berlin is surrounded. I shall retire to my bedroom and await our visitors."

"Martha, they will kill us. They will rape you first, and with your looks, perhaps not once, and perhaps not just one of them."

"I can assure you I will not be raped," Martha replied quietly and distinctly.

Two hours later, she heard the Russian soldiers breaking down the front door. They were shooting wildly as they went from room to room. She heard Hannes run up the stairs and into her boudoir. He stopped in his tracks. She was lying on the bed in her translucent nightdress, underneath which she had nothing on. Martha had decided she would face the door. At her side and in her right hand, a pistol, his service gun.

"What are you doing? Have you gone mad?" he shouted.

He walked towards her and looked at her from the foot of the bed. Martha opened her legs, so he could see her hairy crotch. It was the last thing he saw as Martha Richter raised the pistol and shot him twice at close range in the heart.

"Goodbye, Hannes," she murmured.

Minutes later, a young Russian soldier burst into the room and approached her wide-eyed as she lay there. He was unbuttoning his trousers as she killed him. And also, the man behind him, who was in the process of laying his rifle to the side and struggling to get out of his trousers at the same time.

The first hand grenade that was thrown into the room didn't kill her. It did, however, convince her that the game was up. She calmly put the big pistol into her mouth and blew her brains out.

8

MATTHIAS KRIEGER
1944–1953

MATTHIAS THREW HIMSELF INTO THE ditch as rifle shots zipped over his head like angry wasps. He was about to crawl away into the apparent safety of the trees on the other side of the path when he heard the unmistakeable roar of the T-34 climbing up on the other side of the small embankment. Where the hell were Bruno and Uwe? They had the bazooka and ammo. At the same time, Matthias realised that a bazooka popgun wasn't going to help him, but the ditch might. The roar of the machine was deafening. He pressed himself hard into the dry ditch, hoping that the tank track wouldn't land on him directly. He looked up out of his right eye and saw the left-hand side of the tank dropping down on him. He was gagging on the diesel fumes.

"Mama," he squeaked as the pivoting tracks landed two metres away from his head. He could hear the Russian infantry soldiers coming up behind the machine. Just as he thought they had all passed on down the lane, he felt a boot on the side of his face. Looking up, he simultaneously fired three pistol shots into the face of a surprised, young, blond-haired Russian soldier. *He was merely a boy*, thought Matthias as he scrambled up and disappeared into the woods. Now, where the hell were Bruno and Uwe?

He found them after going further into the forest. They had decided on a call sign that sounded like some sort of bird. None of them knew any real bird calls.

They were a mixed crew. He and Uwe had been prospective university candidates before the war broke out, thus differing from Bruno, who had already completed three semesters of philosophy at Heidelberg before being called up. The army, not being quite sure what to do with these budding intellectuals, decided to put them in military reconnaissance. Their task was to forage and explore the enemy's position, gauge his strength and probable lines of attack or retreat and report back. Now it was the German army doing all the retreating and Matthias and his little troop were lost. *So much for intelligent reconnaissance*, thought Matthias, who, as Leutnant, oversaw what was left of their scattered unit. Bruno had reckoned that they were approaching the Ukrainian-Polish border. They had to get back to the German army, which was unfortunately disintegrating, so none of them knew where the nearest units could be found, but they reckoned they should head westwards, direction Germany. So much for intellect.

They continued their way through the forest, proceeding west until they came into a gully. To their left loomed a wall of rock against which a shot suddenly ricocheted off and flew past them, and then another, much closer. The three of them took cover behind a big boulder in the middle of the trail.

"A sniper, look!" hissed Uwe. Matthias saw the barrel of a rifle peeping out behind a boulder some one hundred metres further up the ravine. In the distance, the rumble of a T-34 could be heard approaching from behind.

They were trapped. If the T-34 was approaching, so was the Russian infantry and that meant air-cover too. As if his thoughts had conjured up the worst possible scenario, he heard the distant snarl of a Jak-9 fighter. They both looked at him desperately.

"Listen, when the fighter sees us, which, in this gully, he will, throw yourselves one to the left, t'other to the right. Our sniper friend will have to take cover too when the strafing starts," he screamed.

"And you, Matthias?"

"I'll be over there diagonally to the right, in the woods."

"You will be seen!"

"It's our best chance. Here he comes! Leap *now!*"

The enemy plane came snarling in, and as he opened up his nose canon and two machine guns, Matthias jumped slantwise to his right and ran for the woods, hoping that the Russian sniper wouldn't pop him before he reached the undergrowth. Out the corner of his eye, he registered Uwe and Bruno diving to their left and right respectively all the while the Yak 9 was hammering away dead centre at the rocks behind which they had been hiding from the sniper, who was nowhere to be seen.

He threw himself headfirst into the underbrush, spat out dirt and grass, set up his elbows, and took aim. The Russian was clearly visible, now slightly from behind and to the side. Matthias took aim. His opponent was trying to get a bead on his comrades. From his now more favourable position,

Matthias had a clear enough view of the man's back. He squeezed off a shot and the Russian slumped forwards and clutched the boulder that had been protecting him. He didn't move again.

The menacing, roaring rumbling of the tank was now frighteningly close. The Yak 9 would be back as soon as he had finished his loop. Without giving it a second thought, Matthias yelled at and sprinted with Uwe and Bruno along the gully past their dead enemy and into the woods beyond.

Taking a zig-zag course, they jogged for some miles until they could hear nothing but the sounds of the forest and of water flowing downhill. Experience had shown that Uwe was the most competent in being able to judge their position; apart from that, he had some rough maps of this area. He reckoned that they were in the mountainous forests of the Skolivski region, approximately fifty kilometres east of the Polish border. After two days, following a river upwards towards its source, they came across a derelict hut near the stream in a wide-open clearing. There, Matthias ordered them to rest.

"I estimate we are safe enough at this point; we'll camp here for the night," said Matthias. The others groaned and let their rucksacks fall to the ground followed by themselves, weary after marching many kilometres in the opposite direction from their last seen enemy.

"Get up and get out!" shouted Matthias. "Secure the area. One of us is on watch as of now. We change guard every two hours, so one of us gets four hours' sleep in one go. I'll take the first watch, but first we check the area and see that it is safe."

"If we see a young wild pig, do we shoot it?" asked

Bruno, quietly. "I think we should – we have got to eat meat again soon."

Uwe, who was now exploring the inside of the hut, poked his head out and answered with a yes straight away. Against his better instincts, Matthias agreed with them; he knew that the men needed a full belly if possible. To be able to fight well, good spirits were essential. Looking around at the surrounding forest with the mountain peaks towering over them, he decided that if the Russians heard a shot, they would not know from which direction it had come. Apart from that, they were well off the main strategic routes heading west.

"Okay, if we see a wild pig, shoot it."

Immediately, a shot rang out and echoed around the surrounding mountains like rolling thunder, followed by high-pitched squealing. Matthias thought the noise would never stop.

"Got it; dropped it!" shouted big Bruno excitedly, who had all the time seen the young pig and had had it in his sights. It had been trailing behind its herd, the rest of which now ran screaming into the forest. Uwe came out of the hut waving two bottles in each hand.

"Look, vodka! They are covered in dust, so they must have been here before the war broke out. Let's put them in the stream to cool."

"Okay, but we are not going to drink all four bottles at once," said Matthias gravely.

"Suit yourself, Herr Leutnant. I say a bottle for each man and one for the road!" Uwe laughed. He strode over to the stream and arranged stones in the water around the bottles with the same care and tenderness as if he were putting children to bed.

Three hours later, Matthias was on the ground propped up against a perfectly rounded boulder, watching the dancing flames of the campfire they had made, comfier than he had been for many a year. His belly, like those of his comrades, was full of roast pork accompanied by roast potatoes and cabbage; products of the neglected vegetable garden they had found at the back of the hut. He reckoned the last time a person had used this hut for hunting would have been about eighteen months ago. The vegetables tasted a bit funny, but better than anything they had had in a long time.

He took another slug of vodka, straight out of the bottle. He didn't really like alcohol and, apart from the occasional beer at suppertime back home, he never touched the stuff. He liked to keep a clear head, which wasn't the case now. The vodka didn't really taste of anything, but he certainly felt relaxed.

One hour later, as dusk was settling in, it seemed to him that the massive green wall of the forest across and around the clearing seemed to have become greener, darker, and menacing. It was so still. Now the green wall was moving towards him, quivering as if it wanted to embrace him with its dark secrets. From out of this bulwark, a form appeared, walking slowly and flickeringly towards him. His mood shifted.

"Bruno," he whispered.

"Oh no! It's my turn to take watch," said Bruno. He looked across at the approaching lanky figure of blond, spikey-haired Uwe. Uwe waved vaguely, grunted, then sat down by the fire, sighed, and stretched out his long legs, as if resigning himself to the massive stillness of the green night in this land of shadows.

Matthias waved weakly across to Uwe and took a deep draw from his vodka bottle, then turned over on his side. As comfort, and as usual, he started to think and dream of Judith. This time, they were at his home sitting on the bench looking out over the golden lake in the setting evening sun. Judith was talking in quiet tones about how she would like to paint this scene using the techniques and style of Gabriele Münter. Matthias turned to give her a kiss and found himself staring into the bloody and torn visage of the young blond-haired Russian soldier, who had trodden on him and who he had immediately killed. He sat up sharply, his face burning, and expelled an explosion of air. He sank back.

"Am I losing her?" he whispered.

The last thing he could then remember until he was shaken awake two hours later was watching big Bruno's broad back disappearing into the darkness.

"Well, what I suppose Nietzsche really meant was that we had freed ourselves from the tyranny of religion and the Church; that man had shown himself to be his own master, the superman and more, if you will. I reckon that's why Heidegger latched on to Hitler, our very own superman – and look where it fucking got us!" Bruno scratched his black-stubbled chin and then his equally black hair, spat into the fire and rolled himself another cigarette with the rough Russian tobacco he had harvested or traded during his travels.

"So, he was a Hitler man, Heidegger, was he?" asked Uwe, looking up.

"Yes, he was a Hitler man alright," answered Bruno slowly.

"Well, Hitler revived our economy, put us back on the map and gave us our pride back. And apart from that, he put the Jews, who betrayed us in the Great War and who then led us to financial ruin in the 1930s, in their place. Namely at the bottom of the ladder."

From the mountains, they heard the lonely howls of the wolves calling to one another across the peaks and valleys. Then the air breathed stillness and solitude.

Uwe shivered, turned away from an unsure, silent Bruno and looked askance at Matthias, who replied slowly: "I don't know. All I know is that Hitler hated the Jews, and my girlfriend was a Jewess. In my family, I was taught that hate is a sin. Hitler also got us into this bloody, bloody mess. So, as far as I'm concerned, he has done me, my girlfriend, my family, and my country no good whatsoever – to put it lightly."

He looked at his two comrades, who were mulling over what he had just said.

Uwe eventually replied, slowly: "But if your girlfriend was a Jewess, then…"

"Shut up, Uwe; it is none of our business. That's another thing I hate about the Nazis; they make everyone's business their business. Fuck that!" shouted Bruno vehemently.

"Very well. Who's taking the first watch tonight?" replied Uwe disconsolately.

"I will, then I can get four hours of sleep afterwards," said Matthias decisively.

"But before we do, I must ask; Matthias, you are the boss, when do we get leave to go home again?"

Bruno guffawed loudly and said: "Look around; do you see a train homeward bound?"

Matthias answered quickly to nip a potential ugly quarrel in the bud. "Uwe, the fact of the matter is that the whole of our army – no, armies! – are on the retreat. All leave has been cancelled. We will be back in Germany, or what is left of it, soon enough."

"What about you, Matthias? You have not been home for a long time, as long as we have been together."

Matthias looked at Uwe for a full minute before he replied: "At home, I feel restless; it is as if I miss being on the front with you, my dear fat-faced comrades. Apart from that, it is too dangerous, and I don't want to cause my parents any more grief."

"I know what you mean about missing being on the front, but why should it be dangerous for you at home, Matthias?" said Uwe, looking very puzzled.

"My girlfriend was a Jewess – not only that, an English Jewess – this could still cause problems, not just for me but also for my parents." Again, he looked at Uwe, carefully measuring his reaction.

"I see," replied Uwe slowly.

Bruno spat in the fire again and said: "Fuck it, lads, let's get some sleep."

It was their second night. Matthias had decided that they should stay put until they had recovered completely from their recent twenty-mile retreat (and their heavy-duty night before with vodka), reasoning they would be fighting for their lives soon enough once they were on their way again.

The evening skies were darkening even more with the gathering rain clouds. The wall of dark green that surrounded their clearing seemed to Matthias denser and more secretive than ever before. He felt the menace of war and the need to move on.

"Okay, enough of philosophy. We will sleep in the hut, changing guard every two hours as per usual. I'll take the first turn," said Matthias – secretly hoping that he would then be tired and certainly sober enough to enjoy his only solace in comfort: Judith Rachel Lareine.

The next morning, they also spent two hours trying to disguise the fact that they had camped there. He ordered them to gather up the fire ashes, rake the area over gently and cover it with grass from the clearing. In the hut, they spread dirt around and created as much dust as possible.

"Well, it would fool the likes of us, but not a trained scout," said Uwe, hefting his rucksack up onto his back.

"It will have to do; let's go," ordered Matthias, and they made their way through the forest at the other end of the clearing.

***

HE MUST REACH THE CREST of the hill. He had no idea how he had come to be carrying this heavy machine gun and a belt of ammunition across his shoulder. Shells were exploding to his left and right from the unseen Russian artillery on the other side of the hill. Time and again, he took cover behind large granite rocks. The hillside provided scant cover otherwise. He had to get to the top to stop the enemy reaching it from the other side first. If they broke through, then they would be slaughtered. Two heavily landing bodies to his left and right told him that Bruno and Uwe were with him.

"I've got the tripod," said Bruno.

"And I have three long and bloody heavy ammo belts," groaned Uwe.

Matthias shouted above the chaos: "Keep crawling; it's our only chance – the others are too far behind, and they are getting pounded by the shelling. Keep crawling; the only way is up!"

The three reached the peak and, between a row of rocks that provided a semblance of cover, unseen, they set up the machine gun. The Russian shelling was thunderous, vicious, and was now zeroing in on their comrades, who were stuck at the base below them. They didn't have to wait long before the Russian infantry started to scrabble up towards them. With steady Bruno working the machine gun, calm Uwe feeding him the cartridge belt and Matthias picking off the officers, they stopped one wave after another of the enemy.

"Change position! Move over fifty metres to the left, otherwise their mortars will get us! *Move, damn you! Move!*" Matthias's voice cracked as he screamed his commands and immediately moved crabwise to their new position.

"My God, what a waste of good men," said Bruno, compressing a cigarette between his teeth. From their new position, he mowed down one row of infantry after another, whose line of attack was dictated by the rock formations on this side of the hill. They had to advance through a natural funnel, which made for easy killing. The bodies of their enemy were piling up on top of one and other, making it even more difficult for their comrades to advance. They had to clamber over them, thus making themselves an even easier target for the three Germans.

"In about two minutes, we will have no ammo left!" shouted Uwe through the noise, the smoke, and the death.

"Let's get out of here and leave the damn machine gun!" commanded Matthias.

They scrambled down the west side of the hill and disappeared into the forest below – always moving away from the battle. At the same time, Matthias was trying to estimate the full strength of their enemy, and to find his western flank. After some time, Matthias designated big Bruno as lead man. Bruno had eyes like a hawk and the ears of a wolf.

Eventually, he said: "I can hear water; come on!" Desperately thirsty, he and Uwe followed him blindly through the dense undergrowth. They both ran into Bruno's massive back, first Uwe and then, behind him, Matthias. It reminded him of a scene in a silent Charlie Chaplin film. What he then saw was not funny.

A German soldier had been tied to a tree, his trousers were down, and his mutilated crotch was covered in dried blood. In his mouth were his testicles and penis, or what was left of them. His rucksack and boots were missing.

"Quiet!" shouted Matthias in a whisper. "I can still feel the body heat of this poor bastard. They can't have got far."

They crept alongside the left bank of the stream and, after a few minutes, heard Russian voices. The scene they came upon could have been one from the French impressionists: five teenage soldiers, no more than boys, were relaxing around a picnic cloth set out on the ground, upon which was bread, sausage, and cheese, and even a bottle of red wine. The soldiers had obviously just finished washing themselves at the riverbank. Now they looked up in wide-eyed horror at the sight of these intruders. Their weapons were strewn around in a haphazard manner.

"Get up!" hissed Uwe, waving his free hand in an upwards motion.

As soon as they did, with hands above their heads, all naked to the waist, he shot the one nearest in the crotch and proceeded to execute the second boy. Bruno opened fire in the same manner on the next two. Amid the deafening screams and the spurting fountains of blood, they looked to Matthias to finish off the last youth in the same manner. This boy looked at Matthias pathetically, pleading with his brown eyes, so clearly could he see him as he fired one round and then another into the lad's manhood.

"Let's go back and bury our man," shouted Bruno.

Matthias, in a shaky voice, ignoring the mayhem around him, replied: "No, it's too dangerous, these woods are teeming with Russians."

Later that day, they came across two more Russians who they ambushed and killed. One of them had a German army rucksack on his back and German army boots on his feet. At his side, a long, evil-looking knife that he hadn't bothered to clean the blood off.

"It was these two, then. They look like deserters to me," groaned Matthias.

"Fuck it, fuck them, and fuck this godless war. Let's go," growled Bruno and spat at the foot of the two bodies.

***

MATTHIAS GROANED. HE COULDN'T MOVE. Only his hands seemed to work. He used these to carefully tap and prod his body; he felt everything. He was intact. Looking across, he saw that Uwe wasn't.

The last thing he could remember was screaming at Uwe and Bruno to get down as the Russian artillery had zeroed in on their squad. He could see Uwe's head, his eyes staring upwards as if to indicate supreme annoyance. The rest of his mangled body lay a couple of metres away from him, flung out like a puppet.

Big Bruno lay on his side to his right, still beside him as if he were sleeping quietly. He was dead; Matthias could tell after watching the giant man for several minutes. His chest hadn't moved, and his left ear was covered with blood. Behind it was a hole.

Then he saw Judith coming towards him. "Judith," he croaked, "how nice to see you."

He looked at her again and gasped. Out of her nostrils, maggots were making their way down to her naked breasts. Around her loins writhed a snake. She advanced towards Matthias, swinging her hips.

As she mounted him, she whispered in his ear: "Now is the time for us two at last."

***

THEY HAD BEEN ON THIS road for days. They were prisoners. The attacking Russians had overrun them. They had surrendered with their arms held aloft. A Russian came up to them and had shot the German soldier standing next to him in the head. He had levelled his pistol at Matthias when his commanding officer told him to stop. "останавливаться!" He would never forget that word.

This morning, Bernd had given him half of a tiny apple. It had reinvigorated him as if he had eaten a full meal. Almost. They had drunk from the ditches at the wayside. The column of prisoners stretched back as far as he could see. The Russians said the war was lost and Berlin had fallen, and that Hitler was dead. As they trudged on, Matthias kept looking at the back of the man in front of him willing him onwards so they could reach their destination alive. At night, they slept by the roadside.

The next morning, as they came through a village, Matthias saw Russian women lining the road. They were crying at the sight of the prisoners' distress and were giving out pieces of bread, fruit, and dried sausage to them. Matthias gratefully garnered a bit of everything. He glanced across at Bernd who, like himself, was of small stature, but not so solidly built. Bernd was eating, slowly and very carefully, as one did.

"Even our guards share their food with us. What the devil! We treated their men like shit," cried Bernd.

"Shut up and eat what you can," snapped Matthias.

He viewed his situation from what he considered to be a compellingly practical viewpoint: he was alive, uninjured apart from his knee, which bothered him on and off and caused him to limp. He was always hungry and always on the lookout for food and water. He was thin; they were all too thin. He drew his reserves of strength from his upbringing. His family had relied on nobody else to get through in life. His father had fought for his country for years in the trenches in the Great War. He and his wife had suffered through the hardships of the post-war years, keeping their small farm and building business going. No matter what. Furthermore, Matthias realised quite clearly that they were god-fearing, decent, resilient people. Matthias wanted nothing more than to get back to them – and to Judith, his English Jewess. How would that be possible?

Recently, his nightly picture of her face was fading, he was always so hungry. His wretched uniform hung loosely from his frame; his muscular build had deflated. He had to concentrate on staying alive, and he sensed and feared he was becoming harsher, even crueller, because of this – because of this war that he had endured for six long years. He recognised that a part of him had died along with those he had seen killed, slaughtered, even. And those he had killed himself. Just of late, deep in the night, the innocent, impressionistic vision of the bathers often came to mind through the veil of his hunger, not Judith.

'Conscience is a blemish that the Jews inflicted on mankind.' Didn't Hitler say that? And, as Bruno had frequently said when faced with a conundrum: "Fuck it! Let's go!"

"Fuck it, Bernd, let's keep up," announced Matthias to his startled companion.

They tramped onwards. Nobody spoke. Everyone was concentrating on the one thing: the next step. The dust, which had settled with their brief rest, was starting to fill the air again. On this trail, it was their continual companion, drying their throats and smothering their senses.

"My dear Matthias, I am delighted to see that you have made it thus far, despite the present conditions in which we find ourselves."

"I know that voice!"

Matthias turned in absolute astonishment and rising joy when he saw the slim-built, one-armed major who had accompanied him on the train for the wounded almost four years ago. Major Warner smiled warmly at Matthias's obvious delight.

"What the hell are you doing here, Major?" asked Matthias in wonderment.

The thrill of seeing the man again who had given him so much encouragement when he had been so downcast was so evident that Bernd smiled with him. Major Warner beamed again with pleasure at this enthusiastic welcome on this hot, dusty, sad, summer's day.

"A good question, Matthias. What on earth is a one-armed German major doing in the middle of Russia? Well, I was working with the intelligence corps as a translator and interpreter for the interrogation of high-ranking Russian prisoners. Although, of late, the shoe has been on the other foot, so to speak."

The conversation died down quickly; they had to save their strength. Matthias had on his right Major Warner and, to his left, faithful protector Bernd. *Together we are strong; we will survive this*, he thought. For the first time in a long time, his heart lifted. He looked up to the sky and saw skylarks flitting fussily to and fro.

Some hours later, he saw the outline of a settlement a couple of miles ahead; not a village, a town. The column was coming to a halt.

At the railway station, they waited for the train to nowhere, as some of the men named it. The train consisted of very many roofed freight trucks with sliding doors. Matthias waited with the major and Bernd until it was their turn. They had used the time as an opportunity to fill their field flasks with water and to rest. Their guards didn't seem to mind them wandering about as long as they stayed in sight.

"You couldn't do this if you were a German prisoner," exclaimed Bernd, stating precisely what they were all thinking. Yet time and again, some of the town inhabitants, who surely did not have much to share, took pity and gave them food and water.

When they finally got into their designated wagon, Matthias realised that it was going to be an exhausting journey, for their wagon was stuffy, hot, and very crowded. The long, long train moved off, and through the slats they could see many prisoners left behind, no doubt waiting for the next train.

After an hour and some discussion, they reckoned they were heading east. Five days later, the train came to a halt outside of the town of Asbest in the Urals. When the doors were finally swung open, many of them fell off the wagons and onto the ground below and crawled their way to the awaiting prison camp. Matthias, in spite of all, noticed that their indifferent guards weren't laughing at their misery – they were hungry, too.

**

MATTHIAS AND BERND PUT THE dead soldier Bernd had woken up next to that morning onto the back of the cart feet first. It was easy that way, but also harder, because you tended to look the dead man in the face. Summoning all their strength, they laid the next starved skeleton feet first next to him. They filled the cart with bodies and, together with the others, pulled it to the pit, where they were dumped next to the other corpses. Their comrades dumped! *There is no other word for it*, thought Matthias. He knew things were more than desperate and continued his deliberations: he realised that if things didn't improve soon, they'd had it. Not even their Russian guards had enough to eat.

Matthias said to Bernd: "We have been here over a year now and there are unmistakable signs of cannibalism."

Bernd replied: "I have my eyes open and my shiv ready for anyone who is going to try anything. Fear not. I hide it well and they don't search us anymore; what's the point?"

"So, I reckon we are safe." Matthias sighed and looked at his tough little friend thoughtfully.

They headed slowly back to their hut and were met by Major Warner who, as a translator, had one of the best jobs in the camp.

"Good news at last!" He smiled weakly at them and leant back against the wall of the hut. "We are to work in, or near, Asbest. We will receive decent food and even cigarettes if we work well. I've just been translating these instructions from the UPV. The camp is going to rent us out to the town of Asbest to do construction work and the like. To ensure we do not die on the job, no joke intended, we will receive as of tomorrow proper food – all of us, the whole camp. The Russians seem to be sorting out some of their agricultural problems. Whatever, food is on its way."

"Thank God," exclaimed Matthias fervently and puffed out his cheeks. "They'll need carpenters. Back home, my father and I made everything from furniture to roofs, to boats. And they will certainly need translators even more, just to keep the ball rolling, Herr Major."

"Yes, my dear Matthias, which will be most satisfactory."

"We are not going to starve. Thank God for that!" said Bernd. He sat down on the step to their barracks and started to cry, tears slowly rolling down his gaunt cheeks.

"Bernd, old comrade, why the tears?"

"I am a barber by trade, and here everyone has shaved heads. What use am I?"

"Have you lost your marbles? You are now a carpenter's mate. I'll need you to help me with the construction work – lifting, carrying, handing me my tools and learning by doing. We can vouch for you, right, Major?"

"I think we can manage that alright. The Russians just want the job done and they know we Germans are efficient, so they usually let us get on with whatever we think is the most resourceful way to complete the assignment. More good news: we officers will be transferred to the officers' camp we have been trying to build. So, with more food to finish that task too, things will become more bearable. The three of us stay *together*. We will continue to share what we have. The trouble is that this starvation kills first comradeship, then each individual; it is every man for himself in the battle for food. Those that die, die alone. But not us. Apart from that, Bernd, you are our protector. I have never met anyone quite so violent as you, my dear friend. I want you particularly to continue keeping an eye on young Matthias – he is somewhat too trusting. This camp is a dangerous place."

Matthias turned and looked at Bernd. Bernd looked up to them both. He sighed deeply and heavily and stood up to face them.

"I solemnly swear that I will do my best to protect you both. And I will do that: safeguard the pair of you. As you both know, I learnt the savage part of myself at the Battle of Kursk. After our tanks had been knocked out and our guns emptied of ammunition, we used knives and spades, as did the Russians."

The three men lapsed into an exhausted and thoughtful silence about what they had become and what had been done to them.

"And, Bernd," announced the major, "officers want to look smart, so they will need haircuts. You will have a supplementary form of income too. Not bad, eh? Better now, my friend?"

Matthias looked across at Bernd, whose face lit up, and said: "Come on, let's get our portion of fish-head soup and stone-hard bread before it's all gone."

Twenty months later, the work on the building site for the huge new asbestos factory had progressed well enough to please their Russian masters, with everyone ensuring that things didn't move along too quickly. The winters had been fantastically cruel with temperatures down well below minus twenty degrees. They still had to work, and, being a carpenter, Matthias ensured that they always had excess wood to burn in the braziers, which pleased their guards as well. The work had to be conducted slowly and carefully – the deep freeze slowed everything down – but the prisoners had stopped dying so frequently and in such vast numbers. A certain degree of normality had ensued. Matthias knew that there were certain guards who would beat you without reason, or spit on you as you passed them by. Others just did their job and let things run their course. But woe to anyone who had been a member of the SS! They were still being winnowed out among the prisoners. They were taken away and never came back. The major explained to Matthias and Bernd that the Russian bigwigs seemed to have decided on a policy of using the millions of German prisoners for rebuilding the country they had so brutally devastated.

Looking up at the huge roofbeam he and Bernd had just fixed into place, Matthias thought back to when he and his father had built the new boathouse. They had then added on the barn cum workshop for repairing wooden carts and vessels large and small. The family business had been doing well before the war broke out.

He now even had the time and the strength to take up carving again. He first made one of a wanderer resting on a tree trunk. He painted the little man a red hat, green trousers, and brown boots. The materials and colours he had bought from a guard, a budding artist no less, for some cigarettes, which he had saved. He presented the wanderer to the chief guard, knowing full well from Major Warner that this man appreciated and returned favours.

Matthias was rooting around in his brain how to bring together a project that would unite him and Judith firmly in his consciousness. The agonies of war, the deprivations of prison camp, the sole will and aim to survive had almost forced her completely out of his mind. He needed her, next to his parents and his home in Eriskirch on the lake, to continue on.

***

"YOU DO NOT WANT TO mess with him, Matthias. He is old-school National Socialist and an unscrupulous, unprincipled, mean dog of a man! He freely admits still that he was a member of 'The National Committee of Free Germany'. He still enjoys many favours from the Russian command, and he doesn't even have to work and gets well paid for doing so."

Matthias was sitting opposite on his bunk bed to Major Warner. He looked across and replied: "Okay, okay. Again: all I wanted to ask Colonel von Heim was if I could have a sizable chunk of oak to carve out a piece I have in mind."

"Unfortunately, they have no real room for artists here, my dear Matthias," replied the major slowly. "I think it would be too risky; von Heim doesn't like us because we don't toe the line. His line. He would be glad of an opportunity to turn a request from you down and then report you to his Russian masters for trying to steal valuable wood."

"But, dammit, the National Committee was for the spread of Russian-style socialism in Germany among our officers, then they turned coat when the Americans first got hammered in the Battle of the Bulge. Why should the Russians stick to him?"

"Because he is useful to them in the running of this camp. He has no loyalty other than to himself. He would gladly betray you in the wink of an eye. As I said, he is a good old-fashioned Nazi. And a lot of the men here like him for that."

Matthias felt his frustration mounting, and he shouted: "What the hell! Why are we still here? It is 1950. Why do they keep us here? All the others have returned home."

"I say, be prepared. This camp is a dangerous place, Matthias. You can't trust those Nazi types; some of them are real killers."

Bernd nodded and took out the evil-looking shiv from his boot holster and started to sharpen it slowly on his piece of gritstone.

"I learnt to use a bayonet, a knife and even a spade at the Battle of Kursk. In this country, it all depends on the situation, especially when guns are of no use at close quarters."

"I'm glad you are with us and not against us, Bernd, your gentle nature hides your warrior instincts most effectively," enunciated Major Warner slowly and deliberately.

"I wish only to be left in peace, to return home and take up cutting gentlemen's hair in my barber's shop in Munich again," replied Bernd softly. He slid the shiv back into his boot, yawned and stretched himself out on his bunk. "And to be able to eat three square meals a day instead of this crap you have to fight over in this shitty prison."

"Quite, Bernd, quite. Matthias, I wanted to say that we are victims of our own strategy of survival. You and Bernd are by far the best carpenters, far and wide. And I am an experienced translator, not only of Russian, but French and English too. They want to hold on to our talents. They know how well we can work. Apart from that, we are pawns in the international political arena."

Matthias groaned, looked up at the major and said, "But they still won't give me that oak I need."

The major regarded Matthias intently. "Oak is very valuable in these parts, and it is not 'they', Matthias, it is von Heim – and he certainly wouldn't. I have noticed, if you have not, that he doesn't like you. You are too good at your work, and he doesn't work. There has been talk about this, among the Russians too. It is well that you have quiet Bernd at your side day and night."

Matthias saluted across to Bernd, then slumped, disappointed and dejected, back onto his bed. He had wanted to carve and form a work of wood, of Judith and himself, that would give him comfort to gaze upon when he returned back to camp after a long day of arduous work. What the heck! Judith would be about thirty-two years old by now. For some years, they had been allowed to receive post and to send letters. His parents were well enough; his mother wrote to him regularly and he to her, asking her to send on his letters to Judith in England. As yet, Judith had not answered, or if she had, her letters had not reached him, or his her. Apparently, back home things were looking up. Since the currency reform in 1948, the economy was booming, in Friedrichshafen too, and he should come home soon and help them out, his father had said.

She had not replied to his letters. She could be long married with a couple of children. She could have died. Perhaps she and her parents had moved away from Lichfield. He sensed she had neither married, nor was she dead. She was waiting for him.

He sighed, got up and looked at himself in the mirror above the washbasin. His dark curly hair had streaks of grey in it, and around his eyes were lines of fatigue deeply etched into his face. He looked down at himself; he had gained back his weight and his muscles to a certain extent. They still didn't get enough to eat. He was thirty years old now. He had given twelve years of his life to his country, to people like von Heim, corrupt, selfish, evil people. People for whom he had killed. Boys at a picnic.

***

THREE YEARS AND TWO MONTHS later, they were marching out through the Russian countryside. They had been marching for hours. Typical for the Russians, nobody told them where they were going. Matthias looked around him, Bernd to his left, Major Warner to his right.

"Come on, Herr Major, tell us where we are going."

"Well, it is always risky to pass on information that you have received in the office of the Russian camp commander, but skilled workers such as you and Bernd, and specialists such as myself, are to be allowed to go home with the others. I shall be looking forward to returning to Cologne."

"Well, that's great news! Why didn't you tell us sooner? Bernd, did you hear? We are going home!"

Matthias and Bernd hugged each other, causing the column behind them to stop. Soon the news spread through the whole centipede of men like wildfire, causing buzzing unrest, which in turn activated their guards to become warier and suspicious – until they realised the cause for jubilation. They then relaxed and nodded their heads. Some even smiled. Prisoner and guard knew each other well enough by now.

"I was not going to impart any information until we were on the train in Gorod Yekaterinburg, which is where we are no doubt marching to."

Matthias smiled to himself at Warner's pomposity, and he looked across at Bernd, who winked back. In doing so, he saw the tip of a stiff cardboard envelope sticking out of the top of the major's rucksack. He thought it to be strange that the major would bring something so office-like with him, and that he had been allowed to do so.

He mentioned this to him, and the major replied grimly: "Oh, they know about this alright. In fact, they gave it to me as a farewell present. I'll show you what's in it soon enough."

Strange, thought Matthias, *it takes a lot to get the major so upset*, and he wondered what it could be that was causing his friend so much disquiet.

As dusk approached, they came to a big lake and 'camped' by the shore. These waters were close to the settlement of Zarechnyy. The Russians had their tents; the Germans slept in the open. Each of them had been allowed to bring a blanket and a store of provisions consisting of the usual hard, black bread, sausage, cheese, a water cylinder and a number of apples.

At Gorod Yekaterinburg, they boarded the train and spent two long days travelling in cattle wagons. The train simply stopped every now and then in the countryside so they could relieve themselves at a suitable spot and refill their water containers. Eventually, they reached their destination: the Central Moscow Railway Station. There they received food packets and were allowed to use the toilet facilities, also to wash themselves. After a day's wait, their designated train pulled up with Moscow-Berlin written on its side. There were carriages for them to sit in.

As luck would have it, Matthias, the major, and Bernd had a compartment for themselves. As the train pulled out of the station, the three of them, filled with hope, pressed their noses against the window, eagerly watching the activities of a main railway station. Matthias wondered why they had been so fortunate. Probably because the number of POWs being allowed home had sharply decreased because there were fewer and fewer prisoners left in Russia, and the Russian railway bureaucracy hadn't caught up with reality – as usual. It was April 1953. The fact that they had a railway carriage to sit in was a luxury to be enjoyed and was a puzzle not worth thinking about.

"Luxury at last." The major sighed, slumping back into his seat. "Okay, men, let's now have a picnic!" he added joyfully.

Bernd got his loaf out and proceeded to divide the portion he had cut off into hard little squares to be enjoyed slowly one after another.

"I suggest that today, to celebrate, each one of us gets a whole slice of bread each and plenty of sausage. What do you think?"

Matthias looked across to Bernd, who smiled back and nodded. "Agreed, let's celebrate."

This they did. They had just finished their celebratory meal when the train slowed to a halt at a station. On the platform was a group of hard-faced-looking men.

Matthias looked across at the major questioningly. The major said: "Look at their armbands," and announced, "they are the NKVD, which is the People's Commissariat of Internal Affairs – the Russian equivalent of the Gestapo. They are after SS men that are still among us and also other war criminals. Hold your breath, men."

The NKVD men boarded the train. Matthias was thinking about the boys they had killed near the river. He heard a lot of shouting from further down the train. They came down the corridor and looked into their compartment. One of them stared Matthias straight in the eye, nodded and continued on.

Looking out of the window, they watched as five men who had been hauled out of the train were lined up against a wall. The man in charge of the action took out his pistol and shot one prisoner after the other between the eyes. The last man in the row made a run for it along the platform towards the field beyond. He got about twenty yards before three shots in the back brought him to his knees.

"Russian justice, Gestapo style," said Bernd.

Hours later, as they headed towards Minsk, the slowly rocking train left the forest region and their temporary view was that of huge sunlit open fields that were being worked by the farmers. Sheep were grazing in the foreground and to the left a typical Russian-style farmhouse could be seen.

"This country seems to go on forever, and in spite of our hardships, there is much that I have grown to like about it," said Matthias as he turned to Major Warner and Bernd, who were sitting opposite him.

"I agree; after twelve years here, it seems to have become a part of us."

"Burned into our minds more like, then frozen. I'll be glad to never see this country again. You can keep it," Bernd said decisively. He folded his arms and looked up at the mirror on the opposite wall.

"Well, there is also that, I suppose," answered Warner slowly and thoughtfully. "And another thing – the padding of this seat could be better; I've had a metal spring poking me in my arse for the last half hour!"

Matthias burst out laughing and looked across at Bernd, who, after a moment's indecision, guffawed heartily and openly with them. It was so unlike and yet typical of the major to keep them together with such an unpredictable statement.

Major Warner then stood up and reached for his rucksack on the luggage rack and pulled out the briefcase Matthias had seen on the trek to Yekaterinburg.

"Gather round, *mes enfants*, I have terrible news for you. These are the photographs the camp commander gave to me. Look."

Matthias craned his head over Bernd's, who, as usual,

was the quickest to be first. To begin with, he could not make head nor tail of the slightly blurred big photo. The first photograph showed people, families on a platform of a place signposted Auschwitz-Birkenau. An SS man pointed them towards various entrances; some people were going to the left, others to the right.

The next photo showed a tall chimney stack emitting heavy dark grey smoke.

How strange, thought Matthias.

The next photograph after that showed a close-up of the burnt remains of a human being lying in an oven. The next one showed the closed metal door of the oven with the imprinted inscription: J. A. Topf & Söhne, Erfurt. Then the sight became all too familiar; starved skeletons of men, but also women and children. So many of them, lying haphazardly in piles. Many more than he and Bernd had had to dispose of in the camp they had just left.

"Virtually all Jews. They just rounded them up and shipped them to this place, and apparently other places like this, worked them, then gassed them, and then burnt them. Day in, day out, year in, year out. Millions of them, or so the Russians told me. Look at this one; it shows the extent of the place. The commander gave me these to show the people back home what we had been fighting for."

Matthias slumped back in their seats, trying to process in his mind what they had just seen and heard.

"Why didn't the enemy bomb this place? They bombed everything else in Germany. It is the size of a city!" cried Matthias.

"You will have to ask them when you go over to England to find your Judith."

"It is a good thing your Jewish girlfriend left Germany when she did, Matthias," said Bernd gloomily.

"So, so, so, now look, look, looky look, look, we have a little Jew lover in our midst."

The three of them turned abruptly to the voice they had heard. Matthias looked up at the imposing figure of Colonel von Heim, who was standing in the open doorway. So involved had they been with looking at the terrible photographs, it had gone unnoticed that the door had slid back open as the train had chuffed up a steep incline.

"No matter now; the time has passed when I would have had you taken away, beaten, and shot, and your little English Jewess too. That is, if you had been fortunate enough for such a merciful mode of execution. Now get out, all of you, at once; I require this compartment for myself only. Out!"

Behind von Heim was the big, menacing figure of Sergeant Toom, whom everyone called the Goon. In his right hand, the Goon held a self-fashioned knife.

"You get out of here; you are a fucking disgrace to us all!" screamed Matthias.

He leapt up and spat in von Heim's face. Before von Heim could react, Bernd sprang at him and plunged his long, wicked shiv under his ribcage and into his heart. Von Heim gasped in disbelief; his face contorted with horror. He sank backwards and Toom, who was struggling to get his own knife clear, had to catch him. Bernd, recognising his chance, put his left foot up against von Heim's chest, pulled his shiv out, leapt again and rammed it into Toom's right ear. Toom collapsed with his master to the floor, as did Bernd. Toom had stuck him simultaneously.

"Bernd! Bernd! Don't you leave me too! Bernd, Bernd, Bernd," sobbed Matthias, stroking Bernd's cheek as well as he could. Bernd was actually lying on top of sergeant Toom.

Bernd looked up and said: "Don't you worry about me, Matthias; the Goon has done me a favour. I died in Kursk. You do me one, too, and go to England and find your Jewish lover and give her a kiss for me." Blood started to bubble up from his lungs and Bernd grasped Matthias's right hand with both of his, groaning with the effort. He sighed. Matthias watched as the light in his friend's eyes faded away.

"Is there no end to it?" groaned Matthias, and he was still kneeling and sobbing next to Bernd when the Russian guards appeared. He heard Major Warner explaining what had happened in Russian. The guards looked at each other, shrugged, and conversed animatedly and in harsh tones with the major.

Matthias feared the worst.

Major Warner translated: "They don't want any more trouble, and certainly no extra work, just because of three dead Germans. When the train stops at a suitable clearing to replenish with fuel and water, we two get out and, with the help of other POWs, bury all three of them. If we work well and quickly, there will be no inquiry. Also, we are to fetch mops and buckets and clean this place of blood. The floor has to be spotless!"

Matthias looked up at the men standing around him and nodded. He got up again.

***

MATTHIAS LOOKED AROUND HIM. HE was headed for Friedrichshafen, the last leg of his journey, but he could not seem to find the right platform.

Berlin had been even more confusing. They had arrived from Moscow in what was called 'The Eastern, or Russian, Sector'. Apparently, the city had been further divided into 'The American', 'The British' and 'The French' sectors. As far as he could ascertain, Germany had been shrunk and divided into East, communist, and West, democratic. He had crossed from the German Democratic Republic into the German Federal Republic, just south of Erfurt. It had been quite an experience, with many guards checking his documents of dismissal. He and the major had parted ways at Leipzig. They had exchanged addresses and shaken hands vigorously; it was not in the major's nature to display more emotion.

He had slapped Matthias on the shoulder with the one hand and said: "Look after yourself, my now not so young friend; there are dangerous waters ahead for both of us. These are not in the nature of rapids, or waterfalls, but are within us and are dark and still. You have my address; it would be good to meet again at some point. But for now, it is goodbye."

Major Warner had turned, hefted his rucksack over his good arm and onto his back, clambered down onto the platform, turned again, waved, and made his way down towards the gates. As the train started to gently pull out from the station, Matthias had watched his upright form until he slowly disappeared among the other travellers.

Eventually arriving in Stuttgart, whose main railway station was one big building site, he noticed other, perhaps more surprising, changes: the women, who were wearing strange clothes that looked nice; the well-dressed men. He felt shabby in his battered uniform. For the first time in many years, he was among civilians going about their everyday business. You could feel it in the air: they were free. He was free. He felt an inner sense of comfort in the realisation of this fact. He was free to go home, and nobody would try to kill him. He felt light as a feather, then with his customary irrationality, he immediately felt sad, heavy, and an inner feeling of unease pervaded his body.

"Where is this bloody platform 10b?" he said out loud, garnering curious looks from passers-by.

Four hours later, on arrival at the battered railway station in Friedrichshafen, he started on the ninety-minute walk to the village of Eriskirch. Friedrichshafen had been hard hit. Everywhere were ruins to be seen and new buildings were going up. There was almost a frenetic activity in every street he observed.

As he walked past a bakery on the main street out of the town, the lady owner came out and, taking pity on his exhaustion and ragged appearance, said to him: "You poor man. Come inside and have a pretzel and a coffee."

"Very kind, but no thank you," said Matthias as he straightened his shoulders and walked on. He needed no pity from anyone.

The walk along the lake of his *Heimat* disappointed him; he could find no comfort in witnessing it, nor the Swiss mountains beyond. He was also blind to the spring flowers that grew at the lakeside, something that he had previously always quietly taken pleasure in. He felt his inner body starting to wind down but, more worryingly, his spirit was sinking. The last stretch on his way home seemed endless.

As he opened the five-barred gate of the entrance to the family property, he heard the lilting laughter of children who were playing on the grass in front of the farmhouse. Suddenly, he could smell the spring air again; the green of the grass became almost too intense to view and the birds seemed almost deafening. The blooming magnolia and cherry trees to the side of the house exuded colour and life so very enthusiastically.

Home.

One of the girls, the smallest, with dark hair and a grubby frock, ran into the house through the front door shouting: "Auntie Anne! Auntie Anne! A ragged old man has just come through the gate and he's coming towards us. You must come at once!"

"Hush, child, let's have a look at this intruder."

Matthias saw his mother appear in the doorway of the house. He walked up to her, and as she put her left hand up to cover her mouth, she started to cry. He took her into his arms and held her and held her. He felt the gaze of the three girls as they stood around them.

The youngest said in a clear tone: "Could you stop making her cry, please?"

"Well, little one, she's making me cry too. She is my mama."

"Oh!"

Over his shoulder, he heard his mother say quietly, "Esther, go around the house and get Uncle Sepp and your parents. Alma, and you too, Deborah, go with her."

The girls did as they were bidden and some minutes later, the Bernsteins stood at a respectful distance as they watched the Kriegers reuniting.

"Mama, Papa," asked Esther once more, "why are they all crying, yet again?"

"Because they are happy to see each other. It is time to go home and leave these good people in peace. Come, children, it is a lovely day for a walk along the lake."

Arm in arm with his father and mother, Matthias looked across as the Bernsteins walked slowly up the drive to the five-barred gate, the two younger girls clambering over it whilst the older one, Alma, slowly opened it and looked back at him with a puzzled look on her face.

***

IT HAD BEEN SIX WEEKS since he had returned, and here he was once again: the community room of the Saint Nikolas Catholic Church. Matthias regarded it with a sense of wonder – it still smelt the same as it did fifteen years ago. That was the day he had been with Judith Lareine for the last time. The day on which he had fought and beaten Hinrich Richter. When he thought about it, it had really been a fight over Judith's affections. Hinrich had never got over the fact that Judith had turned him down some time before. It had been obvious that he was still attracted to her. He just could not show it in a normal way.

Sitting opposite him was Father Donnelly, the visiting Irish priest; he had replaced Father Ryan, who had died in Dachau – murdered was the better term, he thought. So much death, so much death. He felt his mind clouding grey again. Once more, leadenness seemed to blend out all colours.

He was here because his father had urged him to come along and have a talk. He was here because he had returned home after fifteen years of war and imprisonment in Russia. He was here because Judith had not answered any of his letters. He was here because he could no longer say yes or no or do anything except sit on his bed and look at the wall.

Sometimes he cried.

His dear mother was upset. He was here, but he didn't want to be. He was here because he did not want to, above all, hurt his parents. His father, loyal, creative, farmer cum builder, stolid and straightforward, had lines of worry crinkling his already scarred face. Scars from a beating he had received in the war. He had said he had had a bust-up with the SS about hiding some pigs. Enough said, his father had announced. "The SS was always bad news."

He slumped in his chair. Looking across, he thought: *how could a priest help? Was God at Auschwitz?*

Father Donnelly looked across the table at them both and said: "Welcome, Josef; welcome, Matthias."

Father Donnelly was a serious-looking young man. For many years now, Friedrichshafen and Dublin had been exchanging Catholic priests. He spoke fluent German, and he spoke quietly. He was of medium height with a round face, short dark hair, and a ruddy, friendly complexion. He seemed genuine.

"Greetings, Father Donnelly," replied father and son in the traditional Swabian unison.

"Matthias, I thank you for your trust, for allowing me to assist you when things have not been going well for you of late. Your father and mother asked me after church last Sunday if I could be of help."

"The road to hell is paved with good intentions, Father—"

"Come now, Matthias," interjected Sepp. "My son, we are only trying to get you back on your feet again."

Father Donnelly burst out laughing and replied: "There is some truth in what you say, but perhaps we can exchange intentions for deeds."

Matthias felt a liking for this man. "I'll talk with you for a while, Father," he replied.

"Then let us begin. What troubles you, Matthias, why are you so sad that you do nothing?"

"I killed the impressionist Russian soldier-bathers who had no water. I destroyed a young blond boy's face. Without thinking twice, I killed many times." Matthias glanced at his father's honest, now troubled, sad face and continued: "And I came home to find my country destroyed, and up to its knees in the blood of millions. Before the war, I wanted to go to university to study engineering, or even art. Not anymore. What did we fight for? And Judith does not answer my letters."

"Matthias, do you think those young men you call impressionists would have let you live if they had been able to reach for their weapons?"

"No."

"And the young blond boy?"

"No, of course not. We were sometimes surrounded and in the midst of battle, but it is the way I killed, or helped to kill them, that is so terrible. Then so many of my comrades were slain and I have survived. There is a hard, white veil in front of me through which I can see everyday life going on. But I cannot get through it or past it; it holds me back where I am. Behind this veil. It saps my strength. I feel leaden, empty."

"So, you were caught up in a world of war, and did you do your best to be a good soldier and a good man? Auschwitz or no Auschwitz?"

"Sort of, I suppose."

"And you survived. Matthias, remember what Jesus said as he hung dying on the cross: 'Father, forgive them; for they know not what they do.'"

"Do you believe he rose again?"

"I believe he tried to show us that we can overcome the weakness and evil within us and rise up to be our better selves."

"Nobody is perfect, Father."

"Indeed. Although Peter denied knowing Jesus three times, he said to him: 'Upon this rock I shall build my church.' Be that as it may, let us pivot: what did you find most satisfying before the war, Matthias?"

"Being with Judith Lareine, making sculptures, making furniture, helping my father at work."

"I could use a hand now, son," said Josef quietly.

"Matthias, let us suppose – and I am serious now – that a miracle happens tonight and when you wake, all these terrible things that trouble you have been solved."

Matthias felt his mind lifting as if light had entered from an improbable source.

Father Donnelly was not to be stopped; he continued inexorably onwards: "How would your parents know that this miracle had happened to you?"

"They would see me laughing again, helping my father build roofs and furniture. Most of all, I would probably continue making the marble sculpture of Judith. Perhaps I would even go to England and find out why she has not answered my letters."

"So, let us explore this avenue of legitimate thought further. When was the last time you felt like a miracle had really happened to you?"

"Back home, before the war, when I was working outside making a table of best cherrywood for the Fischers, and afterwards, sitting on the bench facing the lake and kissing Judith. Then bathing and splashing about with her, holding her in my arms in the hot June sun."

"And the sculpture of Miss Lareine?"

"That was meant as a surprise. I never finished it."

The priest glanced across at Josef Krieger, who was wiping tears from his eyes and said: "It is beautiful; it was almost completed before he ran away."

"Matthias, again: let us suppose that a miracle happens tonight and when you wake up tomorrow morning, all these terrible things that trouble you will have been solved. Could you not help your father once again and resume work on your sculpture tomorrow?"

Matthias felt enjoyment at the thought of this image and answered: "I could try."

"You can ask no more of yourself than that."

Matthias wriggled his shoulders and lurched forwards in his chair as if he had been released from a cruel confinement. He looked across to the big window and saw, as he had so many years ago, the azure sky and a little sailing boat fluttering along the grey-green water of Lake Constance. He breathed in deeply. It was hardly believable that this room still smelt of musky catechism!

"Thank you, Father," he said.

"You are most welcome, my son. How do you feel now?"

"Better, I think."

186

"A little bit better or a lot better?" Father Donnelly leant across the table and grasped Matthias by both his hands, his dark eyes fixed on Matthias.

"Better, Father, just a little bit whole lot better."

"Welcome home, son," said Sepp Krieger, and pulled his son towards him in an awkward embrace.

"It's good to be home at last, Papa."

"Well, Matthias, I suggest we meet again next week. Same time, same place?" Father Donnelly reached out his hand and Matthias shook it.

"Yes, we will do that, Father. Same time, same place."

9

1ST MAY 1953 – JUDITH LAREINE, LICHFIELD

FROM THE STREET LAMP BELOW, the light shone through the gap between the curtains. This was the cause of her awakening, yet again. Looking up, once more, Judith could just make out the rosette in the middle of the ceiling. In the centre was the flower itself surrounded by leaves. The whole centrepiece seemed to be on a plate, and she could just discern that this was further encircled by more patterns. The last outer decoration was one of leaves again. *Old-fashioned, but nice*, she thought. It added to the stillness and quietude of the bedroom in this flat on Beacon Street, Lichfield.

She could find no sleep, again. For the third night in a row. Professor Reginald Hoskins snored softly and shifted to his left, away from her, causing her a moment of inner relief.

Should she continue with the tree? She had seen it in the late afternoon sun in the woods of Beaudesert, where they often went. It was standing in lonely isolation, its silver so beautifully lit by the golden rays. She and Yolande had spotted it at the same time. They had laid down their bikes and finished off the remains of their picnic in the seemingly magical clearing. She had asked Yolande if she should paint it when she got home. Yolande had looked carefully at the silver birch, bathed in golden light, and then at the sketch that Judith had started. She told her to do what she wanted to do, to follow her artistic instinct.

"What about my agent?" she had asked.

"What about your stupid agent?" Yolande had replied, laughing.

"Well, I've never done anything so… so isolated before." Which had seemed a rather lame answer at the time and as she moved restlessly in bed, she thought it still was – lame.

"What do you English say and are so proud about? This beautiful sunlit tree is in splendid isolation, like you, Judith, with your Professor Hoskins."

"What do you mean? Reginald is a good man and most sociable."

"Yes, he is that, but you are lonely, even when you are with me or your parents. I can feel it."

"Yolande, steady on, he is a good man, and you know I want a family of my own," she had replied vigorously. But, of course, her friend wasn't to be stopped.

"I know, *ma petite*, I know. But look at the men you had before. You told me how passionate and courageous Captain Tom was and this German Matthias, who was, how do you say? The salt of the earth? Strong and honest."

"Yes, and he was also a very good artist – a sculptor, in fact. A German sculptor."

"No matter; he was a young man of substance. What is more, his light is still inside you; I can tell, I am French."

189

At this, they had both burst out laughing and rolled on their backs and watched the clouds moving slowly across their line of vision. They had listened to the birds calling in the trees, which were whispering softly to one another in the late-afternoon breeze.

"You should seek him out. The war has been over eight years now."

"We were last together a long time ago and everything ended badly. We were very young. Two years ago, he sent me a letter from a prison camp in Russia. His parents forwarded it on to me."

"That is remarkable, Judith! What did he say?"

"Oh, he just wanted to know how I and my parents were getting along. He probably wanted to know if we had survived the war. Look, the kites are circling above us again."

Patting down her pillow, Judith remembered trying to divert Yolande's attention away from the subject of her love life, and particularly about Matthias Krieger.

Reginald turned over again in his sleep and said: "I'll be over in a minute," and with that, he turned again and continued snoring lightly.

Judith cast her mind back again to the clearing in Beaudesert that day with Yolande: "Did you write back to this lonely prisoner in the middle of Russia?"

"No, the day after, there was a long article in the newspaper about Auschwitz. It was all so horrible – the war, the bestiality of it. The suffering of the men in the burns unit. I could not reply to his letter. I hate Germany! There, I've said it! And now it is probably too late. If he has any sense, he will have married and started a family."

Yolande had replied with a, "*Je comprends*," and changed the subject back to the painting. She said: "Judith, war or no war, Professor Hoskins or no, I think you should paint this loneliness to reflect that which is within you – not what your bloody agent might like or not."

Judith had laughed and told her once more that her English had become very good.

This was the first time in a long time that she had actually spoken about Matthias. As a girl, no! As a young woman, she had loved him with her whole being. They could converse for long periods at a time or just enjoy each other's company in silence. When it was hot, and Matthias was working on a sculpture outside under the trees and she on her paintings, they would hardly say anything to each other the whole afternoon. His mother would bring out some homemade lemonade and biscuits; then they would sit on the bench and look across the lake at the little boats and big steamer ferries with the Swiss Alps in the background. He would move over and put his arm around her, kiss her lips, and murmur in her ear that she was his princess of the lake.

She remembered, fondly, asking him once what he thought of the Blue Rider Group around Wassily Kandinsky. He had replied that the paintings she had made of the Kriegers' farmhouse by the lake reflected the simplicity and the direct use of the strong and honest colours of Gabriele Münter. He liked them, he had said in English. She smiled inwardly, for he had also asked her, with a big grin, if perhaps she could paint their hogs in the style of wonderful August Macke. She had pushed him off the bench as he laughed helplessly, and a few minutes later, they were fooling about in the lake, gasping at the shock of the cold water on a hot summer's day.

She had loved him so much; his curly hair, his sturdy, strong frame and his natural creativeness and gentility. The quiet man of the lake, she used to call him.

Judith waggled her big toe again, which tended to cramp up when she was overtired. She thought that she could kill a cup of tea to help her relax, but she did not want to wake Reginald. Her next thought was of the fight between Matthias and that brute Hinrich. She had been so frightened. Matthias as well; that had been apparent to everyone at the lakeside school-leaving party.

The memory of the violence made her involuntarily shudder so much that she thought Reginald was going to wake up. His right leg was outside the blanket. It was a long skinny leg inside blue and white striped pyjamas, and she suddenly realised she disliked both the pyjamas and the long skinny leg.

A dawn of revelations, she thought to herself, and, putting off her realisation of her dislike for Reginald for later, she reluctantly continued the salvage of memories she had long ago securely kept down in the depths of her psyche. She wanted to measure them with the life she had led. Or was a more appropriate expression the life that she had experienced until now? She felt intrigued. Judith felt something move within her mind; she had to follow this. She eased herself out of the bed and tiptoed to the door.

That bloody doorknob squeaks every time you turn it, she thought, *I'll pull it at the same time, which should do the trick*. It did. She pulled the cardigan she had gathered up from the chair next to her bedside over her shoulders and made her way quietly out of the room and then into the kitchen. She closed the kitchen door gently and put the light on, which immediately seemed to blaze inside her head; too bright, too much light. She switched it off again. And by the light of the moon shining through the kitchen window, she then put on a pair of woolly socks that had dried on the radiator (Reginald did not approve of laundry in the kitchen) and slipped into her slippers, which she had also carried out of the bedroom with her.

She removed the whistle from the kettle, filled it with enough water and lit the gas ring below it. She reached up for the biscuit tin, took three digestives out and placed them on a plate, which she put on the kitchen table next to the unopened letter from Friedrichshafen, Germany. She moved across to the crockery cupboard and took out a cup and saucer (the big ones). She placed them next to the plate of biscuits – but a tad further away from the German letter that her mother had forwarded to her. The bottle of milk was on the floor in the pantry. She just used a bottle unless she had visitors. However, this time she poured the milk into a small jug that she liked and placed it next to the sugar near the letter on the table. The stamp was a picture of an edelweiss; it looked very nice.

The kettle started blowing steam. She poured some of the boiling water into her brown earthenware teapot, replaced the lid, swirled the hot water within vigorously and emptied it. All the while taking care in the half moonlight. The shadows from the tree outside danced and bobbed on the wall next to the kitchen clock. Its ticking seemed more like a clacking in the early morning stillness.

Taking the tea tin, she spooned in two teaspoons of tea leaves with the silver coronation commemoration spoon, which showed the young, pretty new queen of one year. She filled the teapot, about sixty per cent full for one person. She liked her tea not too strong and certainly not too weak.

In the moonlight, she gazed at the letter, which had been lying on the table these past three days. She wondered if it was from Matthias again. She hadn't answered his last one; that was years ago. This one seemed in a rather formal envelope. Her last memory of Germany had been the horrible fight at the lakeside party and the hurried departure from that terrible country with her mother and father in the aftermath.

Hinrich had drunk too much, and he had been nasty with it. He and Matthias had clashed in the art room that afternoon. He had somehow found out that she was a Jewess. Those had been dangerous times for Jews of whatever nationality. Although Great Britain and Germany had not been at war in 1938, they had been on the brink. German Jews had been completely outcast. They had been beaten up on the street in public, robbed of their work, money, property and, most important of all for Nazis, their dignity. Well, as the saying went: 'If you want to drag a man down into the gutter, you have to get down there with him.' She bit hard into her biscuit, causing crumbs to fall onto her nightdress. What they did later to all the Jews had been unimaginable. Germans disgusted her! She furiously brushed the crumbs off herself.

At a later hour, Hinrich had come up to her that night by the lakeside as they were standing around the campfire. He had planted his big feet in front of her and said loudly: "What's this little English girl doing at our party?" he demanded, swaying heavily from side to side.

"Leave her alone; she has been our guest these past five years!" Matthias had called out.

"You shut your face, Krieger, or I'll shut it for you," Hinrich had hissed back.

Behind him stood two menacing and uninvited visitors in their Hitler Youth uniforms.

"An English Jewess. Well, well, let's see if those fine tits are the real thing."

This scene was burned into Judith's memory. She took a sip of tea from the big cup, nodded, and moved on in her recollections.

"These are not just yours alone to fondle, Krieger."

Hinrich lurched towards her and grabbed both of her breasts and shouted, "Honk, honk, I've got me a Jewish sow!" She remembered the blur of Matthias running at him, leaping, and, in mid-air, punching downwards on Hinrich's face. As Hinrich fell, Matthias had hit him again and again, then he swivelled and kicked one of the HY boys in the groin, punched him so very hard in the stomach and, with both fists clenched as a club, smashed him down to the ground. The third HY boy stood rooted in horror at what was to come next. The flames of the campfire reflected his abject fear.

Matthias had stood – no, crouched – panting before him and said: "Go away and take your Nazi friends with you."

The tea had brewed. She put half a teaspoonful of sugar in her cup, added just the right amount of milk and poured herself a cup of golden liquid. She took a sip and then, eagerly, another one, sighed with satisfaction, reached for another digestive, leant back in her chair and sipped her tea again, pleased. Pleased that she could recall this incident without getting too upset again. However, her next thought caused her to frown.

After Matthias had thrashed Hinrich and his henchman (there was no other word for it) to the ground, the others had moved at last and thrown a bucket of water over the two who were still groaning and bleeding. Hinrich had stood, or rather crawled to his feet, as did the other would-be assailant, with the uninjured one helping. The three of them made to move off. Hinrich stopped on the other side of the fire, the flames playing on his face, and had called out to Matthias, who was standing next to Judith, shaken and dazed.

"My father and I will get you for this, Krieger. You attacked me for berating a Jewess! All of you saw this, a completely unwarranted attack, because as we all know: Jews don't count! Especially English Jewish cunts."

Immediately after he finally departed, all the others did so too. As he was leaving, Freddi Peters came over to the pair of them and said: "Matthias, you have to leave Friedrichshafen; they will come for you, the SS. His father has a pretty high rank now. You know how Hinrich is, you have to go somewhere else, just not anywhere near here."

Judith saw yet again quite clearly in her mind's eye how Freddi had looked at her with distaste and said: "You too, Judith, go back to England where you belong. Hurry, both of you!"

Turning her teaspoon back and forth on the wooden kitchen table, she could still recall her turmoil of emotions: relief, and gratitude to Matthias that he had prevented Hinrich from humiliating her further. Distress and astonishment that he had beaten Hinrich and his friend so thoroughly, mixed with fear and distaste at this exhibition of brutality from her gentle would-be lover. And then, afterwards, they had both stood next to each other, but somehow alone. The fire had begun to die down. A cool breeze was coming across from the lake. Everybody else had gone. She had shaken like a leaf and Matthias had been literally vibrating with shock.

She had wanted Matthias to hold her and comfort her but, instead, she said: "Matthias, you must go home and leave for somewhere safe tomorrow."

"Yes, but what about you, Judith?"

"I will be alright; my father has connections. We were going to return to England soon, anyway. This incident will give the necessary impetus."

After fifteen years, she could still see Matthias's face struggling with this information. It had been probably too much for him. He was only eighteen back then. She twenty. She realised now that what she had really wanted from him was him to put his arms around her, to soothe her, make love to her and then to take her gently back home to her parents. Unfortunately, he had agreed with her that they should both go their separate ways. Some gentleman! But now, she realised, she had forgiven him – well, almost.

Two hours and two big cups of tea later, it was beginning to become lighter. Judith looked up at the kitchen clock. It was 4am. She had arrived at three decisions: firstly, she would paint her tree. Secondly, to place it not in Beaudesert, but on the shore of Lake Constance. With further examination of this mental depiction, she realised she would have to be honest with herself. It would show the bench on which she and Matthias had so often sat, looking out over to the lake. The tree she would place a couple of yards behind it. She would be seated on the bench looking winsome and vulnerable, with a pale, sunlit face. She would be wearing a short red dress, long legs visible, and a slightly see-through blouse emphasising her fine breasts. *Such modesty*, she mused wryly. The lakeward side of the tree would be sunlit orange on silver bark; the rear side of the tree would be dark in the shade, as also the earth and the bushes beyond. The atmosphere was one of semi-erotic stillness, yes, and loneliness too, coupled with a sense of menacing expectation. It was impressionistic realism in style from the beginning to end. It was what she wanted to express, true to herself. She smiled again; Yolande would be proud of her.

"True to myself," she murmured. "What about Reginald? I don't love this man and I'm quite sure he doesn't love me."

Her rigorous instruction and training at the University of Edinburgh Queens Medical School had trained her to think analytically and as precisely as possible. She had qualified as a medical doctor. Three years ago, she had returned to Lichfield to practise as a GP. She was a part-time member of a group practice with two other doctors. Today, she would hold surgery in the afternoon. The mornings were for art.

She had sensed from the beginning that for Professor Reginald Hoskins, she was a trophy partner. She was well aware of her own beauty and had decided early on not to be ruled by it and have her personality soured by empty vanity. In its stead, perhaps she had fallen into the trap of the wish for social eminence. Quite clearly, a love affair this was not; she had been flattered that a professor of such eminence had taken an interest in her. It was a friendship of no real substance, and this morning she had realised that it could no longer continue. How could she have allowed this to happen, so intimate in bed yet so shallow in clothes? From outside the kitchen, she heard the noises of Reginald moving from the bedroom to the hall, shortly afterwards the sound of the toilet flushing. She felt annoyed at having her peace and quiet and her thoughts disrupted. She would tell him.

She looked up as Reginald came into the room, and she noticed with distaste his fussy red leather slippers, his blue and white striped pyjama legs showing below his expensive silk dressing gown. He had even combed and brushed his hair.

"Ah, good morning, Judith. Up early again, my dear. I see you have made some tea, no doubt some time ago. Could you make a pot for me, please?"

Judith felt her distaste for his appearance melding into an almost overwhelming dislike for this man. He maddened her with his what now seemed to her prim fussiness, his never-ending exactitude that no doubt made him such a fine specialist in his field. And if he called her his dear once more, she felt sure she would brain him with the bloody teapot! She then felt her body go limp. Her knees felt weak. She was tired of this farce and tired of him. She did not love him. She did not want him. He irritated her supremely.

"Reginald, you are welcome to use all the facilities of my flat when you are down from Edinburgh for the weekend."

"How do you mean?"

"If you want a cup of tea, make it yourself."

"Well, really! You know I'm used to Mr Phelps dealing with such tasks. I have better things to do with my time."

"Your butler is in Edinburgh, and I am very aware of the fact that you are a very busy and important man."

"At whose side you shone most radiantly at the Foreign Minister's little party last weekend. So be a dear and put the kettle on."

"No, do it yourself."

"Now, please do not be tiresome, Judith. I was thinking, this little flat is barely adequate. We will have to find you something more adequate, methinks."

"Think on, buster. I like my flat, I love my work, I love to paint, but truth be told, Reg, I don't love you!"

"Right! First things first: please, please, don't call me 'Reg'. I'm not a bookie. Secondly, I don't expect you to love me, although I am very fond of you, but love – no. Love is overrated and far too messy. Again, no."

That's it, thought Judith, *that is the difference between you and me.* She abruptly recognised her need to be loved. She loved her parents, and they had always loved her. Matthias had loved her, that she had felt and knew. Once again, the knife of light sliced through inside her as she thought of him, Matthias. He who had left her to run away to that horrible war.

With a start, she came out of reverie and caught the tail end of what Reginald was saying.

"…However, I have noticed that, recently, you don't seem so enthusiastic about us."

She ignored him, for she knew that Reginald was highly regarded within the international medical profession and also outside of it, thanks also to the prominence of his very wealthy family. To have her at his side as a doctor and well-known artist made them a very impressive couple. She realised that he really did like her. How nice for him; so bloody cold upper-class English of him!

"Reginald, you are a nice man, a bit of a snob, but still a nice man. Nevertheless, this collaboration, partnership, call it what you will, will cease to exist as of now. I must apologise for misleading you. I thought we would grow closer to one another. I want children, Reginald. I'm thirty-five. You are ten years older, you don't want children, and you still don't know how to make a pot of tea! This relationship, or whatever you might call it, it does not sit easily with me."

She looked up and across to see and gauge his reaction. She saw a certain slight sag in his demeanour; his long face saddened, and she felt for him.

"Yes, I fear I'm lacking in the tea-making department, and I doubt that I'll change in that regard. You are quite right; I don't want to have children. Unfortunately, in my family, warmth and intimacy were not, and are not, as accessible as in yours. 'Tis a pity. Judith, I thank you for your warmth and intimacy, and I'm sorry I could not give you more of myself. Let's leave it there and part as friends, I hope."

"Of course, Reginald," replied Judith with somewhat more enthusiasm than she felt. Simultaneously, she felt saddened by the realisation that she had deeply hurt this decent man.

"I would like to get dressed and leave at once. I would feel better if you stayed in the kitchen and we said our goodbyes now."

"Reginald, you don't have to leave immediately."

"Yes, I do. Now give me a goodbye peck on the cheek, there's a good gal."

Judith got up and went across to Reginald, who was still standing in front of the half-open kitchen door, now in broad daylight. She stood up to him on tiptoe and kissed his thin, stubbly cheek.

"Goodbye, Reginald, and thank you for such a lovely time."

"Thank you, Judith, I hope you find your knight in shining armour."

Reginald Hoskins turned and left the room, closing the door gently behind him. Judith took her place at the kitchen table. The sun was now shining through the room and as the birds twittered excitedly outside her window, she felt tears running down her cheeks. Glancing down, she saw them mixing with the remaining crumbs of digestive biscuit on her plate.

Two hours and thirty-five minutes later, Judith was in her studio at the edge of Beacon Park. It was really nothing more than a small, converted warehouse that had had two outstanding features: immense south-facing windows and a large wood-burning stove with a long metal chimney that went up and through the roof. It kept the long room warm and cosy. She bought the wood off Jim Cotterill, from whom she rented the studio. It had proved to be a most satisfactory arrangement.

She couldn't paint today; she still felt too agitated, upset. Apart from that, the vision of the tree by the lake kept popping up from her subconscious mind. She sat down at the little table that she always kept free of everything. She was a tidy person and liked to keep her thoughts together too. Experience had proven that only when she had a strong idea could she then pursue it by free association of connecting impulses, and then to seek out the suitable style (and even genre) in which to express her representation. In her mind's eye, she started to review her artistic development (it was all cards on the table today!). Could she, would she, want to move forwards by going back fifteen years, by becoming a realistic painter again? But wasn't what she had in mind more impressionistic? Who cares! Well, Jonathan Leighton-Jones did for a start. Jonathan had 'built her up' slowly and carefully to become a recognised expressionist artist throughout the country. Her paintings were starting to sell for thousands of pounds. Her increasing prominence in the circles of culture and commerce had led to her pairing up with Reginald Hoskins. She realised now that celebrity had blinded her. Judith felt darkness rising within her, the dread recognition of failure. She had not been true to herself. She saw her mother pause on the cello in the midst of playing Bach and her looking up, asking her if she was happy. And not just once. Her father enquiring if she was 'alright'. Her annoyance with them for not fully celebrating her fame and the almost overly polite manner with which they had welcomed Reginald into their 'modest home', as they had called it.

She had started painting seriously when she was at grammar school in Germany. Artistically, the region around Friedrichshafen, where she had stayed, had had a rich creative influence on her. The Nazis, of course, had caused no end of damage, forbidding what they called degenerate art. This had hit hard. One of those who had been struck down was Otto Dix, who had moved from Dresden after losing his professorship at the Academy of Fine Arts to live in Hemmenhofen on the lake. He then painted only landscapes. Through him and her work nursing in the burns unit, she had become aware of the significance of the human element in art. Of pain. The agonies she had witnessed of the burnt men of the aircrews who flew night and day against the enemy, Germany. The Germany of Nietzsche, who Dix so admired. Nietzsche, who dreamt of the unchained, noble savage who roamed the earth free and wild. The very savages who had defrocked him and forced him into exile on the shores of Lake Constance. Such was the pain of romantic irony, she reflected.

In a similar abstract fashion, she had tried to depict the cycle of agonies the men in the burns unit had endured. She thought that the use of the deep reds and blacks of pain had worked well. Alternating with greys and whites of remission, coupled with the deep embalming orange of morphine relief. Their faces and bodies often peeping through the coloured veil of suffering.

Her success was due to a friend of a friend. Jonathan Leighton-Jones was a successful London art dealer. He was almost magically aware what the 'taste of the moment', as he called it, was. Meaning what was saleable in the modern art world – and Judith's work was very much so. Originally, she had been greatly impressed by Gabriele Münter and had made several paintings of the Kriegers' house and property; also, of Eriskirch itself, a small village nearby, where they lived. One summer, with Matthias working on his sculptures under the trees beside her, she had completed a number of pictures of the lake and the Swiss mountains beyond. Before she had left Germany with her parents, she had started to emulate elements of the style of Wassily Kandinsky, also of the Blue Rider Group in Murnau, which was not so very far from Friedrichshafen. Kandinsky took the expressionist depiction of his landscapes and subject matter in general to a different level of form and style; his dashing use of colour and form had inspired her, and still did.

Judith stood up and walked across the studio to the opposite wall, against which many paintings were leant. Her German collection, she called them. After the Luftwaffe had first bombed Birmingham, she had taken down all her paintings of Matthias's *Heimat*. Germany had always frightened her. She picked out the painting of the Kriegers' house with the view of the garden bench looking out over the lake. She picked it up and removed the protective paper wrapping and held it out in front of her. She still liked the one with the blues and whites she had used to depict their house in the snow. She wrapped it up again and carried it across to her worktable. Next to the table was a haversack, a present from an injured pilot who had said that he would not be needing it again. Ronnie had been his name.

"Keep focused," she said to herself.

She took out the sandwiches that she had prepared and the flask of tea. She then slid the painting into the haversack and checked to see that the German letter was still safely in the front compartment. It was. Sitting down, she gazed through the large window and watched as a little boy and his father threw a ball to each other, with their dog running joyously from one to the other. When it went astray, the dog immediately captured the ball and ran off with it. The wind was blowing, and their hair was all astray. Through the big window, she could see the dirty grey clouds scudding across the blue sky and faintly discern their laughter and the dog's yapping as they slowly moved deeper into the park.

Judith unwrapped a sandwich; it was spam and tomato, again. Reginald had often chided her for being so measly, as he had called it. She had shrugged this off and told him that she had been brought up to 'waste not, want not', and that she had no intention of changing a very sensible and satisfying habit just because she was earning a lot of money. At present. She screwed the top off the flask and pored the piping hot tea (she had added the milk before she had poured the tea into the thermos) into the top, which served as a cup. She then settled back into her chair and took a sip. She sighed with pleasure and smiled as she watched father, son and little dog as little dots in the distance, all jumping about in the strong wind.

"It's time for you three to go home, otherwise you may get soaked."

Three hours and forty-five minutes later, Judith stood in the entrance to The Park Medical Practice Lichfield of Doctors Smith, Hodges and Lareine and shook out her umbrella vigorously. She had kept the haversack dry. She greeted Anna, the receptionist, and entered her office. She hung her wet raincoat up and placed the haversack on a chair. She took out the painting, unwrapped it and laid it on her desk. She laid the German letter alongside it.

Judith rummaged around in one of the side pockets and removed a small hammer and a tiny envelope with nails with golden heads. She picked a spot halfway along the wall between her desk and the door. With four little tapping blows she placed the nail firmly into the wall. She hung her picture up. Yes, you could see the house and, beyond, the bench facing the lake with the trees behind.

Anna popped her head around the door and said: "Mrs Wilson is here to see you; she said she has the specialist report for you about her leg. Shall I show her in, Doctor Lareine?"

"Yes, please do. Thank you, Anna."

Mrs Wilson almost tripped over Anna in her hurry to

see her doctor. She limped slightly, and she was also holding her three-month-old baby.

"I'm so sorry, Doctor Lareine, I have no one who could have taken Simon at such short notice. I've left the pram in the hall. I hung my coat up there too. I hope that is alright," she said somewhat anxiously.

"No bother, no concern, Mrs Wilson; it's always a pleasure to be of assistance. Why don't you sit down?"

"I will in a sec. I have to rummage about in my bag to get the specialist's report out. Could you please hold Simon while I plunge into the depths of this bag?"

"Yes, of course."

Judith took the little boy into her arms, and he immediately nestled against her, his head slightly swaying and his delicate blond hairs feathering against her cheek. His gentle scent of babyness filled her senses. She inhaled and her mind went blank; her whole body filled with a deep ache of longing. She looked over the little boy's head and saw the painting of the house by the lake. She felt herself sway.

"Doctor Lareine, Doctor Lareine, please be careful! Are you alright, dear? Here, please sit down, love."

Mrs Wilson gently took her baby from Judith and, with her free arm, escorted Judith the three steps to the chair that had been meant for herself.

"Why, you are crying! My dear Doctor Lareine, here is my hanky. Don't worry, it's clean. There, there, don't take on so. Is there anything I can do to help?"

"I must apologise, Mrs Wilson. For some reason or another, I did not sleep all night. Your beautiful son must have overwhelmed me."

"There is no need for you to apologise, Doctor Lareine;

everybody I know likes you and the way you treat us, your patients. Friendly and competent is what I always say. And another thing: if you will forgive my forwardness, I see you are a natural mother. You are also very beautiful, and that can be difficult when finding a suitable partner. I know, I've been through that myself."

"Yes, I always think you look lovely, Mrs Wilson."

"That's not the point!" replied her patient quite sharply. "The point is that we women who want families have to find a man, a husband, who is honest and sincere about being a father and a husband. Someone who is prepared to go the extra mile for us, and not only once. Oh, now I've said too much!"

"Your frankness is quite refreshing, Mrs Wilson. It makes a lovely change. Now, let us look at this report. It must be good, otherwise Professor Deacon would have given me a ring himself."

Three hours and fifty-six minutes later, Doctor Judith Lareine was ready to leave, to go back to her empty flat. Before she did, she sat down at her desk and opened the letter from Germany with a deft slice of her letter knife. It contained an invitation for her to exhibit her work at an art exhibition called 'Reconciliation by the Lakeside', in Friedrichshafen. The organisers were Father Peter Schubert, Father Christopher Donnelly (visiting priest from Dublin), from the Catholic Church, Friedrichshafen, and Rabbi Chaim Moskowitz, from Munich. The exhibition was to be held in two months' time, from the 4th to the 8th of July 1953.

There was a list of the artists who had been invited. Her name was on it, and so was that of Matthias Krieger.

10 HINRICH RICHTER – SPRING 1953

HINRICH RICHTER SETTLED BACK INTO the comfort of his seat on the Zürich to Munich express. He pinched and pulled at the trousers of his dark-blue three-piece flannel suit to be more comfortable. He preferred flannel to wool, which he considered to be not only old-fashioned but uncomfortable. Apart from that, flannel was the material for men's suits this year. He had to admit the trousers showed off his long legs admirably and altogether the suit fitted him perfectly. He knew he looked good in it. The glances that women regularly gave him confirmed him in his opinion that, at the age of thirty-three, his beauty was still vibrant. That gorgeous thing in the bookshop couldn't stop looking at him! She even started undoing the top buttons of her blouse, as they stood unseen in the philosophy corner of the shop.

"That is the kind of philosophy I prefer, if any," he murmured to himself.

He then stretched out his long legs in the otherwise empty first-class compartment. In the mirror opposite, he observed his handsome reflection with great satisfaction: the aquiline nose, the chiselled chin, the good hair and the blue eyes from his father and mother.

Things were going well for him since he had joined the police. That had been a wise move – leaving the Dachau SS at a timely moment. After waiting the appropriate amount of time, he had contacted people who owed him favours in the Bavarian police. Then, after waiting yet again, joined said force at the rank of senior detective, thus renewing his eligibility for his state pension. Thanks to his service in the Gestapo as a civil servant.

Not that he would really need it. He was already a millionaire. He had made sure that he destroyed all the records pertaining to his person before the 42nd and 45th Infantry Divisions and the 20th Armoured Division of the US Army had freed the remaining thirty-two thousand Dachau prisoners. Well done, America! There was also the matter of the thirty railroad wagons chock-a-block with decomposing Jews – the best sort of Jew, really. He had done well to get out early; the Americans had made such a fuss and then killed many SS guards who had been stupid enough to remain.

Dachau, he thought, had been the perfect move after Brest, where he had nearly, but not quite, had his dick bitten off by that beautiful French bitch, who reminded him of Judith Lareine even today. He couldn't think why she did. He reasoned that Judith (who had turned his previous and persistent advances down) had been the cause of his humiliation and defeat in front of the whole class at the hands of her farmer boyfriend. Plus, the fact she was a foreigner and a Jewess! The French cow had fought him on her own, and nobody had survived to see that defeat. Hinrich started to squirm in his seat. To steady himself, he focused again on his rise from the squalor of Dachau to his residence in the old town in the city centre of Munich.

Almost unwillingly, his thoughts turned again to the concentration camp where he had been stationed for almost three years. Admittedly, he had had some pleasurable moments there, especially crucifying that Catholic priest! Also, he had not been so far from his hometown of Friedrichshafen where they had built weapons, fighters, and bombers. They had also developed the V2 attack rocket there. Unfortunately, the town had been bombed flat. The production had continued underground, thanks to the slave labour, but in the end, the war had been lost. So had been the fate of the rest of his family; they had all died in Berlin. It was a pity that he couldn't see them before they died, and a shame that he couldn't bury them. Still, before the fall of the city, he had managed to get the paintings and most of the silver and jewellery out and hide them beneath the boathouse in Friedrichshafen. That was also why he could afford a big apartment in the centre of Munich and drive this year's brand new 1953 Mercedes-Benz 300S Roadster. That and the fact he was dealing in stolen Jewish art collections. Stolen by the Nazis and amassed and hidden by that half-Jew Hildebrand that Goebbels had authorised to steal and sell what the Nazis considered modern, degenerate art. Hildebrand had 'accumulated' art collections from Jewish art dealers and private Jew collections, paying them just enough to be able to flee the country. Thousands upon thousands of wonderful paintings.

"I do love my work," said Hinrich settling back again into his seat.

"Papers, please!"

Hinrich started, looked about him and saw that a customs official had entered the compartment without him noticing, which annoyed him. The door had been slightly ajar to let in some fresh air on this warm spring afternoon. He should have noticed. It was not unusual for customs officials to check on passengers between Switzerland and Germany. However, he had nine thousand nine hundred Swiss francs in his money belt. A sum he had received this morning from Reichelt, a German ex-Nazi who lived in Zürich. He had got the money from Reichelt simply for keeping quiet about him and his art collection. Origin: *Raubkunst*, stolen Jewish art. Allowed was ten thousand.

The customs officer looked at Hinrich and noticed the bulge around his waist under the jacket.

"Anything to declare, sir?" he asked pointedly.

"No," replied Hinrich quietly. "No, I haven't."

"Please stand up, sir, and show me what you have around your waist."

"It's a money belt, and there is nine thousand nine hundred Swiss francs in it; you can count it, if you wish."

"Yes, I would; as you may well know, this is a favourite stretch for smugglers of all kinds, including currency runners."

"I have nothing to hide here."

Hinrich unbuckled his expensive, nicely tooled leather belt and handed it over to the portly inspector, who was grey-haired with a white moustache and a pot belly. He was a head shorter than Hinrich who, on noticing this, immediately sat down to give his counterpart the psychological advantage of height. He wanted no trouble and was unsettled that he was being examined; the amount was legal, but awfully close to the amount allowed, thus conspicuous. His name would perhaps be noted down. He produced his prepared reason for carrying so much money.

"I'm a policeman, and on my days off, I sell women's jewellery. I have a number of good customers in Zürich and also cities in South Germany: Munich, Freiburg and Stuttgart in the main. Here is my ID card. But please don't spread the word that I sell women's jewellery – my colleagues would laugh me out of town." Taking an envelope from the inside pocket of his jacket, Hinrich said: "Here are the papers regarding the sales I have made. As you can see here, the jewels are kept in a safe-deposit box in the National Bank of Zürich."

After counting the banknotes and examining the proffered papers, the customs officer looked down into Hinrich's openly relaxed face, snorted quietly, closed his notebook without having taken his pencil out, tipped his cap and announced: "Have a nice onwards journey, sir, your secret will go no further than this compartment."

"I thank you, sir, and the compliments of the day to you, too."

As soon as the compartment door slid shut, Hinrich sighed, put his feet up on the opposite seat and looked out of the window at the receding view of Lake Constance in the setting golden sun.

"Old fart," he cursed.

Somewhat later, his trained analytical mind took over and he reasoned that he must be more careful in future. The ruse with the jewels and carefully prepared paperwork had functioned well. However, on reflection, nine thousand nine hundred Swiss francs in his money belt was legal – but suspicious. That was asking for trouble. Greed was fine but must be finessed. Enough of this, he must refocus on his mission and review how he was going to implement his raid and escape route tonight.

"The fact of the matter is that I not only deal in art but am also a collector," purred Hinrich as he adjusted his clothing again, stood up, bent down, and admired his reflection in the mirror.

Two hours and thirty minutes later, after his train had pulled into Munich's main station, Hinrich walked across to the open-air car park and unlocked his vehicle. He loved being seen in his Mercedes-Benz convertible. And he cherished the big muscular car with its three-litre, six-cylinder engine, whose deep grumble announced his approach and caused heads to turn, especially female ones who were gazing through shop windows filled with goods. Times were still hard in Germany in spite of the currency reform in 1948, which had worked wonders for the German economy and had seen the end to the black market.

He turned left into the Theatinerstrasse and, after a hundred metres, left again, down into the underground garage beneath the newly built apartment block. Once in his flat, after putting the money in his hidden wall-safe, Hinrich settled himself into his deep leather armchair. He slowly lit his pipe and gazed at the paintings on the opposite wall. There, next to a Picasso, was a Matisse, which was next to a Degas – on this wall alone! Hinrich once again felt the thrill of ownership over such beauty. He loved the paintings aesthetically, but the ownership of them even more. He realised that this showed a remarkable lack of taste; his booty, as it were, lined up alongside each other as if they were hanging in a cheap second-hand shop.

Hinrich sighed. He thought that it was better to have than to have not – and that he was finished with philosophy for today. He knew he had to switch to what he called his acquisition mode for the coming night. He was ready to pay Mr Boveri a visit and relieve him of a certain Picasso he owned. It amazed him that somebody could own such a painting and live in an ordinary house in the middle of Munich. His own flat was virtually impregnable. The only way in was through the front door, and that was made of steel with a simple crossbar on the inside to further deter a forced entry. Additionally, he had had two strong and expensive locks fitted. So: for tonight, he had planned everything down to the last detail. He decided to take only his big, silver, aluminium torch. The gun would make too much noise; after all, his target was old and defenceless and would not be at home, anyway. Following a further hour of planning and reviewing his escape route, he got up and left.

Hinrich saw the bus chugging towards him in the dusk. He had decided on a nondescript coat that reached down to his ankles, which he needed to hide the painting, a somewhat shabby but decent hat, and a briefcase that had seen better days. He looked like the average worker returning somewhat late from the office. The light was poor, and the hat hid his face. He got on the bus and bought a ticket after he had settled in his seat. The conductor didn't give him a second glance; he managed to look smaller than he was. Defensive and inconspicuous.

He got off the bus at Schwabinger Tor. He then walked along Johann-Fichte-Strasse, eventually coming to the Meyer Strasse, at the end of which was a cul-de-sac. The house of the man he was going to rob was at the end. Opposite the house was a piece of open land that stretched around the end of the cul-de-sac to the back of the building. The home of his prey.

Although he enjoyed perpetrating violence on others, be it raping and torturing in Brest, when he was with the Gestapo, or doing the same in Dachau, he had never actually killed anyone, and he did not intend to start now. Furthermore, Hinrich knew himself well enough to be afraid of getting hurt in a struggle. Therefore, he always liked to avoid direct confrontation when his opponent was on an equal footing. He knew the owner, Mr Boveri, was an old Jew in his eighties. How had he managed to stay alive amidst all the Jew-slaughter, and hold onto his Picasso, was a mystery to Hinrich.

Looking across from the stretch of open land, Hinrich saw a light behind the curtains of the front windows of the big, detached house.

"Damn, the old man is at home. He is usually out on a Tuesday evening! No matter, it's now or never."

Surprised at his own daring, Hinrich went through the open field and around to the rear of the house, climbed over the fence, careful not to snag his coat and tear it. He walked upright across the lawn to the back door. All was dark. Peeping in, he realised this must be the kitchen door. Fumbling in his left-hand coat pocket, he tugged out a woman's stocking and pulled it over his face. From his right-hand pocket, he extracted an iron lever and inserted it into the minute crack between the door and the frame. He pulled across and to the left with one abrupt movement. The door cracked, splintered loudly, and swung open. Hinrich froze. He waited until his hearing settled and his breathing normalised. All was still. Producing his flashlight, he proceeded through the large kitchen with an adjacent storeroom and into the spacious dining room. Under the next door ahead, he could see a sliver of light, which must be the lounge. The light he had seen from outside, he reckoned. To his right, an open door showed the way to a wide hallway that led off to further rooms and a stairwell.

He opened the door and walked straight in, now holding the torch as a weapon. Hinrich reckoned that the element of surprise would paralyse his elderly opponent. It was he who got a shock. He walked boldly into the room and immediately into the muzzle of a large revolver held by a resolute-looking, white-haired old man.

"Stand quite still. Don't move an inch while I phone the police," he said, his voice quavering.

"Don't shoot; I want no violence," wheedled Hinrich, knowing full well that if he didn't act, he would end up behind bars for a long, long time.

Herr Boveri moved towards the telephone, lifted the receiver, and began to dial, thus causing him to fumble and drop the heavy revolver. Instead of bending down to retrieve it, he started up abruptly, clutching his breast, as if shocked at his own clumsiness. Then the old gentleman twisted elegantly to one side and keeled over, striking his head on the corner of the bookcase on his way down.

Hinrich smiled. He walked over and stared down at Herr Boveri and at the pain that was wracking his body. He was bleeding from his temple.

"Call an ambulance, please," he groaned.

"Of course. You just relax a while; they will be here soon."

Hinrich grinned down at the dying man as he pulled him away from the bookcase and the painting of the guitar that hung above it.

He was still holding the dying man by the shoulders as Boveri looked him in the eye and spat in his face, saying: "Burn in hell, dirty little thief!"

"Tut, tut. Now, is that the way to treat a visitor?"

Hinrich wiped the spittle off, knelt down next to Boveri and clasped a gloved hand firmly over his mouth and nose. Boveri struggled feebly and then, after two long minutes, no more.

Hinrich moved back to the bookcase and took the Picasso down from the wall. He pried open the back of the frame with a small screwdriver he had chosen expressly for this purpose. He then removed a copy of the same painting, protected with silk paper and plastic coverings, which he had wrapped around his shirt and under his jacket and coat. Next, he wrapped the Boveri original around himself, using first the layers of silk paper and then the plastic to protect it. He then framed the forgery and hung it back on the wall in place of the original.

For the first time, he took in the room he had illegally entered. It was tastefully furnished in an old-fashioned way. There were walnut bookshelves on either side of the wide fireplace, and in the middle of the room a long, low oaken table with a large, luxurious sofa opposite the fireplace. At the opposite end, a small group of comfortable chairs gathered around another low table, which was stacked with books. In the corner was a secretaire, also of walnut. On the walls were paintings, mainly of the old masters. Could that one be a Dürer? The other a Bruegel? Copies or real? Hinrich wondered about the change of taste for this corner of the room. Why a Picasso? It didn't match or make sense. Hinrich realised that this was of no matter. What did matter was the scene of this crime.

He went through it in his mind: *So, the thief broke in, Boveri had a heart attack, collapsed dead on the floor, the thief ran away afterwards frightened and empty-handed. Perfect.* He cackled. Hinrich could hardly believe his luck.

He straightened the carpet. Looking down, he saw blood on his coat. Blood! He took the coat off and folded it carefully, avoiding getting any of it on anything else. He went through and into the kitchen, fearing to switch his torch on. He fumbled around in the dark until he found a sponge next to the sink and then risked using his torch with his back to the window. He rubbed the blood off as best he could without using any water and put the sponge into the pocket of his folded coat. He peered through the big kitchen window to see if the coast was clear. It was. He eased himself through the door, closed it gently and started to walk across the field in the opposite direction from which he had come. He encountered no one.

Out of an innate sense of security, Hinrich took a different route back. He crossed over to the Englischer Garten and was making his way towards the main road on the other side of the Isar when he saw a policeman standing under a lamppost. Hinrich stiffened, and the policeman saw him do so. Keeping upright to hide the Picasso under his jacket and his bloody folded coat in front of him, he forced himself to relax and continue on.

"Good evening, sir. May I ask what you are doing in the park at this time of night?" The policeman was a big man with a beard; he instantly reminded Hinrich of someone, but he couldn't put a name to the face.

"Well, I must say you gave me a pleasant surprise; it is good to meet a policeman when one is alone in the park at night. Yes, I've been visiting friends, and I thought I would enjoy a walk in the fresh air and catch a taxi on the other side of the park."

"Where do you live? If I may ask, sir."

"In the old town in the Theatinerstrasse." Hinrich knew full well that the officer could ask him for ID, so he kept to the truth – well, almost.

"It has become rather cool this spring evening not to be wearing a coat, don't you think?"

"Really? I hadn't noticed. It was so stuffy at my friends', I was glad to get out into the fresh air. Now you mention it, it has become somewhat cooler. I think I will put it on after all." Hinrich made to start unravelling his coat and noticed that the policeman was fast losing interest. "So, if that is all, I shall continue over to the main road."

"Have a nice night, sir, and take care," said the policeman, turning away from Hinrich and peering in the other direction. He was plainly bored.

Reaching the Piezenaustrasse, he hailed a taxi, and, as he gave the driver his address, he suddenly realised who the policeman had reminded him of: Father Ryan!

"Where to? Are you alright?" the taxi driver asked him impatiently.

Hinrich gave him his address and slumped down into the back seat of the car.

Back in his apartment, he carefully unpacked the stolen painting. Unfortunately, try as he might, he could not appreciate his newly acquired treasure. Instead, he sat down in his favourite chair, lit his pipe, and thought again about Father Ryan, the visiting Irish priest from County Clare who had been caught up in a raid on a gang of Catholics in 1943. He had been aiding and hiding Jews. Ryan had been a soft spoken, gentle man, most serious for such a young age. Serious about his faith and the Jews that he had suffered in Dachau for. Since the end of the war, many people thought that Dachau was an extermination camp for killing Jews.

"What do they know?" Richter snorted out loud.

In reality, although they did do a lot of killing, Jews as well, it had been built mainly for dissenters and misfits. Party members of the German Social Democrats, communists, socialists, many of whom were sent home after it had been considered they had learnt their lesson. Indeed, it was most seldom that any one of them raised their impudent heads ever again. The Russian prisoners they killed immediately on arrival. Up against the wall and *bang, bang*, dead.

They had also been useful for experimentation. The goal of such trials was to see how long they could last before dying in a vat of freezing-cold water. The research was to enable the development of better clothing for German pilots who had bailed out over the sea.

The Catholic priests could cause a lot of trouble. Hinrich, as a good National Socialist, knew that the party regarded

Christianity, and Catholicism in particular, as an organisation whose feeble mewling about the weak and the poor had to be put an end to. Himmler reckoned it would take fifty years to wipe out the scourge of the teachings of Jesus. Father Ryan had refused to give up any information to the Gestapo about the Juden Ring. This was most surprising, since the Gestapo knew their torture methods. Hinrich saw Father Ryan as a challenge. Although his responsibilities involved the planning and organisation of the concentration camp system as a whole, using Dachau as a (somewhat outdated) model, he liked to keep his hand in regarding interrogation.

He had interrogated Ryan for days on end. Allowing the absolute minimum of food and water to survive. Ryan was a big man and had obviously liked his food back in Friedrichshafen. He had become a shrunken effigy of his former self. In the end, Hinrich had him crucified. He forced Father Ryan to pick out a tree that grew outside and next to the camp. He remembered telling him that the one he chopped down would make his cross. Ryan was so weak it took him days to chop down a tree that was suitable for his execution.

Like Father Ryan himself, the raising of his cross with him on it had proved most troublesome. They had tied his hands and feet to the wood as well as nailing them. Just in time, Hinrich remembered that Father Ryan's first name was Paul and Paul had been crucified upside down. So it had been and so it would be. At the northern end of the barracks' square hung the gentle Father, who was, as far as Hinrich was concerned, a bloody and dangerous fool.

Hinrich recalled Ryan hanging there for hours. As evening approached, it was clear he was going to die.

Birds kept gathering round him, anxious to get at his eyes. They would perch on his head and begin to peck away – frightened away only by the screams of the priest in agony. Standing before him, Hinrich had felt the urge to piss in the priest's open, hanging mouth. He was about to unpack his organ when Kapitan Oswald appeared to his left wanting some trivial information. Hinrich made as if he was merely adjusting his clothing, but noticed Oswald had given him a questioning look.

Father Ryan, he recalled further, had mumbled something. Always interested in the last words of his victims, Hinrich had knelt down before him.

"What did you say? What?"

"I forgive you."

Hinrich remembered with embarrassment that he had immediately recoiled and shot up and turned around on his own axis.

"You cannot say that! You must hate me!" He shouted this again and again at the dying priest until the prisoners who were sweeping the yard, the officers, and soldiers on duty all stopped and stared at him. He then stopped screaming. No one moved. The only things to be heard were the birds twittering merrily in the late afternoon sun.

"Free him from his cross; make sure he doesn't die. That is an order!"

After an unsettled night, Hinrich, who had never been given to introspection, wondered what would become of him. His parents and sister were dead. He had no friends; he didn't want any. He didn't want to marry and have a family; he didn't like women much – just the one and she had been an English Jewess. He was a millionaire, and that he did like. He must go down to Friedrichshafen and review the loot beneath the boathouse. The diamonds and silver must be worth a very considerable sum, just by themselves. He would take the new Picasso with him. Better safe than sorry.

Feeling better at the thought of even more riches, but somehow not quite settled (which, he noticed, had been coming about quite regularly in recent months), he made himself some coffee and toast. The thought of wealth reminded him of last night's stolen booty. He had killed that old man. Times had changed. If this ever became known, he would get life imprisonment. Up until yesterday evening, he had never actually killed anyone at all. Well, Father Ryan had died after they took him down from the cross; rather unfortunately, he thought. In the end, he didn't want him dead. He didn't regard himself as a killer; he left that to others. He had, in this area of work, specialised in interrogating women, which had gone well until that bitch Ida had nearly bitten his penis off. She had also killed Frank.

Concluding his brief inner survey, the fact that he had committed murder filled him with dread. If this ever became known, he was finished. There was only one person that the police could possibly receive information from and that was his colleague and fellow detective, Konrad Huber. Huber (also ex-Gestapo) had given him the tip about the old man's Picasso and the information that he would not be at home that evening. But he had been, armed and waiting. He had been set up! Hinrich knew from experience that Huber was just as ruthless as he was, probably more so. He envisioned the future train of events: a man matching his description had been seen breaking and entering the old man's house. The stolen painting would be found in his possession. The policeman in the park he had encountered on his way home… Either he had to get rid of the Picasso or Konrad Huber. He knew he could not do the latter. He got up from his expensive walnut kitchen table and wandered into the dining room. There he stroked the beautiful long oak table decorated with two silver candlesticks and a vase of daffodils he had bought himself (Hinrich prided himself on being a cultivated man of taste. It was therefore all the more disturbing for him that he could not arrange his masterpieces throughout the apartment to his own satisfaction). He frowned at the van Gogh hung next to a Dix and continued on to the lounge, where he picked up the stolen painting, which was lying on the Biedermeier table. The sun caught the painting, and it seem to vibrate with colour.

He glanced across at the window and said to the guitarist: "It's a nice, warm day in April. I shall invite Konrad for a coffee and cognac at the cafeteria in the Englischer Garten. He likes to be hosted, that man. Well, I shall host him and toast him." He picked up the telephone, which was on a shelf of the walnut bookcase behind him.

"*ZUM WOHL*, KONRAD." HINRICH TIPPED his tiny cognac glass in Konrad Huber's direction and tilted it back, swallowing the contents in one draught. Konrad Huber did the same.

"And to your health too, my dear Hinrich."

Hinrich stretched out his long legs and admired his brown leather boating shoes. They went well with his beige slacks and his short-sleeved, blue, summer shirt. He never wore a hat when the sun was out. He bronzed almost perfectly, and his rich, blond, wavy hair set off his self-image perfectly.

"Konrad, old comrade Konrad. Do you know, I had a rather strange dream last night. I would like to tell you about it. I think you may have been in it."

"Most unusual, but please do, Hinrich."

"Well, before we do, let me order us another round of cognac, old travelling companion. Waiter!"

He looked across at Huber, noting that the little man wore a black suit (again) with a grey waistcoat and matching black polished shoes. He had laid his bowler hat on the empty chair beside him.

"The same old, same old," murmured Hinrich, looking Huber straight in the eye. "As you know better than anyone else, Konrad, there is no law against owning degenerate, looted art."

"Well, if that is what you want to talk about, yes, Hinrich, and I cannot help but wonder at the irony of it. The Jews, yet again. Literally at least a thousand paintings have gone missing. They must be worth millions and millions. My department really needs more qualified people to track them all down. However, as you so rightly said, there is no German law against owning looted property. How do we find the original owners? How can they prove that the paintings belonged to them originally? Most of the former owners were Jews and they are either living abroad or dead anyway. 'Tis a muddle indeed."

Huber leant back in his chair and puffed on the cigar he had just happily lit. Together they looked across the park. It was unusually warm for April and there were many families picnicking by the River Isar. The squeals and cries of the children playing wafted over to them. Young lovers strolled along the meandering pathways beneath the trees.

Some of them arm in arm, stopping occasionally to kiss in public.

How times have changed, observed Hinrich, who then replied: "The irony being, Konrad?"

"As we know, Hitler saw Jewish culture as an obstacle to realising his dream of a pure, savage, German race. He was helped in stating his case not only by Nietzsche, who, by the way, was himself a mental and physical wreck when he died at the ripe old age of fifty-four, but also by Nordau. At the turn of the century, Nordau, a physician and social critic, postulated that degenerate art and literature, such as the symbolists and modern-day writers ranging from Wilde to Tolstoy and Zola, were weakening our society."

"Very interesting, I'm sure, but again: the irony being, apart from Nietzsche being a very weak and sick man in mind and body?"

"Nordau was the son of a Budapest rabbi, a Jew, and Hitler used his work to destroy his people."

"Oops! How unfortunate," quipped Hinrich, and both men laughed.

"The point is, Hinrich, there are perhaps even thousands of very valuable paintings that have been hidden away. As an art aficionado yourself, I suspect you may know many exciting contacts. Hildebrand Gurlitt, for example, was Hitler's chief art thief. Hildebrand is still in business."

This is what Hinrich had been waiting to hear from Konrad. He had opened the door to his own dead end.

"Just a moment, my friend, the waiter is coming our way, and this weather is simply splendid; let us celebrate the day before we wander back to our homes."

"Fine by me, Hinrich, order away."

"Waiter, two small beers and two double cognacs."

The two men waited until the drinks were served and, as they drank, Hinrich took only a very small sip of his cognac and an exaggerated large swig of the weak Bavarian beer. He slammed his glass down on the table and uttered a loud 'Ah'.

Konrad did likewise but downed his cognac in one gulp followed by a deep draught of beer and gave a deep and loud sigh of satisfaction.

He belched without apologising and said: "Now, where were we?"

"You wanted to know more about my contacts in the art world, Konrad, but let me tell you about my dream first."

Huber settled his round bottom more comfortably in his wicker chair, looked across at the green and pleasant sunny vista spread out before him and thought he could let Hinrich indulge in his stupid sentiments (to him, Hinrich seemed to have lost some of that wonderful, driving aggression in the last few years).

He exhaled a large cloud of cigar smoke and said: "Pray continue."

"I will. The thing is, I dreamt I was in an old man's house. I dreamt that he would not be there. But do you know what? He was armed with a gun pointed at me! We were standing in his lounge, and he pointed the gun directly at my heart and then said: 'Take down the Picasso and leave this house.' He then went to the telephone and tried to make a call. As he was doing this, he suddenly collapsed and struck his head on the corner of the bookcase on his way down. He died of a heart attack before my eyes. It was most unsettling. All I remember is that he insisted I take the Picasso with me. One of a guitarist, as you well know."

"How very realistic, my dear Hinrich."

"Yes, but there is more. I dreamt that you had given me the information where this Picasso could be found, and that the old man wished me to take it, and that he would not be at home if I went there to acquire it. But he was! Then, suddenly, I was being arrested by you and my key ring lay on the table next to my wallet and ID card. Then you picked up the keys to my apartment. Not only that, but you knew about the boathouse. A real nightmare, huh?"

"Yes, but that's enough now. Let us drink some more," slurred Huber, who was now sitting ramrod straight in his chair holding his beer in one hand and clenching his cigar in the other.

"You are squashing your cigar, Huber. Is that sweat on your brow? Anyway, I also dreamt that I had made precise notes of the information you had given me about the painting: how to get to the old man's house and where the Picasso was hung, and that the house would be empty. I had dated them and had them deposited them in my bank safe. I request that the bank keeps a record of when I make a special deposit, don't you know? Just to be safe. So, anyway, I then dreamt I transferred ten thousand marks to your account with the remark 'for information provided'. So, you see, Huber, if I go down, you go with me. Goodbye, and take care; accidents can happen."

Hinrich stood up, smoothed down his trousers, turned to look to see if any women were admiring him and stepped down from the restaurant patio.

Huber lurched up and called to Hinrich's departing back: "But, but, Hinrich, old friend, you forgot to pay the bill!"

Without turning around, Hinrich continued on his way

and slowly raised his right hand and gave a brief wave. As he walked along the path, he looked to his left and watched a mother duck with a row of ducklings behind her. They were waddling their way to the water. One by one, they settled onto the surface and made their serene voyage to wherever they were headed. He stepped aside to allow a young mother pushing a pram to pass by. He smiled.

That night, he slept well, better than he had in a long time. For some reason he could not fathom, he felt not only pleased with himself, but truly at ease. All he needed was the newspaper. He took the lift down to the foyer in his dressing gown and slippers. From his letter box, he retrieved the Munich newspaper and two letters. Back at his kitchen table, he scanned the headlines of the various articles in the paper. There was still no news of a break-in and robbery in a house in the Meyer Strasse. Good! The police may well have thought that a burglar had fled after Boveri had collapsed and died; apart from that, there was nothing missing. Ha! Laying the paper aside, he picked up the first letter, which was from the electricity company – a bill. The second letter was from the town arts centre in Friedrichshafen. It was an invitation to an art exhibition, 'Reconciliation by the Lakeside', for him as a recognised art expert. *Well, things are looking up*, mused Hinrich contentedly. He scanned the list of contributing artists, two of which stood out: Judith Lareine and Matthias Krieger.

11

THE LAKESIDE ART EXHIBITION, 1953

ALEXSANDER ABRAHAM WAS ENJOYING THE ocean of sky as they sailed across and far above the English Channel, over and beyond the scattered cumulus clouds below, tinged with the sun's golden rays. He felt the calm and warmth of doing what he loved: flying high, softly, and smoothly with oceans of space before and about him. He then realised again: the last time he flew to this location, he had killed an unarmed man (he had killed many men). Indeed, because of this, he was flying slightly more southwest than was necessary.

He leant across to Yolande and said: "We are approaching the position, go behind and fetch Judith, like we said."

Yolande didn't reply, but, nodding her head slowly and thoughtfully, she unbuckled and left her seat, balanced herself by holding onto their two seats and went aft.

Turning his head, Alexsander observed her face that he loved so much. So attractive, despite the disfigurement she had received at the hands of the Gestapo. Her fierce beauty and spirit could never be quenched, he thought happily. And now they had a son.

He glanced at Judith, who was sitting on the bench behind them holding baby Timothé; her face was radiant, and so was the baby's. Above the noise of the Beechcraft Bonanza D35, he could intermittently discern his son's happy gurgling as Judith rocked him gently to and fro (not that he needed it, but Judith obviously did). The sun was shining through the starboard side window, catching the lights in Judith's burnished hair and Timothé's rosy, red cheeks. They both shone.

Alexsander heard Yolande call out: "Judith, we are nearly there. If you still want to, Alexsander will show you."

He noticed, too, how the colour drained from Judith's face, its exquisiteness fading into a pale greyness. She nodded. Yes.

Yolande seated herself next to her and Judith gave Timothé back to her.

Leaving Timothé with his mother, Judith half stood and, grabbing hold of the forward seats, swung herself into the co-pilot's place. Alexsander signalled to her to pick up the earphones and microphone.

"If I remember correctly, the U-boat pens from La Rochelle were exactly ten miles from this point due east," he said. "You can just see the Île de Ré. This is where Tom died. To see his wonderful grave, Judith: just look down. Now."

Which she did. He looked across and saw the tears welling up and trickling down over her face. He listened and, over the earphones, heard her chanting 'El Malei Rachamim'. She had once told them that she had learnt this from her parents as a child. It had helped her through all the

232

terrible deaths she had witnessed as a nurse in the burns unit in Lichfield.

She began the prayer with the sentence: "Merciful God who dwells above, provide a sure rest on the wings of the…"

Alexsander bowed his head, closed his eyes, and chanted the prayer with her. They were flying blind. The Beechcraft suddenly started to buck and bounce as they hit a band of turbulence. Alexsander held course.

Judith finished with the words: "The Lord is his heritage, and he shall rest peacefully on his bed. So let us say, Amen."

In that moment, Alexsander, the Jew from Lublin, turned to her and also said, "Amen." The aeroplane promptly resumed its previous steady, droning progression. Dipping his portside wing, he said: "Look down over there, where the land begins in that field before the woods start: I killed the man who killed Tom. He was a bad man."

Judith stared down over Alexsander's right shoulder at the expanse of grey-blue sea with the white ripples of the waves making their way to the Île de Ré. Tom was down there, his fierce spirit at peace at last.

Judith looked across at Alexsander and realised what this gentle, gawky man, who was nodding grimly into his microphone as he adjusted their course northeast for Friedrichshafen, had done. What he had had to do. As a fighter pilot. Alexsander felt her gaze upon him as she looked across and nodded, stood up and swayed her way over to Yolande and Timothé.

***

THE NEXT DAY, AT NINE o'clock, Judith felt the warmth of the gentle early morning sun gradually heating her up from left to right. How curious. She had made a good decision in wearing a cardigan over her summer dress. No shorts today; this was a formal occasion. She had left Yolande and her family behind at the hotel and after a simple continental breakfast had walked about a mile to this most unusual, pleasant, and courageous location. Brave in so far that it was a location most apt for the exhibition 'Reconciliation by the Lakeside', the opening of which was scheduled to begin at one o'clock. She joined the little queue at the entrance and was surprised to see that she could walk straight through the pavilion and onto the grounds. On the right was a table at which sat a young Catholic priest in black with a round, friendly face and of ruddy complexion; next to him, a tall, thin, elderly man in a dark suit, and on his head, a kippah – a rabbi, no doubt. On the table in front of the two men were name plates. Father Christopher Donnelly and Rabbi Chaim Moskowitz – how nice!

She smiled and said: "Good morning, Father Donnelly; shalom aleichem, Rabbi Moskowitz." She presented her letter of invitation.

"And the top of the morning to you, dear Miss Lareine; we have heard so much about your fine work. Welcome, welcome, my dear."

"Thank you, Father Donnelly."

"Shalom, Fräulein Lareine, shalom. You must excuse me; my English is not very good."

"We can converse in German, Rabbi Moskowitz."

"Ah, we will do that; my colleague Donnelly speaks excellent German too."

"I'm so glad to have made both your acquaintances; thank you very much for the invitation."

"You are most welcome, my child," replied the rabbi. "Is that not so, my dear Donnelly?"

"On this lovely morning, indeed it is, Rabbi Moskowitz, indeed it is."

"Would you think that the weather would make any difference to the quality of the people we have invited?"

"Certainly, that is a very good question for this time of this beautiful morning."

Judith laughed and then realised she was holding up the people behind her, so she moved on in order to let these individuals enjoy their welcome from these two lovely men. She walked out and onto the expansive exhibition area.

The venue was situated at the lakeshore on the grounds of the public beach, which was made up of an expansive grassy area, interspersed with groups of trees, which led gently down to the water. This breadth of green was normally reserved for sunbathing and picnicking. *Not today*, she thought. The organisers had invited the artists to choose their own spots to display their paintings and sculptures. The weather forecast had been perfect: an average of twenty-two degrees Celsius. So much the better! The alternative venue would have been in the pavilion – and safer, probably. From the start, she had noticed the police. Always in pairs: two at the entrance, two at every artist's display stand and two pairs that patrolled the whole area at a leisurely pace.

She suddenly realised that her misgivings (which she had shared with no one) about coming to the lakeside again after the disaster of fifteen years ago had evaporated. Everything was so normal in the sunlight, and quiet of a

Sunday morning. She suddenly heard a booming horn, looked across the glassy, clear waters and spotted a ferry making its way towards the town of Romanshorn on the Swiss side. The occasional small sailing boat scurrying to get out of its way, everything so utterly ordinary, picturesque with the snow-capped mountains on the horizon. She asked herself again: *How could all of the horror that had emanated from this country, which loved middle-class order above all things, have come about? Are all Germans evil? If not: how could they have voted a man so full of hate into power?* She felt her disaffection for this country seeping up within her yet again. This was not the way to think! She remembered her Shakespeare, which she had studied at school in this very country of thinkers and poets, and quoted out loud from *As You Like It*: "The fool doth think he is wise, but the wise man knows himself to be a fool."

Two men carrying tool bags looked across at her in puzzlement. One of them took his cigarette out of his mouth and said something to the other, who laughed heartily as they continued their way on past her. This morning was meant for the installation and setting up of the various artists' work. Each artist had been asked to display five pieces of work.

About two and a half hours later, she had just finished overseeing the setting up of her paintings. Each artist had chosen an area below a group of trees, which provided protection from the direct sunlight. At first, she had been sceptical, but when the men had finished positioning her paintings – two from Eriskirch, two of the burns unit and her latest piece, all of which were behind a cordon for viewers – she was satisfied enough. Each picture was affixed at head height to a small, moveable trolley which could be moved according to the incidence of light conditions (that was how the curator, Herr Leger, had described it), and she was, again, pleased with this solution. In the sometimes-dappled sunlight effect, with the occasional breeze rippling through the quivering leaves, the paintings came to life. The earlier ones of this region seemed to gleam, and those of the Kandinsky-like nightmares of the men in the Lichfield Burns Unit seemed to draw you in all the more. She was especially pleased with her latest picture of the lonely young woman sitting on the bench staring outwards across the lake, with the sunlit tree behind her and, beyond, the ominous darkness of the unknown. The critics could go to blazes; this was what she felt.

She was in formidable company; it was a diverse group of Jewish and non-Jewish, of local and international artists of world renown.

Now she was hungry. Judith sauntered across the grass to the entrance area in front of the pavilion, where the ladies of the Catholic Church had set up a coffee and sandwich stand under a large colourful awning. On offer was not only fresh, hot coffee but also buttered pretzels and a choice of cheese and ham rolls. There was even a variety of cakes to choose from.

She eyed the Black Forest gateaux intently, looked up to the kindly lady who was serving her and said: "I'll get back to this one later."

"Shall I put you a piece to one side, madam?"

"Yes, please," and then, thinking of Yolande and then Alexsander, "you better make that two slices – no, three."

The overweight lady laughed and deftly cut the cake into quarters and eighths, put three slices on one large white plate, covered them with a transparent dome for said purpose and said pleasantly: "Please don't forget them. I can't eat them all by myself at the end of the day!"

"Don't worry, I certainly won't; they look far too delicious. For now, I'll have a buttered pretzel with my coffee."

Judith sat herself down at a small round table set up outside the pavilion and observed the hurrying to and fro of the other artists and their entourage. The line-up was impressive, she mused. Jews and Gentiles alike: Dix, Gabriele Münter (her favourite), Sepp Mahler… all of whom had been banned by the Nazis. The artists of Jewish origin were also most striking: Rothko! He had come down from Paris especially for the exhibition, followed, no less, by Willem de Kooning and herself, which was most flattering but rather odd. They probably couldn't get anybody else. Nevertheless, she had earned enough money from her painting to invest in Alexsander's budding commercial air delivery venture. The Beechcraft Bonanza would be paid off in another five years, and Alexsander had proved himself to be a level-headed businessman as well as a superb pilot and was reimbursing her on a regular basis as agreed. She was a passive partner, a cool-headed decision to provide an alternate avenue of income for herself. Yolande kept the finances in order and was keen to buy a second aeroplane to deal with what she viewed as an expanding market. Indeed, business in Europe was flourishing in the after-war boom.

Feeling the need to move, she finished her snack and started on a tour of the exhibition. The very first station was beneath the three beech trees to her right. Aha, Gabriele Münter, no less. On seeing Münter's painting of the house in Murnau, the slight flutter of inner agitation that had been all the while slumbering at the back of her mind came to the fore with a force that shocked her. She had to see Matthias! She wanted to know what he looked like, how he was, how much he had changed, if she could still like him. He used to be so lovely. She couldn't concentrate on Münter's paintings, so she moved on, feeling the coffee and pretzel churning in her stomach. She felt heat burning up from within and without, stopped to steady herself, and took off her cardigan.

"Keep calm and carry on," she muttered and continued on her way.

Passing by Berthold Müller-Oerlinghausen's exquisite figures beneath an enormous oak tree, which she thought was too shady for its purpose, she realised that she had arrived at the outer western perimeter of the exhibition. She stopped in her tracks at the sight of herself sitting on a bench in the shade of a tree. She was gazing out across the lake. At the other end of the bench sat a man, who was slightly bowed forwards. At the water's edge, several paces in front of him on a low table, were two headpieces, probably of stone. Next to them were what seemed like two stone bottles. To the left and right-hand sides respectively, between table and bench, were two larger headpieces positioned on the ground: two to the left, two to the right. The whole representation was circular in form. Her statue was of pure white marble. It was an exquisite piece of a young girl – no, of herself – gazing out wistfully into the distance with both her feet positioned on a marble football. She had used to do that after kicking a football around with Matthias: sit on the bench and enjoy the view. She was dressed in shorts, sandals, and a singlet – exactly how she used to be.

As she came closer, she realised that the stocky man was Matthias.

"Matthias!" she called and hurried towards him.

Matthias Krieger turned to see his dream had come true. His face lit up and he said: "So, you have come back at last, Judith."

***

HE WAS LATE. IT WAS 3pm exactly when Hinrich put his foot down and the Mercedes-Benz 300S convertible's six cylinders roared back at him, and he flew past the lumbering bus full of passengers who were probably heading for a late afternoon at the lake. He loved the power of the engine and the sleek lines of his racing-green coupé. He glanced briefly up to the right and saw a young woman staring hungrily down at him, his blond hair ruffling in the wind. Truly, all was right with the world.

Ninety minutes later, he arrived at the exhibition venue, carefully parked his car in front of the pavilion and, remaining seated and motionless behind the wheel, he said out loud: "How am I going to proceed?"

He got out and decided to leave the hood down; nobody was going to steal this baby in broad daylight in provincial little Friedrichshafen. He pocketed his keys and stood still in the pleasant late-afternoon sun. He wasn't quite sure why he had come: to view the works on display, obviously. Many were still to be had at reasonable prices, in spite of the Americans buying up everything in sight. The European market was still comparatively weak, but that would change. At the present rate of economic growth, there would soon be more and more money pouring into the market. Apropos, new money: the work of Judith Lareine was in demand. Apart from that and, moreover, he couldn't bury the itch at the back of his mind that he wanted to see her again; her, yes, but not Krieger. How the hell he had survived the war was just a stroke of bad luck. That he had been invited to display his work was inappropriate – he was small fry. No doubt the Jewish-Catholic organisers needed some local talent to make the exhibition 'hit home', as it were. To a certain extent, the same applied to Judith: an English Jewess, former inhabitant of Friedrichshafen, returns in peace. *And my peace I give you. Ha!*

He walked over to the wooden pavilion entrance, displayed his invitation card and entered the grounds. At 5.30pm, he was standing in front of a painting of a child playing with a doll in a dream-like landscape. He was immediately reminded of his little sister, Birgit, and how she loved to play with her dolls in the garden. One sunny Sunday afternoon, just like this one, she had got herself all dirty. Their mother had become extremely angry and had rushed across the garden shouting at Birgit to get in the house at once. She had raised her hand to slap the little girl, and Hinrich had grabbed her arm to stop her, causing his mother to shake him off furiously as she continued with her efforts to beat Birgit. Hinrich had again hung onto her arm until she had calmed down – sort of.

Not for the first time recently, a feeling of unease clouded Hinrich's thoughts. Birgit, the priest in Dachau, the old man in his home, Birgit. How had she died? Why did she die before his parents? He realised that he had now reached the outer edge of the exhibition. In the late-afternoon sunlight, he looked up to the trees, whose rustling in the breeze seemed to whisper back his uneasy thoughts. So, he switched his view and looked across the area to his right and suddenly perceived Matthias Krieger sitting on a bench surrounded by sculptures holding hands with Judith Lareine in a paper bag.

***

ONE HOUR BEFORE

JUDITH STOPPED, BENT DOWN TO him, took his face in her hands and kissed his forehead. She took a step back and surveyed the silver-grey in his curly dark hair, the creases of worry below and around his eyes, the deep furrows in his cheeks, the result of years of deprivation and, no doubt, starvation. The strange glint in his eyes and, above all, the sense of weariness that hung about him, as if he wore an invisible cloak of lead.

"Matthias, it is so nice to see you again. I never thought it would be possible."

"Well, Judith, I had very nearly given up hope that we would ever meet again."

"Well, against all odds, here we are!"

"Judith, I have seen pictures of your paintings in the newspaper, and they are most impressive. I always thought that you were very talented."

"Thank you, you are very kind. You always were gentle and sympathetic."

"Not always; I did some bad things in the war, and bad things happened to me."

"I'm so sorry to hear that, Matthias. Yes, it was horrible. I worked in a burns unit in a specialist hospital as a nurse, then I went on to become a doctor. I work in Lichfield. I have a flat near my parents' house."

"Throughout the fifteen years, I thought of you every day, Judith, but when you seduced me as a whore in a pit, and then, when I got home, you didn't answer my letters, I almost lost the will to think of you. Why did you not answer my letters?"

"What on earth! Matthias, how could you say such things straight off the bat?" Judith turned and looked out over his head; she felt anger, dismay and disappointment welling up inside her. She turned back forcefully and said: "I don't know what to say. Well, for a start: I simply could not reply to the one letter I received from you after we had been at war for six years. Our families at war! How terrible! And after the war ended came the dreadful reports about the concentration camps and the efforts to exterminate us Jews completely. I just could not."

"Yes, I witnessed that in action, too."

"You didn't take part in it, did you?"

"No! Of course not! I sort of helped stop an execution commando in Russia. What sort of man do you think I am?"

Judith stared at him, bit her lip, and blurted out: "You were the sort of boy who didn't walk his very frightened girlfriend home after a Nazi had attacked her! You are a very violent man, or at least one part of you is. What do you mean, me being a whore?"

"That's how I once dreamt of you, Judith; you kept me going day by day in every way. Unfortunately, one afternoon we got pinned down again by the Russian artillery. I woke up next to my dead and decapitated comrades and you came to me as a horrible apparition. It was the devil trying to destroy that which had kept me alive. That which I loved. I'm sorry I hurt you just now, and I'm so sorry that I didn't walk you home that night."

"If you had done so, I would have taken you to my bed and never ever let you go again." She reached across and gently laid her hand on his tired cheek; she felt his tears trickling down over it and down to her elbow. "Matthias," she said softly, "all these years I haven't been true to you. I have not been true to myself."

Matthias sat up abruptly and gently removed Judith's hand from his face and laid it in her lap.

"Please understand, Judith, when I returned home some months ago, I became ill, not so much in my body but in my mind. I did something about it, thanks also to my parents, and now I'm on the mend again. Look at this beautiful statue of you as I knew you fifteen years ago. I was inspired by the magical sculpture of 'Pan Comforting Psyche' by Reinhold Begas. But enough about me; tell me about yourself and how you became a doctor. What was it like, nursing in a burns unit? It must have been very difficult. How did it affect your art? How did you become a doctor? Are your parents well? Tell me all."

Judith sighed and looked at Matthias for a long time. Then, finally, she said: "Matthias, that was a lot to take in; pain, horror and disappointment seems to have been the tenor of our youth. I'm so sorry you had to go through what happened to you. Why did you join the army to fight for this horrid cause? Couldn't you have joined the Resistance or fled across the lake to Switzerland?"

"Resistance! What resistance? Around here, anybody who spoke against the Nazis got beaten up or ended up in Dachau or one of its subsidiary camps. There was no Resistance, woman! You should know that; you were here then! Anyway, I thought the best place to hide from the Richters would be in the army. Switzerland! I had no friends there. My father fought for his country in the Great War. I didn't think I would be involved in a world war in 1938. Nobody did! So, I joined the army to hide from the SS! Can't you or won't you understand that?"

He was now standing in front of her and was shouting so loudly that the ducks nearby all flew away in one sudden movement, quacking and carping noisily.

Judith felt as if a hard white wall of aggression was howling in her face. As soon as Matthias had ended his outburst, she arose and walked towards the tableau of the two figures in front of her. She glanced at the headpieces to her left and right; she had an uncomfortable feeling of being trapped within Matthias's nightmare. She walked away from him and his world of pain, into the water, and waded back along towards the main area of the art exhibition.

Matthias groaned as he watched her receding back. He made to get up but sat back again, not knowing what he would say to her. What more could he say? She was obviously upset with him. He was still upset with himself (or, to be more accurate, within himself). He sat back down with a bump on the bench, causing his statue of Judith to shudder.

He leant across and said: "I'm sorry, Judith." He felt his heart sinking and disappearing into his lower abdomen.

He peered across the grounds and could no longer see her. She had gone. He then looked out across the lake and shouted out at Switzerland: "Well, you made a right mess of that, Krieger!"

It seemed to him a weak and echoless sound.

How could he have poured out all that vile vitriol onto a girl – now a woman – who he didn't really know, who he supposedly loved? He dimly realised that she was trying to understand his position from the perspective of an Englishwoman. How could she? He barely understood it himself. He was a loyal German youth from Lake Constance. Like everybody else, he had hated the Nazis (well, almost everybody). Now he couldn't even move; he felt too heavy, too tired.

Later on, he realised his name was being called from a distance. At first, he thought it was a cry of a tern, then he realised it was a voice, and he looked up and saw Judith wading along the edge of the lake towards him carrying a tray laden with food and drinks. He laughed out loud with delight and relief and sprinted across to help her by removing the precariously balanced two bottles of beer.

"Do you think you can manage that? How typical of a man to grab the booze first." She was smiling. "As you can see, I bought two fried sausages, one pork for you and one beef from the kosher stand for myself, and a portion of what they called French fries and beer for us both, so that we would have something in common."

"Fair enough," answered Matthias, and set the bottles down on the ground in front of the bench. As he turned to take the tray off Judith, he knocked one of them over, its contents spilling out over the already bald patch of hard earth in front of the bench. "Oh, we will have to watch out; that's created a slippery patch there, so be careful."

"Yes, Dad." Judith grinned in reply. She became serious again. "Please tell me who these stone figures in front of us are. To my right, I recognise your mother and father – and on the opposite side to my left?" She looked across at Matthias and waited.

After a while, he replied, "The first one is of Major Warner; he helped me stay sane and alive, mostly when I was a prisoner. Next to him, Bernd; he watched over me, over us, in the prison camp. He was very fierce. The war had crippled his mind. He saved my life. On the table next to the stone vodka bottles are Bruno und Uwe, two comrades I drank with and who died next to me."

He stopped and looked down at the ground. Judith noticed that the hairs on his left wrist were white; on his right, dark. His hands around the beer bottle were still beautiful with long, tapering, strong fingers. He smelt of wood and tiredness.

Matthias stirred out of his reverie and said to his companion: "Now please share with me what you went through."

And she did.

One hour and fifteen minutes later, Judith looked at Matthias and said: "Let us try again and go back to our first conversation, Matthias." Looking him straight in the eye, she added, "Perhaps without the outbursts of fury. I was thinking, as I roamed the exhibition before I returned, about you, about us. If there is going to be an us. As I wandered, these lines occurred to me, from 'The Waste Land' by the American poet T.S. Eliot."

Judith, switching to English, spoke slowly and clearly:

"Who is the third who walks always beside you?

When I count, there are only you and I together
But when I look ahead up the white road
There is always another one walking beside you
Gliding wrapt in a brown mantle, hooded
I do not know whether a man or a woman
—But who is that on the other side of you?" [1]

"Do you understand, Matthias?"

"I understood the text and, I think, the meaning. Do you think that I have such a shadow, Judith?"

"Yes, I do, Matthias."

"Do you have one?"

"Yes, but perhaps not quite one so unnerving. My painting helped me, but now I'm alone again and I am unsure if I can ever be anything else other than that – alone."

Matthias looked down at her exquisite legs and her delightful form, her perfect high cheekbones and deep-black hair, which she now kept short in contrast to her schooldays. He felt as if his future happiness was slipping away from him.

He dipped into the paper bag of French fries at the same time as Judith; as they touched fingers, they both pulled back instinctively and then, embarrassed, both dipped in again.

"Well, well, would you believe it: here we are again."

The setting sun bathed the lithe, handsome form of Hinrich Richter in gold as he strode towards them, his jacket leisurely hooked with one finger over his shoulder. Matthias felt a bolt of electric alarm surge through him. Simultaneously, he heard Judith gasp with shock. Instinctively, he stood up in front of her and assumed a protective stance.

---

1   'The Waste Land', T.S. Eliot, 1922.

He snarled: "What do you want, Richter?"

"You! You! Stop!"

Hinrich turned in the direction of the yelling and saw Yolande Abramovic, who he once knew as Ida, striding towards him looking dark and furious. She had left the pram standing with a puzzled Alexsander beside it.

Matthias watched Hinrich turn towards the voice, his brow furrowing until he obviously recognised who Yolande was. He swivelled and, in doing so, slipped on the wet, slippery surface he had reached. He fell headlong. His head hit the marble football under Judith's sandals with a sickening crunch. A fountain of blood immediately spurted out of his left temple. His eyes were wide-open, stricken with disbelief.

Matthias rushed over to him and instinctively tried to stem the fountain of blood with his hand, causing to it spray over himself and Judith, who had knelt down on the other side of Hinrich. Hinrich reached up and grabbed Matthias by the hand and raised his right hand towards Judith. She took it, frightened, and reached across to Matthias and held his free hand.

Hinrich whispered: "I could not love as you."

So, they knelt. The three of them joined in hands until Hinrich's heart stopped its mad pumping.

Judith stood up, and, letting go of Hinrich's lifeless hand, but not that of bloody Matthias, she led her former lover into the deeper waters of Lake Constance. As she waded out, she felt the cool water slowly rising up to her thighs. She led them further onwards. She stopped, turned and wordlessly took Matthias by the shoulders and pushed him under the surface, held him there for a number of seconds, and then released him. Matthias surfaced, gasping. In turn, she felt his big hands on her shoulders as he pushed her down forcefully beneath the surface and held her there. All was grey. He released her. She shot up, also gasping and spluttering in the sunlight, washed clean of Hinrich's blood, and embraced Matthias fiercely and passionately.

"Never let me go!" she cried into his ear as she felt her tears mingling with the waters of the lake. "Ever."

From a distance, Father Donnelly from Dublin and Rabbi Chaim Moskowitz from Munich looked upon them.

Chaim Moskowitz turned to Christopher Donnelly and said quietly: "There is hope for us yet. All of us."

LAST PAGE SOURCES AND REFERENCES

THANK YOU –

To William Manchester, for his *Goodbye, Darkness* for relating to us the horror of his devastated warrior-youth. His scenes of himself and the sniper and also in the bomb crater inspired me to put Matthias into similar predicaments.

To Andrea Wulf, for her *Magnificent Rebels* in which she depicts, shortly after the French Revolution, the meeting of the minds of Goethe, Schiller, Schlegel and many more of the great free German intellects in Jena, near Buchenwald.

To Rafael Seligmann, for *Lauf, Ludwig, Lauf!* (*Run, Ludwig, Run!*) a part of which Siggi relates in chapter 5.

To Tom Holland, who describes so graphically in *Dominion* Hitler's aim to destroy Christianity and Judaism.

To Anthony Beevor, for his extraordinary account of the battle for Berlin in his book *Berlin: The Downfall 1945.*

To James Hawes, for his excellent *The Shortest History of Germany.*

To Eugen Kogon for his definitive account of the SS in *Der SS-Staat.*

The description of the nurses and auxiliary nurses' uniforms and badges can be found online at: ww2civildefence. co.uk/nursing-uniforms.html.

The treatment of severe burns by McIndoe and Gillis is described in Severe Burns in World War II: https://www. ncbi.nlm.nih.gov/pmc/articles/PMC5845992/.

As far as I know, there was no burns unit hospital in Lichfield during WWII and also no such theatre that I described in chapter 3.

'The Waste Land' by T.S. Eliot. Published by *The Criterion* in 1922. It can be found online at: https://www. poetryfoundation.org/poems/47311/the-waste-land.

Avinu Malkeinu: Rachel's version was taken from Leat's Sabbah's beautiful rendering: https://www.youtube.com/ watch?v=mHGbSvOuOSg.